# MISS WOODLEY'S KISSING EXPERIMENT

A Lady's Lessons

*Book Three*

Jade Lee

Book design by eBook Prep
www.ebookprep.com

Cover design by The Killion Group Inc.
www.thekilliongroupinc.com

May, 2017
ISBN: 978-1-61417-965-8

*ePublishing Works!*
www.epublishingworks.com

# DEDICATION

For the man who has suffered through
a great many of my experiments,
has always made me tingle,
and is the love of my life:
My husband Dave.

# A
# LADY'S LESSONS
# SERIES

# CHAPTER 1

"Lud, you foolish boy! You do not expect us to believe that you have been languishing in the Yorkshire wilds, do you?"

Geoffrey Rathburn, Earl of Tallis, winced at the lady's strident tones and dodged her fan as she playfully rapped him on the arm. He had barely entered his mother's ball ten minutes earlier when the lady and her daughter literally cornered him between the staircase and a huge towering column.

"Truly," he said, his bored drawl showing distinct signs of wear. "I am afraid I must disappoint you, but I was—"

"Faith thays you were thpying for the Home Office," said the woman's pasty-faced daughter who, unfortunately, had not mastered the art of a fashionable false lisp without spitting. "How romantic," she crooned as she fluttered her eyelashes at him.

"Nonsense, Anora," snapped the poor girl's mother. "No doubt his lordship was enjoying masculine pursuits."

The girl pursed her thick lips, forcibly reminding him of the Yorkshire sheep he had just left two days ago. "Oh," she said with a sly wink. "Mother hath explained all about men'th needth. I'm thure I understand. Explithitly."

Geoffrey had the grace not to choke, but it nearly cost him his tonsils as he suppressed his natural urge to gag. Finally, when he was able to draw breath, he managed to give the girl and her domineering mother a weak smile. "Then I am sure you will understand that I must wish my mother a happy birthday." He bowed as politely as he could manage and began pushing his way through a veritable tide of matchmaking mamas and their ever hopeful, ever hopeless daughters.

If only he had known his mother planned to put him on the marriage block tonight, he would have worn a nose ring and a saddle instead of his last good set of fashionable evening wear. And to think that two days ago he had been missing London!

Struggling to maintain his sense of humor, Geoffrey maneuvered his way through the female throng until he caught up to his mother. She was gracefully holding court in one corner of the rented ballroom and looked elegant as always, her silvery hair caught up with ivory combs that perfectly matched her cream-and-burgundy gown.

"Many happy returns, Mother," he said as he dropped a light kiss on her cheek.

"Geoffrey!" she exclaimed, twisting her diminutive frame around to see him more fully. "You made it after all!"

He dropped into his best courtly bow. "In the flesh, Mother."

"Oh, darling, you sound glum. You are not going to spoil my birthday just because I decided on a slightly larger celebration this year than usual, are you? With that monster Corsican running wild on the continent, I felt we all needed a little extra cheer."

"How very patriotic of you," he offered.

She gave him a searching glance, then pouted prettily. "You are angry with me."

He sighed, knowing his mother was incorrigible when it came to restraining her expenses. She was a society butterfly through and through. It was part of her charm. So he smiled, reminding himself they were finally getting their financial heads above water. If his mother celebrated in a slightly larger than appropriate style, it was only in anticipation of the successes to come.

After five years of dedicated labor, the Tallis fortune was beginning to recover.

He felt himself relax, his gaze traveling over the expensive hothouse flowers, the full orchestra, and elaborate dinner buffet. "No, mother, I am not angry," he said, surprised that he did, in fact, mean it. "Truth be told," he added with a cheeky grin, "I am in the mood to celebrate."

"Excellent," she said as she snared an elegant crystal flute from a nearby table. "Because I have wonderful news of my own." She wormed her arm through his and drew him aside, her eyes alight with secret information.

He tugged lightly on one of her curls, which had escaped her elegant coiffeur. "Let me guess. You have found the elixir of life and have grown twenty years younger." He leaned forward, whispering into her ear, "That is not a secret, my dear, because you do not look a day over thirty."

"Oh, you foolish boy," his mother said, blushing to the roots of her silver hair. "Drink up." She pressed the crystal flute into his hand, and he obediently sipped, savoring the best champagne—the only champagne—he had tasted in the last five years. "It is Sophia," whispered his mother. "She is to wed Major Wyclyff in four weeks!"

Geoffrey stopped mid-sip, the champagne going sour in his mouth. He slowly lowered his glass. "What did you say?"

"Isn't it wonderful? We shall announce it tonight." She was smiling, her face glowing with delight. "In truth, they have already wed in secret—after a romantic drive to Scotland—but the formal event shall be in four weeks."

His sister was already wed?

"I swear I had begun to lose hope," his mother continued. "I am practically beside myself with delight."

Geoffrey was happy for his sister as well. After five seasons, Sophia deserved to find love and marriage. It was just that everyone, including the girl herself, had come to regard Sophia as a sweet, *maiden* woman. She'd told him she would never marry. She'd insisted he use her dowry to purchase new sheep stock.

By God, she'd *insisted*!

Now she was to marry in four weeks time. Where would he find her dower money?

"Drink some more, Geoffrey. You look pale."

He barely heard his mother. "Can they not wait at least until next year?" If he had a few months, perhaps he could scrape together some of her portion. "They need not wed immediately," he repeated, speaking as much to himself as to her. "I can manage something in a few months."

Gradually, his mother's prolonged silence penetrated his mind, numbing it with added fear.

"Mother?"

"They cannot wait, Geoffrey. Sophia is…" She glanced quickly around to make sure they were alone, then dropped her voice to the barest of whispers. "She is in an interesting condition."

Geoffrey gaped at his mother. Pregnant? Sophia, the woman he once dubbed the Ice Queen, was pregnant? His blood started to boil in brotherly anger. By God, he would show—

"They are in love, Geoffrey."

"But—"

His mother's voice suddenly turned sharp. "Geoffrey Lawrence Thomas Rathburn, I have approved this match. If you do anything to hurt your sister or Major Wyclyff, I swear I shall never forgive you!"

Geoffrey turned to his mother, his eyes pulled wide in shock at her tone. She had not called him by his full name in twenty years. Slowly, his indignation began to ebb. "You want this marriage?"

"Absolutely."

"And Sophia?"

"Is in alt."

Geoffrey saw the finality of it in her eyes. His sister would wed. In four weeks time. "Then I suppose all that remains is for me to provide her dowry," he said bleakly.

He drained his champagne, his eyes burning from the unfairness of it all. Four weeks. How would he find Sophia's marriage portion in so short a time?

"We do not have it, do we?" His mother's voice was low, almost fatalistic.

They both knew she referred to Sophia's dowry. As much as she pretended to know nothing more than the latest on-dit, his mother was not stupid nor willfully blind. She was well aware of their financial circumstances.

"No," he answered in equally low tones. "We do not have it."

"Well"—she averted her eyes, leaning over to grab another glass of champagne, which she pressed into his hands—"I believe Major Wyclyff will still marry her without—"

"No!" His one explosive word drew the attention of more than one curious guest, and Geoffrey quickly moderated his tone. "What kind of man would take his sister's marriage portion?"

"She insisted!"

"I should not have done it!"

"But you did, and rightly so. Sophia does not blame you in the least."

"Confound it, Mother." He ran a hand through his hair. "It is her money."

"Speak with Wyclyff. I am certain he will understand."

"Absolutely not! Wyclyff needs the money almost as much as we do." His hand clenched spasmodically around his glass. "It is Sophia's money. She should have it." He just did not know where he would find it, short of selling off everything he just worked so hard to achieve. Getting that money, in four weeks time no less, would put them back to where they were five years ago when nothing would have saved them but an heiress.

Oh, God. He glanced around the room with renewed understanding. He saw the glittering jewels, the rich fabrics, the money represented in each and every young girl in the room.

"Good God, Mother, you have filled the room with heiresses."

She sighed, confirming his worst suspicions. "I knew you would go prickly," she said. "Men are so fastidious when it comes to their honor."

Geoffrey bit back his retort, knowing acid remarks would not help the situation. Instead, his gaze followed her gloved hand as she gestured at all the flowers of polite society. "They are all here, awaiting your slightest attention."

"And they shall fall prostrate before me at the altar, no doubt," he said, frustration making his words too sharp. Why had he worked his back to near breaking these last years if not to avoid the Marriage Mart? He felt like one of his own sheep at a county fair.

"Come along, dearest," said his mother as she drew him toward the edge of the ballroom. "There is one young woman I especially wish you to meet."

Geoffrey allowed himself to be pulled, but his steps became heavier and slower with each passing moment. It had been bad enough five years ago when he had tried his hand at winning an heiress. He nearly succeeded, the delectable Amanda Wyndham hand and hand with him at the altar. Except that Amanda turned out to be Gillian Ames, a girl desperately in love with Stephen Conley, the fifth Earl of Mavenford. Bowing to fate and his own second thoughts, Geoffrey quietly stepped aside, annulling his own hasty nuptials so Gillian could marry her true love.

A parting gift from Mavenford had given Geoffrey the breathing room to rebuild his family's finances. Except now, five years of heart-breaking labor later, when Geoffrey had finally wrested the family clear of debt, he suddenly had to find his sister a dowry commensurate with the Tallis name.

Which meant Geoffrey once again needed to wed an heiress.

For the first time in years, Geoffrey felt a great fury build within him. He was angry at the greedy mamas who pushed their nursery-pure daughters at him in hopes of winning his title. He was angry at his father for throwing his children's inheritance away at the gaming table. But most of all, he was furious with himself.

By all accounts he was an intelligent man, a financial genius willing to spend long days shearing sheep and long nights studying how best to maximize his yields. Yet for all his labor, he'd still failed. It was a bitter taste in his mouth.

Geoffrey dug in his heels, stopping directly in front of a side doorway. "No."

His mother paused, turning to him in surprise. "What?"

"I said, no."

"No what, dear?"

"No more champagne, no more dancing, no more insipid girls."

"But—"

"I am tired, Mother. And not in the best frame of mind to tease smiles out of frightened young heiresses."

"But—"

"No." Geoffrey allowed his mother to study him with her intense green eyes, letting her read the fatigue on his face and the worry that had etched fine lines into his features. He was at his limit. She needed to understand that.

"Very well, Geoffrey," she finally said, her smile fading. "Perhaps you should go upstairs and enjoy a brandy in peace. The music room is decidedly pleasant this time of evening."

Geoffrey smiled, gratitude welling up inside of him for the temporary reprieve from the Marriage Mart. Dropping a quick kiss on her cheek, he ducked into the side hallway and bolted up the stairs. He needed time to think. To plan.

God, four weeks!

He reached the room and poured himself a brandy, not even bothering to light a candle. Taking a deep breath of the surrounding darkness, he loosened his cravat and wondered what he would do. He knew the answer. He was intimately acquainted with every aspect of the Tallis fortune—or rather lack thereof. Though he searched for an escape, mentally reviewing every sheep, every acre of the family land, he knew there was no hope. There was no way he could provide Sophia's dowry and still pay the mortgage.

He had to find a rich bride.

But he could not bring himself to accept it. Not yet. The very thought was like a noose tightening around his neck. He had only just poured himself a second glass of the restorative elixir when he glanced at the open window.

Was that a leg?

And a hand braced on the sill?

A girl was climbing in the window. Bloody hell, they were mounting the greenery to get at him!

He was torn between the equally desperate urges to laugh hysterically and to flee screaming in terror. Was there no end to the female determination to get him wed?

Like a man drawn to probe his own sore tooth, Geoffrey's gaze slowly returned to the intrepid woman. The leg was actually quite lovely, curved nicely and shining with pearly whiteness in the moonlight.

In the distance, he could hear the murmuring of his mother's guests, no doubt milling through the ballroom searching for him. There was nowhere for him to run, he realized with a distinct sense of fatalism. He might as well enjoy the show.

Dropping peacefully onto the settee, he gave himself up to total enjoyment of the lady's wiggling as she tried to squirm in sideways through the narrow window. He caught a glimpse of brownish-blond curls escaping an elegant chignon, heard the gentle rustle of white silk, and then all was eclipsed by the sight of the shimmering skirt pulled taut against a nicely rounded bottom.

In truth, it happened quite quickly, but Geoffrey knew those few seconds would be forever etched upon his memory. The mysterious woman had given him just enough of a view to enflame his senses, and then, with a final whisper of white silk and a couple tiny hops, she was inside, everything covered and in its proper place, her back toward him.

"Oh, do pull the stick out of your hair," he drawled. "It quite spoils the effect."

The girl gasped and spun to face him, her eyes wide with shock.

Was it possible? Had she truly not expected anyone in the room? Geoffrey shook off the thought. Why else would a girl climb the greenery if not to find him?

"I congratulate you on your ingenuity," he commented, his sense of humor softening the bitterness in his voice. "Consider my curiosity well and truly piqued."

The girl frowned at him, her brow furrowing in thought. "Thank you," she commented, though her words seemed a bit distracted. "I am counted quite clever."

"I could not agree more. So clever, in fact, that I cannot wait to know more." He leaned forward and, with a quick flick of his wrists, lit a nearby candle.

"No!"

But it was too late to stop him. The candlewick caught and they were both bathed in the soft glow of its light.

She was a pretty thing, older than he first guessed. In the semi-light, her eyes appeared rich blue pools fringed by impossibly long lashes. Her lips were the dark red buds of a woman who…had just been kissed?

Yes, he thought, as he felt his body tighten in response. She had kissed someone. And, she was definitely older than he first guessed, perhaps as much as twenty-one. His gaze dropped, following the graceful curves of her fashionable dress, noting the small, pert breasts and an enticingly slender waist. The rest was hidden beneath her skirt, but his mind had no difficulty replaying his delightful memory of her creamy white thigh and slender leg. It was not until he noticed her slim foot tapping in annoyance that he returned to the present.

"My apologies for staring, fair vision, but it is not often I get to look on a woman brave enough to flaunt Mother Nature herself."

"Then you clearly do not have any sisters," she said congenially.

He nearly choked on the thought of his sister, the cool Sophia, forgetting herself so much as to climb a ladder, much less a tree. "On the contrary, my sister is the epitome of serene consequence." He grinned. "I much prefer the leaf-strewn variety." Then he gestured to the rose-and-orange colored leaves still clinging to her hair.

She gasped, her hands quickly flying to her coiffeur as she tried to find the offending objects. Keeping his wicked grin in place, Geoffrey uncurled from the settee and moved closer to her. "Please, allow me."

He was quite careful not to disturb her coiffeur as he withdrew the fall colors from her hair, but he could not help noticing the silky texture of her golden tresses. Then, suddenly giving in to a wicked impulse, he deftly pulled out two of the pins anchoring her chignon.

"Oh, dear," he said with false chagrin as her curls tumbled free. "How clumsy of me." Then he sighed with delight as he touched the riotous glory of those locks.

Unfortunately, he was not allowed to linger for she quickly backed away from him, her mouth pursed in disgust. "Oh, bother. It is forever doing that."

Geoffrey had to choke back his laugh, unaccountably pleased when she had little success repinning her hair. Stepping away lest he be tempted to pluck out the remaining pins, he gathered his brandy. "Come, fair vision, share a drink with me."

"And I have lost my fan!" she cried, oblivious to his offer. She began scanning the floor for the missing item. When it did not present itself, she ran to the window to lean out, peering into the darkness. Geoffrey knew he must say something quickly or she would climb back out to find it.

He stepped forward, taking her slender hand as he drew her away from the opening, which, he now noticed, was disconcertingly high off the ground and the tree a rather precarious step from the window.

"Please, allow me to introduce myself. I am Geoffrey Rathburn, son of your hostess."

"The earl?" The words were apparently startled out of her, and she leaned forward slightly as if to get a better look at him.

"One and the same." He released her to bow in his best courtly manner, his smile widening as she stumbled into an awkward curtsy.

"Good evening, my lord," she stammered, her eyes drifting back to the window.

He could not mistake the meaning. She intended to search for her fan despite the depth of the plummet if she slipped. He quickly poured her a glass of brandy. "Please, I suddenly find myself unaccountably lonely. Will you not share a glass with me?"

She hesitated a long moment, and he held his breath waiting for her response. It was truly wicked of him to keep her there. He ought to encourage her down to the ballroom, via the doorway, but he had yet to solve the puzzle of her unorthodox entrance. After all, she might be a beautiful thief come to rob his mother's guests. It was his duty to learn more about her.

"Come," he coaxed. "What harm can there be in a simple glass?" He raised his eyebrows, quietly challenging her adventurous spirit.

She did not seem to notice. "I think I should go back out in the tree."

He felt his mouth go slack. "Just to find your fan?"

"My fan?" She frowned, then suddenly her expression cleared. "Of course not, silly. To think."

"You think in trees?"

"Usually. I have the most wonderful tree house at home, and so I suppose I just developed the habit. Aunt Win says it is very odd and I must try not to do such things in London, but sometimes I cannot help it." Her eyes once again wandered to the towering oak. "I feel certain that in this case Aunt Win would understand, except in the moonlight my white dress would be rather conspicuous. And though Aunt Win has been most tolerant of what she calls my unusual nature, she has warned me that others might not forgive so easily."

Geoffrey nodded, strangely enchanted by the ebb and flow of her lyrical voice. Her every word was spoken like an individual note on a page, almost with scientific precision, even when her thoughts wandered in chaotic directions. But taken all together, especially when mixed with moonlight and brandy, her words seemed to mesmerize him, luring his thoughts to places he never would go on his own.

"So you see," she continued, "when I saw the open window, I decided it would be best if I thought in here."

Geoffrey frowned at the sudden stop to her conversation. "So you were not looking for me," he stated, oddly piqued at the thought.

"I had no idea the room was occupied. I will go back to the tree." As if that resolved the matter, she stepped to the window and lifted her skirt in preparation of climbing the sill.

"No!"

She paused, her eyes wide with surprise, and he racked his brain for a suitable reason to keep her with him.

"I, uh, cannot let you go out. You might fall—"

"I never fall."

"But you might."

"Do not concern yourself, my lord. I admit I did fall once. My father said I bounced quite nicely, and although I did break my arm, it healed in a few weeks. In fact, the confinement forced me to catch up on my studies. So, all in all, it was a positive experience."

When he had no response to that, she nodded politely to him and jumped neatly to the windowsill.

"No! Uh, just think of my mother."

She frowned. "The countess?"

"Why, yes," he continued, finally thinking of something suitable. "It is her birthday today, you know. And although you might bounce quite nicely, it would give her the vapors just to think of it."

Her frown deepened. "Why would your mother have the vapors if I fell?"

He shrugged, a smile pulling at his lips. "I have no idea, but I assure you, she would. Therefore, as her son, I must insist you refrain from climbing the tree. At least during the remainder of her ball."

She sighed heavily as she nimbly dropped back to the floor. "Oh, very well. But then where am I going to think in peace?"

"Why not right here? I assure you, I can be quiet."

She eyed him narrowly. "Promise?"

He nodded, his lips pressed tightly together to hold back his smile. Then he pushed the brandy into her hand. She took it, but did not deign to drink. Instead, she settled neatly into a nearby chaise as he returned to his place on the settee.

Unfortunately, despite his promise, he found it exceedingly difficult to sit in silence with the odd creature. She stared down at the floor, idly tugging at her hair as she apparently fought with her thoughts. Then, every once in a while, she released a sigh so heavy it seemed to press her deeper into her chair.

He could not stand more than ten minutes of it. "Perhaps you would do better if you thought aloud," he offered.

Her body jerked slightly as she glanced up at him. "You promised to be quiet," she accused.

"I did not realize you would be so very loud."

She tilted her head, clearly confused.

"You are sighing. Quite loudly. I am surprised they have not heard it downstairs." He was teasing her, although he kept his expression somber, and suddenly she smiled, her entire face lifting with an inner delight.

"Do not try to gammon me, my lord."

"I would not think of it."

She sighed again, and her long lashes closed over her eyes making dark half moons on her cheeks. "It is nothing really. My aunt would tell me it is undoubtedly all my fault."

Geoffrey touched her hand, pushing her brandy toward her mouth. "Take a drink, angel, then you can tell me what happened."

She opened her eyes, obediently sipping from the snifter. Then she spoke, her voice trembling with self-recrimination. "It is my fault, my lord. I am cursed with the most insatiable curiosity. Or perhaps," she added on a softer note, "it is the weakest of wills. It has gotten me into more trouble than I can count."

Geoffrey narrowed his gaze, noting for the first time her hands trembled slightly as she held her brandy and that her throaty whisper was not a seductive affectation but a sign of true distress.

He silently cursed himself for his stupidity, suddenly remembering the rosy blush of her just-kissed lips. The girl had not been running him to ground, but had been escaping something—or rather someone. Someone had just accosted her, and at his mother's ball no less.

Anger burned within him, and he silently swore to avenge this odd creature before him. He barely gave thought to such uncharacteristically gothic behavior on his part. It was simply necessary. But first he had to ascertain the facts, and as delicately as possible.

"I am counted quite discreet," he offered softly as he reached forward, capturing her small hand in his. He had not intended to touch her, merely wanted to discover the name of the boorish gentleman, but somehow he found himself possessing her small hand, caressing its velvety softness. "Tell me from beginning to end what happened."

She gazed at their entwined hands, slowly tilting her head as if considering the sensation. Then she abruptly stood, pulling her hands away as she began to pace. "Do you know Alvina Morrow? She is to wed Baron Heise next month."

Geoffrey blinked, wondering if she were trying to distract him with an on-dit or whether it was important. "I have only recently returned to London and have not had the pleasure."

She shrugged slightly, her gown shifting in the soft light, giving Geoffrey a distinctly unchivalrous thought. "It makes no matter. She is a dear friend of mine. She had an offer from an earl, but turned him down for the German baron."

Geoffrey remained silent, his attention focused on the shifting planes of her face. He had not realized a person's features could be so totally expressive.

"We were having a comfortable coze just yesterday," she continued. "And I asked her about her choice. Her mother had been mad for the higher title, you understand."

She glanced up at him, and he nodded, silently encouraging her to go on.

"She said she loved the baron. Actually, she said it quite a bit more eloquently than that, with a great deal of heartfelt sighs and doe-eyed looks, but that was the essence of it."

"Then I congratulate her on her good fortune."

She glanced over at him, clearly catching the cynicism in his voice. "You do not believe she was in love."

"As I do not know either party involved, I am unqualified to judge."

She shrugged and again his gaze wandered to the shifting fabric of her gown. "I did not believe her either. I asked her how she knew she was in love, and…" Her voice faded, and she frowned down at her brandy. "She said he made her tingle when they kissed." Even in the soft candlelight, he could see the blush staining her cheeks as she continued speaking.

"Naturally, I thought it was all nonsense, but I did check my father's library, especially the Greek love poems." She looked up, pinning him with her dark gaze. "Did you know that literature offers hundreds of references to various physical responses?"

He gaped at her, not quite sure how to respond. "I, uh, believe I am familiar with some of the references."

She nodded, as if pleased with his intellectual abilities. Then she spoke again, her words punctuated by the swish of her skirts as she paced to the window and back. "I have never been kissed, you understand. Harry's and my family have had this understanding since we were born. Our properties connect, and so I wondered if…if—"

Geoffrey finished her thought, his tone excruciatingly dry. "If you would tingle when he kissed you?"

She shrugged, her gaze back on her brandy. "I was curious."

He sighed and tried to keep his voice bland despite the anger still hot within him. "Angel, did he hurt you? Do I need to summon a doctor?"

"Oh no!" she exclaimed. Then she bit her lip, and he was sure she struggled to restrain a grin. "Unless it is for Harry, er, Lord Berton, that is. I am afraid I hit him rather soundly. I…I may even have broken his nose." She paused to gulp some of her brandy. "It is quite ironic really as he is the one who taught me to punch in the first place. We did grow up together, you know."

Geoffrey did not know what to say. Here he was delicately trying to ease her past the trauma of an over-amorous beau, only to discover the girl handled the situation quite neatly on her own. And with fisticuffs, no less. "Please, tell me what happened," he urged, suddenly more relaxed.

Her hand strayed to her lip, touching it lightly. "We were taking a turn about the garden, and then I asked him to kiss me." She frowned as she continued. "Do you know, he never gave me a moment to explain my interest when…" She blinked and looked directly at Geoffrey, her eyes growing wide. "When he kissed me!"

Geoffrey felt his eyebrows rise in surprise, fairness compelling him to defend the unknown Lord Berton, ham-handed though the boy must be. "You had requested as much."

"Well, of course I asked him to kiss me. But not with such…such…"

"Enthusiasm?"

"Wetness!"

Geoffrey was grateful he had set down his own brandy otherwise he surely would have spilled it.

"It was like pressing my lips to a wet fish," she said. "Then when he put his hands…" She raised her own hands and waved them about the area of her bodice. "Well, that is when I hit him." She glanced at him with an impish grin. "Knocked him flat, I fear."

"I feel certain he deserved it," Geoffrey commented, startled by the grim satisfaction he derived from the image.

She shook her head, her eyes filling with genuine distress. "Oh no. I did truly ask for him to kiss me. It is not Harry's fault the experience was so…" She wrinkled her tiny nose. "So repellant. Truly, my lord, if this is a foretaste of marriage, I am afraid I shall not be able to bear it." She poured herself some more brandy before delicately sipping. "It was not at all pleasant." Then she looked back at the tree, its leaves fluttering silently in the moonlight. "You see now why I went in search of a tree."

Geoffrey smiled, amused by her phrasing even though he did indeed see the crux of the problem. It was not that the woman had been heinously attacked, although clearly the overeager Lord Berton had much to learn about the gentler sex. It was that the poor girl contemplated a lifetime of carnal relations with a boy who could not even make a first kiss pleasant.

Geoffrey mulled over the situation, a wicked thought stirring his loins. She was beautiful. And curious. He could do no less than teach her that Harry was definitely not representative of his gender. In fact, was not that what riding instructors taught—to get directly back on the horse that threw you?

Lifting his brandy, he kept his voice lazy with just the slightest hint of challenge in it. She would not know that inside his blood pounded in his ears.

"I would not worry about marriage overmuch," he said. "It was just one kiss, you know, and a bad one at that. There are other men who are less, um, wet in their attentions. One might even say you could find someone to make you tingle."

He smiled at her, a long, lazy smile borne of too much brandy and a beautiful girl who'd turned to him for advice on kissing. She responded in kind, her sweet lips lifting in a delicate curve, her eyes alight with curiosity as she considered his words.

Suddenly, she nodded. "You are quite right, you know. It was only one kiss. Certainly not enough evidence to warrant a lifetime of chastity."

"Heavens, no."

She tilted her head, her gaze wandering over him in a way that made his skin heat with a sensuous hunger. "I suppose there must be others who could handle the situation with more skill."

"Scores." His voice was rough with desire.

"It is not as if Harry and I are engaged. There was merely an understanding. In fact, my aunt financed this entire season just so I might have the opportunity to meet other eligible gentlemen."

He watched her take another sip of brandy, her perfect mouth pressing against the edge of her glass, parting to allow the entrance of that dark liquid.

"I, myself, am counted quite an eligible gentleman," he commented, his gaze still on her moistened lips. "And quite good at kissing."

Her eyes sparkled with the candlelight. "Indeed, my lord?"

"Absolutely."

"And do ladies tingle when you kiss them?"

He set down his glass, only vaguely aware of the impropriety of this conversation, more deeply aware of the rosy glow of her skin in the candlelight, the gentle lift and lowering of her breasts as she breathed, and the slight part to her sweet, red lips.

"I have never thought to ask," he replied as evenly as possible. "Perhaps we could try an experiment."

"Why," she suddenly exclaimed, "that was exactly my thinking. Exactly what led me to Har—"

"Forget Harry," he said abruptly. "Focus on gathering more information."

She set down her glass with a determined click. "An excellent suggestion. Stand up, my lord."

He blinked. "I beg your pardon?"

"Stand up. Harry kissed me standing up. I feel that in the interest of fairness, we should duplicate the situation as closely as possible."

Geoffrey frowned at the half-full brandy glass in his hand, wondering why he suddenly felt completely foxed. "I beg your pardon?"

"You do wish to know if your ladies tingle, do you not?"

Geoffrey looked back at her, his mind feeling slow and dull. Suddenly, he had an odd surge of sympathy for the unknown Harry. "Uh, yes," he began. "I suppose I do."

"Well, I promise to share all my information with you."

He grinned, delighted that she had taken up his suggestion with such alacrity. Except that honor required him to mention the unusual nature of her plan. "You do realize this is most improper."

"Nonsense, my lord. This is science."

He nodded, pleased with that explanation. This was science, he told his conscience. He had his duty to perform in the name of investigative research. He pushed himself upright. "You wish me to stand?"

"Yes. Right about there." She pointed to a spot directly beside her left shoulder, and he dutifully stepped forward, his body tightening with anticipation.

"Do not forget to touch my bodice," she reminded him.

"I shall endeavor to remember."

She peered at him, apparently confused by his dry tone. "Unless you would rather not. I would not wish to impose. You are being most helpful."

His grin widened. "I shall attempt to force myself. In the interest of scientific discovery."

She returned his smile with a pleased one of her own. "Excellent, my lord. I was sure you were a game one." She lifted her head. "You may begin."

He looked down at her upturned face and had the oddest sensation of falling, sinking deep into the swirling sparkle of her dark blue eyes.

"My lord?"

"My name is Geoffrey."

"Geoffrey." His name was like honey on her lips, dizzyingly warm as it heated the air between them. She lifted her chin a bit more, raising her lips to his, but he did not take them. Not yet. Instead, he traced the curve of her face with the tip of his index finger, noting the exquisite lift of her cheek and soft brush of her eyelashes. She was clearly startled, her mouth parting in surprise that he had not simply claimed her lips.

"Harry did not do that." Her voice was thick, and he grinned at the indication of his effect on her.

"My apologies." But he did not stop. He let his hand trail lower across her brow, skating across the tip of her nose until he outlined the gentle flare of her lips. He felt her breath, warm and seductive as it caressed his fingers. Pressing downward, he let his thumb trail inward, soothing the jagged flesh torn by the impatient Harry.

He felt her breath catch, and her body melt against him. His restraint gave way. His resolve not to frighten her crumbled beneath the silken heat of her body pressed against him. He claimed her lips abruptly, almost savagely. Her lips tasted of the brandy they had sipped, dark and rich and full of promise. She tasted sweet, her innocence fresh, her response open and easy.

He deepened the embrace, pulling her harder against him, opening her to his plunder. He took it all, tasting, exploring, touching her totally with just this one kiss. She responded eagerly, learning his movements and adjusting to them, meeting them, then adding her own unique flair.

It was a kiss to enflame passion, and he nearly lost himself to it. Only the muted sounds of the orchestra beginning another set kept him from disgrace. With a supreme effort of will, he broke away, stunned by the pain the movement caused, shocked by the raggedness of his own breath.

His only comfort was that if he was discomposed, she was even more so. Her eyes were dazed, turned dark and wide with ardor, and her lips were a haunting red, urging him back to their forbidden depths.

"Angel," he rasped. "I think we had best return you to your heavenly realm."

She blinked, clearly coming back to herself with an effort. "What?"

He smiled, pure masculine pride salvaging what the kiss's unexpected intensity had stripped away. "I asked if that was a satisfactory experience." He was teasing her. Her answer was written clearly across her face and body.

She appeared to rally her scattered thoughts, straightening her shoulders and smoothing down her skirts. "I believe you are right, my lord. I will definitely have to conduct more research before committing to a lifetime of chastity." Then suddenly she frowned at him. "Especially since you forgot to touch my bodice."

He gaped at her, then suddenly the ridiculousness of the situation overcame him in a wave of hilarity. Lord, but the woman was a complete hand. Standing before him now, she was as cool and composed as the most proper matron in his mother's ballroom. Only he knew what fire lay just beneath her calm exterior. Whatever man was lucky enough to marry her would enjoy a lifetime of ecstasy in his marriage bed. Assuming, of course, the man was not too stupid to discover it.

He reached out a hand and smoothed a curl away from her eyes. "You almost tempt me, my dear. But now, I think, I should call your…aunt?"

She nodded, though disappointment clouded the dark crystal of her eyes. "Mrs. Winnifred Hibbert. She will be with the dowagers."

"And what is your name?"

"Oh!" She colored slightly in embarrassment. "I am Caroline Woodley. My father is Baron Alfred Woodley."

He bowed in his best courtly manner. "Then I am most pleased to meet you, Miss Woodley. Now I shall fetch your aunt."

It was not until much later, after the orchestra played the last dance, after the candles were extinguished and the ballroom doors closed that Geoffrey relived the exquisite moments of their kiss. In the darkness of his bedchamber as he gazed out on the delicate rose of a new dawn, he recalled her words.

*I will definitely have to conduct more research.*

More research? Into kissing? She could not be serious. Could she?

# CHAPTER 2

His kiss was like fine chocolate, smooth and intoxicatingly rich. No, it had been like hot, spicy apples, burning her mouth with a delicious fire. No, it had been like—

"—sheep manure."

Caroline blinked rapidly, her thoughts jerked back to the present. She focused on her short, young man of affairs who looked politely back at her.

"I am dreadfully sorry, Mr. Ross. I am afraid I was not attending."

He colored slightly at her frank gaze. "Quite all right. Perhaps I should attend to the specifics myself."

Caroline hesitated, torn between her responsibilities to her father's estate and the urge to just hand over the whole mess, lock, stock, and barrel to her sweet man of affairs. "I do not know. Do you think—"

The library door burst open cutting off her words as a statuesque beauty in dark burgundy stalked into the room. "Are you not finished in there yet, Caro? We shall have callers any minute."

Caroline looked up from the desk, smiling fondly at her ever-hopeful aunt. "Who would call for me, Aunt Win?"

The dear woman paused, pulling self-consciously at her lace collar. "I suppose Harry—"

"I am not in the best of charity with Harry right now. If he calls, you may tell him I am indisposed."

Her aunt brightened. "Have you two fought? Your father will be most annoyed, but I cannot say I am surprised."

"It was not a fight exactly..." Caroline let her voice trail away, unsure how to describe the situation. She was not truly angry with Harry. He had been overly enthusiastic. The problem was she could not possibly think of Harry without her mind skipping straight to their horrid kiss, which brought her directly to the much better, much more exciting kiss later on. And there her mind halted, firmly obsessed with the man who had occupied her thoughts incessantly for the last twelve hours.

How could she face her almost-fiancé when thinking about the splendor of another man's touch?

"Caro! Has my newest shipment arrived yet?" boomed a deep voice from somewhere above them. Caroline winced. She should never have told her father she could hear him through the ceiling. Ever since then, he had taken to screaming at her from above stairs.

Caroline sighed, sending Mr. Ross an apologetic glance.

"Caro? Can you hear me?" repeated the deep voice.

Abandoning decorum in favor of peace, Caroline screamed at the ceiling. "Your chemicals have not arrived, Papa. I am sure they will be delivered soon."

"What?" came his muffled response.

Caroline sighed and stood, her head tilted toward the ceiling. "Not here yet!"

"Perhaps, Miss Woodley," came the slightly nasal tones of her man of affairs, "it would be better if I returned at a later date." Caroline heard the telltale sounds of paper rustling and spun around.

"No, no! Please, Mr. Ross, just bear with me for a moment. All I need is a little peace." She looked significantly at her aunt who stood just inside the library door, her arms folded across her fashionably plump bosom.

"Perhaps you could make sure all is ready, Aunt Win. Then call me if there are any visitors."

Aunt Win released an indecorous snort, and Caroline realized she would have to be more forceful. "I only require another half hour with Mr. Ross. At most an hour." She stood and crossed to her aunt, trying to gently usher the woman out the door. When gentle did not suffice, Caroline resorted to firm and almost rude as she pushed the woman into the hallway.

"I think you spend altogether too much time in here, Caroline," Aunt Win said with a disdainful sniff. "I think that Mr. Ross should—"

"Aunt Win, please!" She took a deep breath. The center hall was not the place to make speaking comments, but sometimes she had to be quite plain with her relative. "You must understand, it is only because of Mr. Ross's expert management that we—"

"Caro! I am going to send 'round a footman." Her father's voice preceded his appearance at the top of the stairs.

"Papa, please do not bellow like that—"

"It is a matter of setting priorities," continued her aunt.

"Never mind, Caro. I shall go myself."

"Papa!"

"Caroline, you are not attending!"

"Aunt—"

"Caro!"

"Miss Woodley…"

Caroline sighed and closed her eyes, wishing herself in the silent boughs of an elegant maple tree. She had only just placed her imagined body in her favorite spot when her very real father barreled into her, knocking her flat against the wall.

"Oh, beg your pardon, my dear." Her father's swift, lean hands caught her, setting her upright.

"Papa—"

"Cannot talk, my dear. On my way out." Then he smiled and dropped a kiss on her forehead before clapping a hat onto his thin, gray hair. Though tall, her father gave off the impression of being short, almost squat with his disheveled, stooped appearance. His hair was constantly in his eyes, his shirts forever sported stains, and even his trousers had burn holes. Only his coats were immaculate, but that was because he never remembered to wear them.

Not even now when he was about to go outside.

"Papa! You are not dressed—"

"Miss Woodley," interrupted Mr. Ross, as he joined them in the front hall. "Has your father signed those patent papers I gave you? You know I can do nothing without his signature."

"Of course, Mr. Ross. Papa—"

But she was once again interrupted, this time by the heavy thud of the front knocker. Thompson, their aging butler, was apparently delighted with this most unusual event and wasted no time in flinging open the door with a flourish that belied his sixty years. It was on the tip of Caroline's tongue to reprimand the elderly retainer when she caught sight of their caller.

Geoffrey, the Earl. Elegant in riding breeches and a tight coat of dark brown superfine, he stood on the step with a posy of white roses in his hand. Then his eyebrows lifted in surprise when he caught sight of the chaos in their front hallway.

For her part, Caroline could only stand and blush, her reason suddenly deserting her when faced with the object of her most secret fantasies in the flesh. Unfortunately, Aunt Win had no such difficulties.

"See! A caller—"

Caroline could only moan in mortification.

"And you are still in that dreadful gown with ink stains on your fingers!"

She did not bother looking down. She whipped her hands behind her back, tucking them out of sight as much as possible while she tried to restore some sort of decorum. "Thompson," she began. "Would you please—"

"Good afternoon, sir," interrupted her father, as he tried to shoulder past the earl. "Must excuse me. On my way out—"

"Papa!"

"Really, Albert!" exclaimed her aunt.

Her father spoke over his shoulder as he squinted into the afternoon sunlight. "I shall go roust the man and find out what he means by holding up my chemicals."

"Fine!" exclaimed her aunt, apparently fed up with the entire situation. Turning imperiously to her butler, she gave her commands as only a statuesque beauty can. "Thompson, Earl, parlor," she ordered. "Caroline, change. Mr. Ross, leave."

But Caroline's eyes were still on her distracted father, now beginning to descend the steps. "Papa! You are not suitably dressed!" she called desperately.

"That is entirely his own fault," sniffed her aunt as she gestured sweetly to the earl. "My lord…"

Fortunately for family dignity's sake, her father heard Caroline's call and stopped abruptly, glanced down at himself, then began to laugh with loud, good-natured enthusiasm. It was one of the things she liked most about him—his ever-present good humor—but at the moment, with the earl watching everything with his keen gray eyes, she was hard put not to wince at the vulgarity of it all.

"My goodness, girl, but you are right. Cannot wander about in my shirtsleeves." He pushed through the door again, shouldering past the earl who obligingly flattened himself against the side wall.

"Papa," Caroline moaned. Then with a sigh, she leaned forward and lifted her father's glasses from a nearby table. "Here. Maybe these will help you avoid obstacles in the future."

"Oh yes." He obligingly put them on. "Cannot seem to keep the devilish things in sight," he added on an aside to the earl. "Now what—"

"Miss Woodley," interrupted Mr. Ross in a more urgent tone than she had heard from him all morning. "The patent papers? Has your father—"

"Oh my, yes." Caroline spun on her heel to catch her father before he mounted the steps back upstairs. "Papa! Did you sign—"

"Never mind that, Caroline," her aunt interrupted. "Mr. Ross, you may return in the morning."

The young man paled.

"But—" Caroline spun around. "But—"

"Silence!" Aunt Win bellowed.

Caroline sighed, recognizing the signs of Aunt Win in a temper. She cast a mournful glance at the earl, but he, like the butler, was enjoying himself far too much to politely disappear into the parlor.

"In the morning, Mr. Ross," her aunt continued. Then with a nod of dismissal, she smiled politely at the earl and gestured him into the front salon.

Which left Caroline in the hallway with her visibly upset man of affairs. "I am sorry, Mr. Ross," she began, trying to soothe the man's clearly agitated nerves. "I am afraid we shall have to speak in the morning."

"See that your father signs those patent papers, Miss Woodley," he intoned, his voice betraying a clear tremor. "I can do little without his approval."

"I understand. What about—"

"Caroline!"

Both Caroline and Mr. Ross jumped at the angry hiss directly behind them.

"Aunt Win!" How had she gotten out of the parlor so quickly?

"You have a caller, my girl. Now get upstairs and change." Then she glared again at the man of affairs. "Good day, Mr. Ross!"

"But Aunt Win, I must speak—"

"Not. Now."

Caroline felt her shoulders droop, bowing to the inevitable. Clearly, no amount of discussion would persuade her aunt that the family's finances were more important than a visit from the earl. She had little choice but to give in gracefully. "Very well, Aunt Win."

Ever the gracious woman, her aunt inclined her head regally. Then, with military precision, she rounded on the butler. "Thompson: tea. Caroline: five minutes exactly. Do not forget." Then she disappeared into the salon.

Caroline bit back the rest of her words, taking a deep breath to make sure her disposition remained serene, though she thought her aunt absurd. How could anyone forget the handsome, interesting earl waited in the parlor, no doubt wearing that disgustingly amused expression?

"Will you be able to study those figures before tomorrow morning?" Mr. Ross asked, once again cutting into her thoughts of the disturbing earl.

"Yes," she said on a weary sigh, absently rubbing her temple against the headache building there. "Come at nine. I shall have the patent papers for you then."

"Excellent," he said in his most stiff tones. Then he bowed briefly and left the house in his steady, measured paces. His dignified exit was lost on Caroline. She had already started up the stairs, her thoughts once again filled with images of her unexpected guest.

Goodness, what must he think of herself and her family? Of all the times for him to visit, he chose to present himself when they were all in the hallway at sixes and sevens. Of course, they were always at sixes and sevens in this household. Her mother had been the only one who could keep order, and until now, Caroline had not thought it important. In the country, one could be as wild as one wished. But here in London and with the earl visiting...

Lord! She tugged at her hair in mortification as she recalled his expression, one eyebrow arched in surprise, his gray eyes twinkling with delight. In her fantasies, she was always perfection itself. She was cool, poised elegance—a suitable match to his dark refinement. In her dreams, he swept her onto the dance floor for a waltz and everyone remarked what a wonderful couple they appeared. She would gaze into his eyes, feeling the powerful draw of his arms as he pulled her improperly close. Then, as they swirled about on the floor, he would whisper words of praise, devotion, maybe even love.

Yes, that is how she pictured it from the first moment she saw him enter the ballroom last evening. Of course, that was before Harry had suggested a turn about the gardens. If only she had said no to Harry. Then she could have been presented to the earl as a demure girl with her aunt, as an eligible woman who could converse intelligently. But no, she had gone with Harry, then appeared before his lordship hind-end first as she wiggled in through the window.

Was there ever a more mortifying situation?

Ducking into her room, Caroline quickly stripped out of her old gown before literally scrubbing her fingers raw trying to remove the ink stains. From this moment on, she resolved, she would be perfect. Absolutely, totally, wonderfully proper and with just the right touch of sophistication mixed with her natural sweet temper.

But what would she talk about with the earl? she wondered anxiously. She was hardly adept at social prattle. Fortunately, her maid chose that moment to arrive, interrupting her whirling thoughts. "You rang, miss?"

"Annie, find me a gown. Something nice."

"Yes, miss."

Thank God Annie had a perfect eye for clothing. Too bad the poor girl was stuck choosing attire for a woman with blue fingers. With a slight moan of disgust, Caroline gave up scraping at her flesh. She would just have to keep her hands demurely folded or somehow pressed behind her back.

As she stepped into a beautiful confection of palest blue, Caroline ran through a list of possible conversation topics. Thanks to her father, she was well-versed in scientific methodology and chemical research, but that was hardly fit for polite banter. It would be like mounting a large banner with the word bluestocking printed on it.

Perhaps they could discuss the latest rumor that the Duke of Cumberland had murdered his valet. No, young ladies were not supposed to be aware of such unsavory things. Besides, she did not wish the earl to think she doted on such gruesome thoughts.

The Regency bill? Too political.

Lord Whitley's latest paramour? Too salacious.

The theater? Too much like begging for an invitation.

What? Her mother would know, she realized with a sigh. Her mother had always known what to say. Until she went mad, that is.

Suddenly, Caroline knew the perfect conversational sally. Rumor had it Lady Hester Stanhope was about to sail for the Middle East. They could discuss that. It had just the right amount of social interest without being too childish or too eclectic. It would be perfect.

And just in case his lordship failed interest in Lady Stanhope, there was always the Regency bill.

With conversational topics firmly in mind and hands firmly tucked behind her back, Caroline sailed out of her room and down the stairs. She would be perfect. The afternoon would be perfect. Life would be perfect.

If only she could survive the next half hour without descending into silliness, erudite lectures, or, heaven forbid, carnally impure thoughts. Definitely no carnally impure thoughts, she repeated. That was the root of her mother's madness. And nothing whatsoever about kissing.

No kissing thoughts.

"Oh, my?" her aunt's voice drifted to her as Caroline approached the parlor. "She has always been interested in scientific discovery, but to do that…"

Caroline paused just before the parlor door, her jaw going slack in astonishment. He could not have. He would not dare tell her aunt about her experiment in kissing. Would he?

Aunt Win continued, her voice carrying quite clearly through the doorway. "Why ever would my sweet Caro do such a thing?"

She could not stand it any longer. Caroline burst through the door, her gaze flashing across the room in search of the Earl. "How could you? I thought you were a gentleman!"

"Why, Caroline!" gasped her aunt, one plump hand raised to her bosom in shock. "What a way to present yourself. I am sure I do not know what his lordship will think."

"I am sure his lordship has already detailed exactly what he thinks," she snapped, finally locating him and fixing him with an angry glare.

Unfortunately, she was unprepared for the sight of him, relaxing in her father's favorite chair, and her eyes widened in shock.

The seat was a large leather thing that dominated the room. The earl looked born to it. Though the chair was huge, the man filled it to perfection, making both seem reasonable for the room. She could see the corded strength in his body, the lean power of his masculine frame, but combined with the chair, he seemed not intimidating as much as reassuring. Almost comfortable.

Add to that his twinkling eyes and general air of mischievous delight, and the effect was bewitching. Even the delicate teacup balanced precariously on his knee looked at home there. If she had been fifteen years younger, she would have climbed up in his lap. Even now, at the ripe age of twenty-one, the temptation was urgently strong, although for entirely different reasons.

For a heart stopping few moments, all she could think about was curling into his arms for another one of his wanton kisses. And from the looks of his blatantly sensual smile, he knew exactly what she was thinking.

Caroline felt herself blush from the bottom of her toes all the way to the roots of her hair. Tearing her gaze away from the handsome earl, she addressed her aunt. "Really, Aunt Win, I can explain."

"Explain what?" drawled the earl from behind her. "We were discussing your youthful predilection for explosives."

She turned, her mind whirling. "I beg your pardon?"

"Yes," piped in her aunt as she picked up the teapot to pour herself a cup. "I was telling his lordship about that time when you assisted your father in his cannon experiments. I swear the entire countryside was deaf for months."

The earl chuckled in polite appreciation of her aunt's comment, but all Caroline could do was stare. "The cannon experiments?" she mumbled.

"Why, yes," he commented with exaggerated innocence. "What did you think we were speaking of?" His wicked grin told her he knew exactly what she was thinking. And dreaming. And wanting ever since that moment she first stepped into his arms last night.

"Caro dear, do you want any tea?"

Caroline started to reach forward, doing anything to cover her embarrassment, only to recall her stained fingers. "Uh, no thank you, Aunt Win." Then she swallowed and made a hasty retreat to the settee where she took an especially long time to arrange her skirts so as to not draw attention to the fact that she was sitting on her hands.

Her aunt frowned at her, but gamely continued. "I, uh, I am afraid Caro's father has encouraged her to learn more than is proper about science. Heaven only knows where her next experiment will lead us—"

"I understand Lord Whitley's latest paramour is a lovely blond actress." The words were out of her mouth before she could stop them. She had been so desperate to change the topic that she twisted her conversation list all around, jumping straight to the most scandalous topic imaginable.

Her aunt's shocked gasp reverberated in the silence.

"I—I mean," she stammered. "Have you heard about Lady Hester Stanhope?"

The earl leaned forward, and she would swear his eyes were laughing uproariously. "Lady Stanhope has become Whitley's latest paramour?"

Caroline gulped. "Oh no!"

"Ah. Then she has taken up the boards. I am not in the least bit surprised. She always had quite a dramatic flair."

Caroline felt herself pale. Good God, what had she said? She could have totally ruined the poor lady's reputation. "No, no, I do not believe she has taken up treading the boards."

"You are not saying Whitley has! Why, he is so fat, there will not be room for any of the other performers."

"Oh no…I mean—"

"Just imagine the poor boy doing Hamlet, prancing about with his belly jiggling and his corset creaking. No one would be able to hear him say, 'thoo be or not thoo be.'" The earl lifted his hand in a delicate wave as he mimicked Lord Whitley's false lisp.

He had the tone of voice down so perfectly that the ladies were soon giggling with delight despite their combined mortification at Caroline's faux pas. Fortunately, by the time Caroline could catch her breath, she had relaxed enough to attempt to explain herself. "I have not heard that Lord Whitley is to brave Hamlet nor make any other thespian attempts," she began.

"Ah, well you greatly relieve my mind. Whitley is a congenial ol' fellow despite his peccadilloes. I would not wish such horrors upon him, nor upon his audience."

Caroline felt her smile grow wider despite her resolve to remain cool and sophisticated. Geoffrey seemed to delight in the outrageous, and somehow he brought her right along with him. "What I meant to say was," she began again, but her voice trailed away as she noticed a delicate piece of ivory tucked in his left hand. "My fan!" she exclaimed.

"My, my!" he responded with teasing smile. "What an odd thing to say, especially when I have come to say just the same thing to you." He held her fan aloft. "My fan! Or rather, your fan." He leaned forward to pass the lacy item to her. "One of the servants found it this morning, and I, um, guessed it was yours."

Caroline felt her face heat once again. What he really meant was one of the gardeners probably found it in the shrubbery. She must have dropped it just before dropping Harry with her right cross.

"Thank you, my lord." Then she reached forward, intending to grasp the tip of the fan. But just before she touched it, he stood, moving forward so abruptly her hand closed about his. It was much larger than hers.

Odd, how a hand could tell one so much about a man. In that one instant, Caroline felt hard ridges and strong tendons flex beneath her fingertips. Where other gentle men's hands were soft and effeminate, the earl's was large and almost bony, with a power that pulsed just below the surface.

Then he twisted in her grasp, turning his palm upward as he gave her the fan. But as he moved, her fingertips brushed calluses created by hard work, and she knew her first impression had been right. His lordship had done more than practice gaming and polite banter.

She looked up at him, chewing on her lower lip as she studied him closely, seeing him as she never dared before. Earlier she recognized the beauty of his muscular legs; now she saw that his shoulders needed no padding to emphasize their width. Neither did he sport a girdle to draw in his narrow waist. She suddenly realized that though he was ever gentle, even fashionably weak- limbed in his gestures, he possessed a hidden power in his body.

The earl was no simple dandy, but a man hardened by work, so compelling that he stirred her every sense. And he was looking at her, smiling with that teasing all-knowing humor, as he no doubt read her every thought straight off her face.

Caroline gasped and felt her face heat with a fiery blush.

"Uh, th-thank you, my lord," she stammered, clutching the fan as if it were a lifeline. Then she glanced down and belatedly noticed her blue fingertips again. "Oh, Lord," she moaned, whipping her hands, fan and all, behind her. Then she felt herself blush again while his dark gray eyes sparkled like firecrackers on a foggy night. "I, uh—"

"Caro! Where the devil are you?"

Caroline twisted around as her father's agitated voice carried loudly from the hallway.

"I am in the parlor, Father," she called, relief coloring her voice.

"Caro," he said, bursting through the door, his wispy gray hair flying wildly about his face. "There is a to-do about our account at the chemist's. Fellow says we have not paid in months. Of course I told him it was all rubbish, but the man would not believe a word I—"

"Albert, really!" interrupted Caroline's aunt in strident tones. "Can you not see we have a visitor?"

"Well, of course I see that, Winnifred, but this is important!" He turned to pull his daughter out of her chair. "Come along, Caro. You must set everything to rights. I need that magnesium directly for this afternoon's experiment."

Caroline sighed, seeing that her father would not be put off. It was just as well, really. She was making a complete muddle of this visit with the disturbing earl. Perhaps what she needed was an afternoon's distance.

It could hardly make things worse.

"Very well, Papa." She stood as gracefully as possible, given that her father hovered impatiently beside her. Then she turned to the others. "I am sorry, but it appears my father needs me. Thank you for bringing back my fan."

Though she spoke in the general direction of the earl, she did not dare look at him, afraid she would see condemnation or perhaps pity in his eyes. She knew her father was considered eccentric at best, a mad half-wit at worst, and she could not bear to see confirmation of that attitude in his lordship's eyes. In under twenty-four hours, the earl's opinion had come to matter more than she cared to admit. So she kept her gaze down and her expression reserved as she ducked out of the room.

Geoffrey watched Caroline Woodley go, his thoughts confused even as he observed the graceful sway of her lips before the door closed out the sight. Only when Mrs. Hibbert released a loud sigh did he shift his gaze from the door.

"Is something amiss, Mrs. Hibbert?" He turned to her, his gaze suddenly sharpening with wariness.

A society woman in her element could spark panic in the bravest of men, he realized suddenly. Like his mother, Mrs. Hibbert appeared to know nothing but the fashion plates that patterned her dresses, but in one unguarded moment, the image of idiocy could be quickly wiped away. Now was such a moment for Mrs. Hibbert.

She was studying him, assessing him with the swiftest of minds, the keenest of glances. And he was frankly terrified, already scrambling for a way to speedily exit the Hibbert household. Then the older woman began speaking, and he knew he'd been trapped.

"I have known your mother for ages, you know," she said.

"Yes, I know," he responded as he straightened in his seat. "You and Mother attended school together. I am sure she would love to call upon you soon, but I am afraid I must be go—"

"It is only in the last few years that we have become intimate," Mrs. Hibbert continued, forestalling his departure. "It is why I feel so familiar with you, my lord, even though we have barely met."

Geoffrey was careful as he placed his teacup on the table. Not by the merest tremor did he betray the sinking feeling of dread within him. "I am terribly sorry, Mrs. Hibbert. But I seem to have forgotten an appointment—"

"Because your mother and I are so close, I feel I can be quite blunt with you and still rely on your discretion."

He knew the expected response. In fact, the words spilled free without thought. "I assure you, I am counted most discreet," he said as he gained his feet, his eyes on the door.

"Good, then perhaps we could discuss a problem."

He froze. He didn't want to ask. To give in to his curiosity now would put the last nail in his coffin. He knew from his mother that Mrs. Hibbert could be horribly encroaching. Indeed, this conversation had all the earmarks of a woman intent on leaping pell mell over the normal rules of polite society. Except his mother also found Mrs. Hibbert to be "refreshingly true"—whatever that meant. And she had urged him to view the Hibbert household with leniency.

On the other hand, he told his conscience, she had not urged him to remain in the household in order to get trapped into whatever scheme Mrs. Hibbert had in mind. He was a bare three steps from the door. He could still make his escape. He was sure of it.

He would have done it, too, if only the problem had not involved Caroline. Whereas he could care less about any woman's matchmaking schemes, bosom friend of his mother's or not, he had a great deal of curiosity about the Woodley chit. Part of him truly wanted to know what Caroline's aunt had in mind.

So it was that, with a true sense of dread, Geoffrey straightened his shoulders and faced Mrs. Hibbert. "Problem?" he asked.

She needed no further prompting. Mrs. Hibbert heaved a sigh worthy of the stage. "It is Caroline," she said in heavy accents.

"She is a lovely woman," Geoffrey inserted, hoping a compliment would deflect the more maudlin aspects of the coming drama. He hoped in vain. If anything, his words seemed to push the older woman into further expressions of disgust.

"Well, of course she is!" Mrs. Hibbert exclaimed. "And that makes it all the worse!" She pushed up from the settee to pace the room, her skirts twitching to and fro with her movements. "Do you know I shall not see her again until long after dinner? Even then it will be to forcibly remove her from her father so that she can attend Lady Castlereigh's ball."

Geoffrey settled back down into his chair, knowing he had already committed himself to hearing the whole of it. "Caroline assists her father in his experiments?"

Mrs. Hibbert nodded. "And she manages this household and keeps the accounts and supervises the Essex estate."

He took a deep breath, his esteem of Caroline's intelligence rising by the second. "She is quite an accomplished woman," he responded truthfully. He, more than most, knew how difficult it was for one so young to carry so much responsibility.

"Exactly!" The older woman threw up her hands as if he had just spouted an elemental truth. "You clearly perceive the problem."

It took a considerable effort for Geoffrey to keep his tone bland, his expression mundanely polite. "What I see is a beautiful woman who does not smile nearly as much as she should."

Mrs. Hibbert pivoted on one heel, then fixed him with a steady gaze. "Exactly, my lord. She is beautiful and graceful and possessed of a modest dowry. Everything needed for a successful, if not stellar, season."

Geoffrey waited in silence, his attention drifting to Caroline's many charms.

"She was a disaster this spring, my lord. No one took the slightest interest in her. And now the Little Season is fast slipping away."

"But—"

"She is shy, my lord."

This time he could not control his reaction. His eyebrows rose in shock. *Shy* was not the word he would use to describe the woman who had so boldly engaged in kissing experiments the night before. *Brazen* was much more appropriate. Or perhaps *spirited, brash*, maybe even *wild*.

"I think perhaps you exaggerate the situation," he opined, his mind still on their passionate embrace.

But Mrs. Hibbert was not to be put off. "No, no, I am not. I have given this a great deal of thought, my lord. Whenever Caroline becomes uncomfortable, she begins talking science or politics or something equally inappropriate. Lord Whitley's paramour, indeed!" She rushed forward, only to sit heavily on her settee before taking a fortifying sip of her tea. Only after all that was accomplished did she continue, her words even more dramatic than before. "But that is not the worst of it, my lord." Her voice dropped into the lower registers, her every word filled with dread. "Sometimes she goes off on one of her own experiments, and then heaven knows where she will end up."

That, at least, he could verify. One of her experiments led her to his arms. And from there into his dreams last night. He shuddered to imagine what would have happened if she had begun her kissing experiment with an entirely different sort of gentleman. That thought alone had him frowning at the delicate china in Mrs. Hibbert's hand. Lifting his gaze, he fixed the older woman with his unwavering stare. "I understand your difficulty," he said with absolute truthfulness. "But I fail to see how you expect me to improve the situation."

Suddenly the woman was up and pacing again, her skirt twitching left and right around her ample lips. "I perceive in you a friend. A friend in whom I may confide, and more importantly, a friend to Caroline."

Geoffrey remained silent. Mrs. Hibbert would soon reveal the role she expected him to play. He had already decided to deny her. He had enough difficulties of his own without adding the delightful Caroline into the mix. Certainly she was charming, and were she an heiress, he would already be planning his campaign. But she was not, and so he had to bring this conversation to a halt. Soon. Before he got dragged in any deeper.

"What Caroline needs," Mrs. Hibbert continued, "is someone who will encourage her to enjoy herself, to enjoy her season."

"To wrest her away from her father, you mean," he commented dryly.

She clapped her hands, her eyes twinkling with delight at his understanding. "Exactly!"

"No."

It took a moment for his response to penetrate the lady's zeal, but eventually it did, and Geoffrey watched as her expression fell into shocked dismay. "But—"

"You are asking me to squire Caroline about. To encourage her in—"

"In levity, my lord. I would not ask, except that your mother and I have been so close all these years, and I am desperate for a solution. Caroline is much too serious."

Privately Geoffrey thought the last thing Caroline needed was encouragement in bold behavior, but he did not tell her aunt that. Instead, he merely shook his head as he leaned forward over her clenched hands. "From everything I can see, Caroline is quite happy as she is—"

"But she is not. She is desperate for some alternative to that awful Harry."

Geoffrey looked up. He had not yet had the pleasure of meeting the much discussed Harry. An omission he intended to correct as soon as possible. "Lord Berton is not appropriate?"

"Good Lord, Harry is the epitome of appropriate. He is upright, moral, good English stock."

Geoffrey frowned. "Then I fail to see the difficulty."

The lady dropped her hands on her hips, glaring at him as if he were the veriest idiot. "Harry is boring, my lord. Deadly dull, to be exact. Together Harry and Caroline would rival stoneware for liveliness."

He frowned, absorbing the image and trying to fit it to the Caroline he knew. "I see," he said slowly.

"No, you do not," the woman shot back with a delicate shudder. "Harry would allow Caroline to do whatever she wished, so long as she did not disturb his horses. She would start simply, of course, with just a few experiments. But, before long, disaster would strike."

Geoffrey raised his eyebrows, waiting for the awful pronouncement. Mrs. Hibbert did not disappoint him. She clutched her hand to her bosom and heaved another dramatic sigh. "Before long, Caroline would become *just like her father*. Locked in a laboratory all day, elbow deep in God only knows what, ready to blow the house to kingdom come in a heartbeat."

Geoffrey nodded. That, at least, sounded like the Caroline he knew.

"Can you not see the problem, my lord? She could do so much more than that. She could *be* much more than that, if only she would try. She needs to learn there is more in life than chemicals and account books."

Like kissing? The thought entered his thoughts in a lightning flash of traitorous lust, and he banished it just as quickly. The time had come for him to end this farce, and he could only accomplish his escape by blunt speaking. He pushed upright, out of his seat, emphasizing his words with the powerful force of his body.

"I will not marry Caroline."

Mrs. Hibbert spun around, her mouth dropping open with shock. "Why, my lord, I assure you, nothing was further from my mind." She spoke with heartfelt sincerity, but he could see the disappointment in her eyes. She had been hoping for a match.

"Your concern for your niece does you credit, Mrs. Hibbert," he said. "But I fear you must seek other prey for the delectable Miss Woodley."

"You still need an heiress, then," the woman said softly, arresting his movement toward the door.

He considered denying it, but could not quite bring himself to lie. He looked significantly at her, keeping his voice cool. "I trust I can rely on your discretion, Mrs. Hibbert."

She drew herself up to her fullest height, which indeed considerable. "Of course you may," she said indignantly. "I would not hurt the family of my dear friend."

He nodded. "My apologies. I meant no offense."

His response was automatic and she waved it off, her hand moving in a gesture reminiscent of his mother. Her attention was clearly centered on her niece. "Caroline has an adequate portion," she began. "Perhaps you could—"

"It is not nearly enough in the long term."

Mrs. Hibbert held silent for a moment, her serious expression suggesting deep thoughts at which he could only guess. Suddenly, she brightened, her eyes latching on to him as if he were her last chance of pardon before execution. "Perhaps you could introduce her to some appropriate gentleman? Someone who laughs and would understand her…her peculiar scientific interests?"

Geoffrey folded his arms across his chest, his emotions knotted within him as had not happened since his wastrel father finally died. On the one hand, the urge to flee this entire business was deeply ingrained. On the other, Caroline did need someone's help, and her aunt had been unable to manage it after nearly two seasons.

"I have only newly returned to London," he began. "My acquaintances are limited."

"You were not gone so very long. And you move easily throughout all of society. Surely there is someone you know…" Her voice trailed away on a hopeful note.

He stroked his chin as he thought. There was that young Perry Fairfax, a scamp if ever there was. And Jonathan Ludlow. Both harmless boys enough past their youthful wildness to be thinking about looking for a wife. Both had a respectable portion and were just what Mrs. Hibbert was looking for. But would they be able to control Caroline's more unorthodox notions?

Or would they encourage them?

He couldn't be sure without a great deal more thought. He looked back at Mrs. Hibbert, noting the lines of strain around the woman's eyes. Though still a handsome woman, this situation had clearly taken its toll.

"You are the only one who can do it," she urged. And though he recognized that she was manipulating him, he also heard the note of desperation in her tone. She truly was at her wits' end.

"Certainly you have some relative who could squire her about…" His voice trailed away. He already knew the answer, even before the lady began shaking her head.

"No one," she admitted mournfully. "You are the only one I can think of."

He had no choice but to agree. He had the right social access, sound judgment in evaluating potential suitors, and most of all, he was the only one, except for the bungling Harry, who had the slightest inkling of exactly what experimentation Caroline had begun.

"Very well," he said, acquiescing despite a legion of misgivings. "I shall take her to the park in four days' time. Have her wear her best frock."

Mrs. Hibbert stepped forward, her hands clasped together in gratitude. "Oh, thank you, my lord. I knew I could count on you. She shall be ready, never fear."

Geoffrey brushed aside her effusive thanks, suddenly anxious to be gone. He could only guess the disasters that awaited him now that he'd given his promise. "Do not thank me yet," he said heavily. "Not until the chit is safely wed."

Then he quit the house as if fleeing Hell itself.

# CHAPTER 3

Geoffrey entered his mother's home quickly, moving directly into the parlor and searching the sideboard for brandy. There wasn't any. Given their straightened financial circumstances, his mother rarely entertained at home. She spent her time visiting others, drinking from their sideboards, eating at their tables.

Which meant that Geoffrey could do no more than glare at the empty space that should have been filled with the best French brandy money could buy. It had been once. When his father had been alive. Or rather, the sideboard in the Tallis family London residence had always stocked excellent French brandy because it was his father's favorite.

But the London town home had long since been sold. His mother resided in a small, poorly furnished, minimally staffed residence well away from the fashionable elite. And this household served nothing but lemonade.

Stomping away from the empty sideboard, Geoffrey headed for the back parlor where he had set up his desk on a pocked table. He didn't get that far. Instead, he nearly slammed into his mother who was just coming down the stairs, obviously dressed to go out.

"Geoffrey?"

"Mother!" He caught her just before she toppled to the floor. "My apologies. I had not realized you were home." When she at last regained her balance, he dropped a kiss on her cheek by way of greeting. "You look lovely." And indeed, she did. Beautiful, fashionable, and most of all, happy, Lady Tallis looked a far cry from the drab, heartsick woman he recalled from his youth. Looking at her now, he realized that marriage to an heiress was not too large a sacrifice if it kept his mother smiling. She had suffered more than anyone from his father's profligate lifestyle. That she could now face the future with such clear happiness filled his heart with warmth.

Except as he watched, her elfin face shifted to a worried frown. "Geoffrey, you look pale. Whatever is the matter?"

He quickly smoothed his features, pulling on a smile for his mother's sake. "Nothing. I am merely feeling daunted by the coming task."

"Really, Geoffrey, some of the girls are quite nice. I am sure there will be someone for you this season." She leaned forward, a twinkle dancing in her blue eyes. "You might even fall in love."

Geoffrey released a mock groan. "Please, I am not in the mood for fairy tales." She was about to comment. Something optimistically female, no doubt, about true souls and wedded bliss, but he stopped her with an upraised hand. "But if you wish to aid me, I have a question for you."

She perked up immediately, clapping her hands with delight. "Oh, you've found someone already, and you wish me to investigate?"

This time Geoffrey did not sigh. He merely tugged on his mother's hand, using all the diplomacy within him as he placed it on his arm and escorted her to the parlor and their single, shabby settee. He was rewarded by her beaming smile even as he disappointed her. "I have not 'found' anyone, Mother. I simply wish to ask about your friend, Mrs. Hibbert."

"Mrs. Hibbert? Or her lovely niece Caroline?" she returned, her gaze trained on his face. "I understand Caroline has an adequate portion."

"How adequate?" he asked, startled that the thought of marrying Caroline did not produce spasms of horror. But then his hopes were quickly dashed as his mother's expression sobered.

"Probably not adequate enough. Besides," she added on a dramatic sigh, "there is some question as to her sanity."

"Truly?" Geoffrey made sure his expression did not betray his interest. A tendency toward insanity might just explain Caroline's odd behavior. As expected, his mother eagerly launched into her tale.

"Daniella, Caroline's mother, was quite the thing, you know. Beautiful. Vivacious. Everyone adored her. But she fell madly in love with that bookish Mr. Woodley and ran off with him. No one could understand why at the time. We all assumed it was some grand passion."

Geoffrey nodded, wondering what this ancient history had to do with Caroline's madness, but he knew better than to interrupt. He simply smiled encouragingly and allowed the story to unfold naturally.

"Well," continued his mother, "Daniella never came back to London, but wrote letters to all of her friends. Long letters filled with how terrible life in the country was. Some people visited her, of course, but the whole place was hideously dull. And her husband had no conversation whatsoever."

Thinking of Caroline's eccentric father, Geoffrey could readily understand how he would not show to advantage at a country party. "But surely Daniella knew to expect this before they married. Unless his…chemical interests are a symptom of his madness."

"Chemical interests?" his mother asked. "Whatever are you talking about?"

"Mr. Woodley. Caroline's father."

Suddenly, his mother's trilling laugh filled the room. "Oh no, Geoffrey. The father is not insane. It is the mother,

Winnifred's sister. Seems her passions quite overset her mind. Daniella constantly ran away. First with this Mr. Woodley. Then, again"—she leaned forward to impart her scandalous secret—"with a gypsy!"

Geoffrey pulled back, shocked to his core. Caroline's mother had run away with a gypsy? "But why?"

"Madness, of course! It is the only explanation."

"How long ago was this?"

"Years. Caroline could not have been more than nine."

Nine? Geoffrey shuddered. To lose a mother, and in so scandalous a way, must have been hell itself. Especially at a tender age when Caroline probably understood a great deal of the talk but was too young to defend herself. "What happened to the mother?"

"Oh, she died! Her sort always does. Of some gypsy ailment, I am sure, just a few years later. The body turned up on their back doorstep. Scared some poor scullery maid right out of her wits. There was a funeral, of course. A quiet family affair, but it was the talk of the town for weeks."

Geoffrey shuddered at the thought, his heart going out to the young Caroline, thrust not once, but twice into such painful chaos.

His mother shrugged sadly. "So you see, Caroline's only defense has been to become a bluestocking, thereby proving that she is not prone to her mother's fits. It hasn't helped, of course. Somewhat like refusing to wear black in favor of dark brown. They both look like mud and neither will get you married."

Geoffrey nodded, amazed that he not only understood what his mother meant, but appreciated the sentiment. Of course Caroline would throw herself into the highly intellectual world of a bluestocking. She was fighting the impression that she was ruled by impulsive emotional fits. And yet, somewhere, her passionate nature required expression. Hence her current interest in kissing.

He frowned, unhappy with the thought that Caroline was in any way mentally unbalanced. She was certainly unusual, but any woman of high intelligence deserved that label. Besides, he decided, given what he now knew of her family, she ought to be congratulated on what social skills she possessed, not condemned as an insane bluestocking. Indeed, he saw nothing wrong with her except a certain nervousness around the social elite. And that, he decided, could easily be fixed with a little experience and a guiding hand.

In short, all he needed to do was expose her gently to society until she gained a little confidence. Once she felt more comfortable with the social whirl, her other interest— namely her bizarre kissing experiment—would naturally fade.

Suddenly smiling, he gave his mother a tender kiss on her cheek. "Thank you. You have told me exactly what I wished to know."

His mother colored delightfully at his show of affection, but even that could not distract her from the question of his future. "Why this sudden interest in Caroline?"

He shrugged, keeping his expression nonchalant. "Her aunt has pressed me into duty." He shot his mother a stem gaze. "She called upon your long association and begged me to help squire the girl about."

"Encroaching," his mother confirmed with a nod. "Did I not warn you? Still, I cannot help but feel for dear Winnifred. She and Daniella were always so emotional, following their hearts not their heads. And now Winnie is trying to do her best for Caroline with barely the money or skills to sustain herself. It is all very sad. Do say you will help them."

"I have already agreed, but only out of love for you," he lied.

In truth, he had agreed because Mrs. Hibbert had seemed desperate, and he had never been able to refuse a woman in distress. The thought that he wished to spend more time with the intriguing Caroline barely entered his mind before he dismissed it as ridiculous. He had no time for even fascinating women—unless they came with a very large dowry.

"And now," he continued as he rose from the settee, "thanks to you, I understand the challenges I face in bringing Caroline into fashion."

"Oh, Geoffrey," his mother sighed as she, too, stood. "You always were such a tenderhearted boy. And I am sure Winnifred appreciates your assistance on behalf of her niece." She reached up and patted his cheek with motherly affection. "Mind that you do not get distracted. Wooing an heiress is not so simple—"

"I know what I am about, Mother," he interrupted peevishly. "And I do not need reminding of my duties to the Tallis name."

She waited a long time before answering, her expression slipping into a sadness he could not explain. "No," she finally agreed. "I don't suppose you do." And with that, she pulled on her gloves, waved airily to him, and left the house. Geoffrey remained where he was, watching her go, wondering at her sudden shift in mood. And more specifically, why he felt an answering melancholy of his own.

Caroline did not go to the Castlereighs' ball that night. Neither did she go to the Winstons' rout the next evening nor any other form of entertainment for the next four nights. Between sessions with Mr. Ross and her father's experiments, she barely had time to think, much less suffer the anxiety of polite society.

She had expected her aunt to fight. Aunt Win was a master at subtly making Caroline's life so miserable that the older woman eventually got what she wanted. But, contrary to what Caro expected, her aunt made no complaint whatsoever. All Aunt Win said was that very soon there would be a social outing she would expect her niece to attend without complaint and in her best dress. She would not reveal what this mysterious outing was, and at the time, Caroline was too relieved to object.

So she'd spent the last three and a half days closeted away and was only now emerging from her private purgatory.

To see Harry.

He had called every day since their ill-fated kiss, but she had steadfastly refused to see him. Until today. Her change of attitude was quite simple. It came to her in the early hours of this morning as she sat in the tree just outside her window. In fact, it was so clear she was stunned she had not thought of it earlier.

Since she and Harry were expected to marry, it was only fair he be given another chance to make her tingle. Perhaps the first trial had been somehow spoiled. Pursuant to that thought, she sent around a note requesting he call at the precise hour of three o'clock—when her father would be deeply engrossed in his afternoon experiments. As for her aunt, Caroline managed to create a minor crisis that required an immediate trip to the Mantua makers. Aunt Win never returned from there in less than two hours.

Harry would have more than enough time and privacy to make her tingle.

She quite looked forward to the second attempt.

Knowing preparation was the key to any endeavor, Caroline took special pains with her appearance. Since Harry was a stickler for the proprieties, she knew better than to appear in anything other than white. Despite the fact she was one-and-twenty, she was still in her first year of her come-out and needs must wear white. That restriction, however, did not prevent her from selecting a gown of the most clinging material, outlining what modest curves she possessed. In addition, the fabric had strands of the deepest burgundy woven throughout in the most feminine of patterns. All perfectly proper. All properly seductive.

If Harry were able to make her tingle, she wanted to give him every inspiration.

So, at five minutes to three, her mind on seduction, Caroline descended the stairway intent on scientific experimentation. She arrayed herself on the couch and took extensive pains with the placement of her legs, stretching them out beside her like a Greek goddess, her every curve outlined, if not exactly visible.

Harry arrived seven minutes late, four minutes after her legs had gone to sleep. But Caroline did not mind, especially when he rushed in the parlor door with a gratifying show of anxiety. She gave him her most sultry smile, noting with satisfaction that his nose was only slightly discolored after her blow the other night.

"Caroline, thank heaven you are in all right."

"Hello…" She tried to make her voice husky, but Harry was having none of it as he crossed to her and tried to pull her off the couch.

"When you would not see me for days, I thought you had taken ill."

"No—"

"You look wonderful. Beautiful, in fact."

"Thank yo—"

"How do you like my new waistcoat?" He dropped her hands and twisted a bit, puffing his chest out to the sunshine. "I got it just yesterday."

"What? Oh, it is—"

"Why the devil are you reclining like that on the couch?"

Caroline sighed. Clearly her attempt at seduction was not having much effect. After years of dealing with her father, she recognized the signs of a man much too self-involved to notice the subtler methods of gaining his attention. It did not bother her overmuch. Men, in her experience, required plain speaking. Or rather, plain action. With that thought in mind, she brought her legs to the floor and tried a different tack.

"That is a handsome waistcoat," she responded, gasping as the blood began rushing back to her legs. "It is most…most geometrical." She eyed the rather dull gray-and-silver thing with boredom. In fact, she thought, as she eyed Harry's entire figure, that was exactly what his physique inspired: boredom. Odd how she had never noticed it before.

His chest was not very broad, his muscles not enticingly pronounced. His hair was a nondescript, rather earthen brown, his face a rather youngish, softish sort. Even his eyes, probably his very best feature, were large, almost bulbous, and…watery.

It was not that physical attributes mattered significantly to her. It was just slightly disconcerting to look at her longtime friend and suddenly discover that, physically at least, he was somewhat, well, froglike.

She folded her hands in her lap, her gaze dropping to the floor as she strove to understand this new thought. "Uh, Harry, I, uh…" she began, wondering what indeed she wanted to say.

"Hush, love; it is I who should be begging your pardon for the horrible way I treated you at the Tallis rout. I have been racked with the most hideous guilt." He knelt down in front of her, grasping her hands in earnest enthusiasm. "I do not know what came over me. I swear, sweetheart, I shall never let it happen again."

She raised her gaze and smiled at him, her heart softening at his earnest words. "That is just it, Harry. I wish it to happen again. Right now. I have especially arranged for Aunt Win to be gone so you may attempt it again."

He recoiled from her, his jaw dropping open in shock. "But—"

"I was startled before. I am sure if only we try it again, you shall make me tingle. It must have been because you were touching my bodice before." She frowned at him. "Make sure not to do it this time." She suddenly stood, pulling him up alongside her. "Stand over there, just like last time." She pointed but, to her consternation, he absolutely refused to move.

"What are you babbling about?" He pushed to his feet and to her surprise, she realized he was not as tall as she recalled. Or rather, he was as tall as he always was, but for some reason she'd thought he was larger. More like the earl.

She shrugged, pushing away the thought. "Pray do not be difficult, Harry," she said impatiently. "You know how serious I am about scientific inquiry. One must absolutely get everything perfect in order to draw the appropriate conclu—"

"Scientific inquiry!" He stiffened, his expression pained. "Do you mean to tell me this has been another one of your blasted experiments?"

She dropped her hands on her hips in consternation. She understood how Geoffrey would be surprised by her actions. After all, he had just met her. But Harry had known her all her life. It was not like him to be so bull-headed about things. "Harry, please be so good as to kiss me this instant. I have to know if I tingle—"

"I most certainly will not!" he bellowed into her face.

"But—"

"Damn and blast, woman, as if I did not have enough pressure in my life!"

"But—"

"No buts, Caroline. I am the man in this relationship—"

"Well, of course. That is obvious—"

"I blundered all over you five nights ago—"

"I know. But I have reasoned out the problem. If only you had not have touched—"

"Blast your blasted reason!" Suddenly he pushed away from her, pacing off his energy. "I was a damned idiot. Overwhelmed your maidenly modesty and all that."

"No—"

"Of course, I did. Tallis told me so the next night. Said he found you most distraught."

Caroline blinked. "The earl spoke with you?"

"'Course he did. Said you were beside yourself."

"But I was not."

"That is what *I* said, but did he listen to me? Of course not." He fingered his slightly swollen nose. "Damnit, Caro, but must you go around telling people I accosted you?"

"I never said such a thing."

"What will people think? Why, even Matilda was telling me I must take greater care with the business."

Caroline felt herself go cold inside, and her voice dropped to a lower, softer tone. "Who is Matilda?"

Harry colored slightly and resumed pacing, the back of his neck turning the color of a young cherry. "Uh, no one important. The point is, I should not have kissed you. That sort of behavior is not what one expects of a wife, and you most appropriately brought me to task for it."

Caroline did not respond. She simply watched his neck deepen in color with every word.

"But now everything is fine," he continued as he lifted his chin. "You can rest assured I shall not touch you in anything but the most chaste of ways until our wedding night."

"But I want you to kiss me."

"Nonsense," he blustered, his voice higher with each word. "You do not know what you are talking about."

She bit her lip, tilting her head as she studied him, trying to find some way to work around this new conviction of his. "I promise I shall not be overwhelmed."

He swallowed, his Adam's apple bobbing up and down as he looked more and more like the childhood friend she remembered. "You-you cannot know that, Caro. I...My kisses can be quite overwhelming."

She grinned, seeing that he was weakening. "Of course they are. But I just wanted to know—"

He cut off her words with an emphatic shake of his head. "Damnit, Caro, I will not discuss this! And I certainly will not risk your regard or Tallis's anger by attempting it again!"

She stopped and gaped at him. His face had now ripened to deep burgundy, and his eyes were so wide they nearly popped out of his head. She had seen him like this before and knew that no amount of cajoling would work. When Harry went all pompous like this, it was like trying to get cooperation from a Grecian statue. One with starched collar points.

"Very well, Harry," she said, adroitly changing tactics. She was determined to get some answers from him, even if she had to move obliquely at the problem. "Then tell me why you wish to marry me."

Harry blinked, clearly surprised at having won so easily. But then her question penetrated his mind, and he frowned even harder. "Damn, Caro, but you are acting queer today."

Caroline sighed, her patience wearing thin. "Damn, Harry," she mimicked, "but you are being remarkably evasive today."

They glared at each other for a moment longer, then as usual, Harry broke first, running his hand through his hair in a familiar gesture. "Lord, Caro, but this is not the thing to talk to a girl about."

"When has that ever stopped us?" she returned. "Come on, Harry, why are you marrying me?"

He sighed and shuffled his feet, looking younger by the second. "You know why we are marrying. In fact," he said with an awkward shrug, "you know the estate better than I do."

She stepped forward abruptly, her hands going out to touch him as she had years ago, when they were children and she last felt comfortable with him. "But don't you want to know, Harry? Don't you want to see if there is a true love out there for us?"

She had not expected the frown that creased his forehead. It was an old expression, one that reminded her forcibly of his father, the viscount. In that one moment, all traces of her childhood friend were erased, and she thought she saw a man in his forties, not a youngster of twenty-two.

"I thought you were too intelligent for such girlish nonsense. It is that aunt of yours, you know, who has put such things in your mind."

Caroline stiffened and for the first time this afternoon, her tone matched the chill in her blood. "I quite like Aunt Win, Harry. You had best come to recognize that fact if you wish to wed me."

He rounded on her, his dark eyes clear and focused as they sighted her. "Yes, I realize you have a weakness for the woman, and I do not deny that she is a charming one. But in your fondness for your dotty old aunt, do not forget who you are."

For a moment she did not want to know what he meant. She could see it in his eyes and knew it would be unpleasant. But suddenly it was very important to her to hear the words out loud. "Just who am I, Harry?"

He sighed, his expression relaxing into one of chagrin as he once again pushed his hand through his hair. "Pray, do not make me say it out loud."

She clenched her teeth. "Say it."

"Very well, but I did try to warn you." He sighed, then took her hands, trying to soften the blow for her. "You are a bluestocking." She winced, but he tightened his grip on her hands, refusing to release her. "Yet I have known you forever, and I have gotten used to it. I think we shall deal well together. I let you play with your chemicals, don't I?"

"You have never been in a position to stop me," she retorted.

"True, but I will be after we are married. My point is that I will not. You can even take one of the servants' rooms for your things."

"But—"

"There's more," he continued. Then he held her gaze until she faced him directly. "I also know all about your mother."

Caroline winced, trying to draw away, but he held her fast. "She has nothing to do with me. I am just like my father. You say so repeatedly."

"Perhaps," he said slowly. "And perhaps not. You do spend a great deal of time in trees."

"My mother never did that."

He nodded. "True, but it is odd nonetheless."

"Oh," she returned softly. "But the doctors say that insanity comes from a disordered mind. I am a woman of science, which requires logic and clear thinking."

"Only in men, Caroline," he said sternly and with his customary level of pomposity. "Science pushes the female mind to madness."

"Poppycock!" She would have said more, but he stiffened his chin and glared down at her.

"My father has said so quite explicitly." Then he fell silent as he tried to intimidate her with a frown. Caroline could only look away in consternation, not because he was fearsome but because she knew from experience that whenever Harry quoted his father, she would never change his mind. Still, even with her eyes turned demurely down, she felt compelled to defend herself.

"All my experiments are organized, reasoned, and well documented," she said softly.

"You see!" he shot back. "Women do not perform experiments, well documented or not. And if I wished proof of madness, all I need do is list your areas of study."

"Harry—" But before she could continue, he began listing her research sins as he had done so many times before.

"First there were those cannon experiments."

And as she had answered so many times before, she folded her arms across her chest meeting him glare for glare. "Those were my father's."

"But you began the sheep soap inquiry."

"Father took those over."

"But you began them, didn't you?"

She bit her lip, knowing it was true.

"You once showed me a mathematical paper proving the existence of imaginary numbers."

She squirmed even as she tried to explain. "They weren't imaginary so much as extremely precise."

He snorted in derision. "You tried to invent a machine to milk the cow."

She threw up her hands in disgust. "Sally's hands were chapped and sore. I merely sought to help her."

"You nearly killed the cattle."

"Harry—" she began, but he held up his right forefinger, and she had little choice but to fall silent. He was not in the frame of mind to listen to her no matter what she said.

"Where is it, Caroline?"

She looked up at him, pulling her eyes wide with feigned innocence. "Where is what?"

"Your ridiculous scribbling."

Frustration welled up in her, making her shrewish as she yelled at him. "They're notes, Harry! Scientific observations. Facts. Notes." And they were hidden just behind the settee so she could write down her deductions on Harry's kiss while it was still fresh in her mind. If he ever got around to kissing her, that is.

"And you keep them with you everywhere. Scribbling away like some damned monk. Caro—"

"Stop it! Just stop it!" Tears burned her eyes and for the first time in a long time, she found herself completely outdone by Harry. The man simply would not listen to reason. She took a deep shuddering breath, trying to calm herself. Trying to show him the truth. "I am not insane," she said firmly.

She looked up at him to see that his expression had softened. "I am not trying to hurt you, you know," he said gently. "It is just that all of it, all these experiments and inquiries and scribblings, they're all damned odd. You should be learning the pianoforte or stitching seat covers, not probing into the geometrical nature of dirt."

She sighed, her response coming automatically just as it had the hundred or more other times he'd brought it up. "Geological nature, Harry. And it's important if you intend to grow crops."

"Perhaps," he returned. "And perhaps not. My point is that I am willing to risk marriage to you provided your strange behavior does not get worse." He leaned forward, trying to look down at her though they were nearly the same height. "You must be guided by me, Caro, because you are not a lady. You are a bluestocking with madness in her family. But you are an endearing madwoman who comes with property and a fine head for sheep management."

She softened, seeing that at least he appreciated her one talent. There was a time when she'd wondered if he would allow her to continue handling the estate after they married. "Then you will let me manage all the properties?"

He nodded. "If you want to."

"Of course I do."

"You will have to consult me in all significant decisions."

She never hesitated. "Naturally," she returned. After all, she would decide what was significant and what was not. As far as she was concerned, it was a perfect arrangement.

"I expect we shall get along famously," he pronounced with a grin.

"Famously," she echoed, wondering why she felt so glum. Harry would let her continue with the estate management, he would give her a room for her chemical experiments so she could help her father as necessary, and he knew all the scandal surrounding her mother. Since Caroline already understood how to manage his tendency to pomposity, she expected her comfortable life would continue without much interruption. What more could she want? Truly, many ladies received a good deal less than what Harry offered her.

"So, Caro, are we agreed?"

She smiled, her expression as warm as she could make it. "Of course, Harry. But…But could you please just kiss me?" she asked wistfully. "Just once. So I would know."

He sighed, clearly giving in against his better judgment. "Oh, very well. But no barring the door for days on end."

"I shan't. I promise." She smiled as a shiver of excitement coursed through her. Finally, she would be able to tingle in Harry's arms.

"Very well, then. Come here." He pulled her forward by the shoulders, and she went willingly, expecting to be enfolded in his embrace. But she never got that far. Instead, just as she started to close her eyes in anticipation, she felt his lips on her forehead. A slight press, not nearly so wet as last time, and then he pulled away.

"There, puss. And no more until the marriage bed." Then he took his leave.

Geoffrey stood in the doorway of the salon and watched her. She did not move. She stood staring out the window as if it were some oracle. If he had not looked for the slight lift of fabric as she breathed, he would have thought her a porcelain statue left forgotten in the half-light of the parlor.

She was dressed beautifully—all in white, but with faint strands of burgundy drawing a man's eyes where they should not go. He wondered briefly who supervised her wardrobe. Somehow he could not quite imagine Caroline spending much time on fashions. She would chafe at the interminable hours reviewing patterns or fitting dresses. She would tap her foot in irritation, her mind on her father's experiments or her aunt's household, or...on kissing.

That thought alone propelled him into the room. Closing the doorway softly behind him, he kept his footfalls silent, enjoying the play of sunlight in her hair. When he first saw her that night at his mother's ball, he thought her hair the color of wheat or rich golden honey. But now, with the afternoon sun touching her, he saw streaks of blond so white they seemed like tiny strands of light.

Almost, he could think her a heavenly creature. If it were not for the frown of concentration on her face, he would indeed be checking her for wings.

"So serious, Caroline? I hope your Mr. Ross has not lost everything on the 'Change.'"

She started at his low tones, her crystal-blue eyes widening in shock. "Oh! My lord, I had not realized you were here."

"I know," he said gently, enjoying her open expression, amazed once again by the way her face revealed her every thought and feeling. "I hope my presence is not an unpleasant surprise." He had not realized he was worried until her beaming smile set him at ease.

"Oh no! In fact, I was just thinking about you."

"Indeed?" Taking her hand, he drew her down onto the couch next to him.

"I was thinking that of all the people I know, you would be most likely to understand what has occurred." She practically glowed with excitement, and he leaned back, enjoying the sheer pleasure of watching her.

How could a man resist such a creature? "Then, by all means, please tell me what has happened," he urged.

"Have you ever found something so completely enthralling that it nearly takes your breath away?"

"Oh yes," he drawled, his gaze lingering on her flushed cheeks and bright blue eyes. "Passion is something I understand quite well."

She blushed at his blatantly sexual appraisal, her cheeks flaring to a bright red even as her eyes shifted away. "No, my lord. I mean a passion of the mind."

"Ah." An image flashed through his thoughts of him as a small boy sailing his favorite toy boat. He had been practically obsessed with nautical studies, even reading ship blueprints, scattering them about the nursery floor. But then his father had lost the last of their productive land, and Geoffrey had been forced to learn sheep husbandry to survive. "I am sorry," he said, working hard to keep the bitterness out of his voice. "I am afraid my deepest passion regards the cut of my coat."

"Nonsense, my lord. You are simply still searching."

He looked away from the sympathy that lightened the color of her eyes to rain-washed waters.

"I, too," she continued, "have spent the better part of my life wondering if I shall ever have that type of passion. My mother did not, and…" He could hear the tremor of fear in her voice.

Curious, he studied her face, urging her to continue. "Was your mother very unhappy?"

She was not looking directly at him, but even so, he saw the wariness in her eyes as she chose her words. "Yes," she said softly. "I believe she was very unhappy. She died many years ago." Then suddenly Caroline brightened, the light falling full on her face as she turned back toward him. "But my father is not unhappy. In fact, he fairly overflows with joy every time he talks of his chemicals. And when Aunt Win is not managing the social whirl, she is an absolute genius in botany. Everyone about Hadleigh consults with her, even the gardeners. But as for me…"

Her voice trailed away, and he recognized tiny lines of strain in her expression, the barely noticeable marks of frustration. He had seen them too many times in his own reflection to miss them in another's. "You have been too busy running your father's household to wonder about grand passions," he finished for her.

Her ready smile rewarded him for his perception. "That is it exactly. I knew you would understand!"

He leaned forward, wanting to clasp her hands, but his sense of propriety kept him from touching her. "And have you found something to inspire you?"

"Oh yes," she enthused, her face animated with delight. "And it is the most fascinating subject."

"I am so glad," he responded. More than glad, in fact, because it would distract her from that ill-conceived kissing experiment. "Tell me, what has caught your intellectual fancy?"

"Why, human carnal relations, of course. And you are responsible for the inspiration!"

It took all his ability from a lifetime of control for him to keep his expression composed. She was gazing at him, her face alight with intellectual fervor, her eyes fairly begging him to share her delight. He could not bring himself to crush her completely, especially since any objection was more likely to entrench her determination.

But…"Human carnal—"

"Relations. Yes, exactly."

"But…" He took a deep breath. "Whatever for?"

"It was your idea, actually. I merely expanded the scope of the research." She leaned forward, her voice dropping as though she wanted to spare his feelings. "I feel that kissing alone could certainly sponsor a whole treatise on its own, but I am more interested in the broader scope. The whole experience, so to speak, and how it interrelates to the heart."

He did not understand half of what she said. His mind was still focused on the suggestion that this fiasco was his idea. "I beg of you, Caroline, please do not lay this at my door."

"Nonsense," she cried, her eyes twinkling with God-only-knew-what mischief. "You are much too modest."

"But…But…" he stammered, desperately scrambling for some way to dissuade her.

"I do hope you are not going to go all priggish on me, are you? I shall be most discreet. And the subject truly does fascinate me."

"Priggish? Me?" He had been called many things, but even his mother would never accuse him of "priggishness." In fact, he felt rather insulted by the thought.

"Good," she responded, apparently pleased by his affront. "Because I am quite dedicated. I have always been interested in the human body, you know."

"No," he said weakly. "No, I did not realize."

"Oh yes. I often assist our surgeon in Hadleigh, but the niceties of cutting and sewing of any kind have always escaped me. I am more of a scientist, you know. Like my father," she emphasized.

"I see." With Herculean effort, Geoffrey managed to rally his flagging intellect. Clearly the woman was insane. Unfortunately, she was also clever and would be able to disguise her madness quite effectively. Therefore, short of forcing her family to commit her to Bedlam, he had to find some way of saving her from herself. Of saving her from blaming him for whatever monumental disaster lay ahead. But in order to do that, he required more information.

He forced a congenial smile as he leaned back against the settee. A glimmer of a plan had just begun in his mind, but he needed more time to properly enact it. Fortunately, his gaze happened to land on the clock, giving him the perfect excuse for lingering. "Caroline, perhaps you could ring for tea while we discuss your plans?"

She clapped her hands in delight. "I knew I could rely on you, my lord. You may present yourself as a dandy to the rest of the world, but I can see the intellect within you."

She smiled sweetly at him and rang for tea while he shifted uneasily in his seat. Except for his mother, no one had ever bothered trying to see beyond the London fribble he presented. His expensively tailored clothes and family's titillating history were enough to occupy most of this city. In fact, it was an image he worked hard to maintain. Fashionable heiresses tended to look askance at a man who wanted more in his life than the social whirl.

But Caroline had pierced his determined front in less than a week. He supposed he should have expected it. She was a scientist, no doubt trained from the cradle to observe rather than just assume. He would be well advised to guard himself more closely around her, he realized. Otherwise, she might make him an object of study, and then God only knew what havoc she would create in his life.

"Tell me, Caroline, what exactly is your planned route of inquiry?"

She frowned, pausing to think as her aging butler inched his way inside with the tea tray. The man moved so slowly, his steps almost infinitesimal, that Geoffrey was positive it would take well into next week before the butler crossed the room. Caroline did not hesitate. She stood and went to him, taking the tray while smiling with almost motherly affection at the old man. "Thank you, Thompson. Why don't you go rest for a while? I can see your joints pain you."

He bowed stiffly, his bones creaking with the movement, as he turned to inch his way back out the door.

Caroline shook her head as she watched him retreat, her frown returning as the minutes slipped by. Then finally, blessedly, the man was gone, though the door remained distinctly ajar, and Caroline was handing Geoffrey his tea. "He thinks he is fooling me, you know."

Geoffrey merely raised an eyebrow in inquiry.

"Thompson. He is much too old to continue as butler. It is plain as a pikestaff his rheumatism pains him. I feel sure he would be much happier in Essex with me and Father, but Aunt Win will not hear of it. She practically swears by the man, and I have not been able to persuade her otherwise. It is just so hard for me to watch him try to cover his infirmities."

Cover his infirmities? Good lord, the man had not even bothered to shut the door. If Thompson were not the house snoop, faking an infirmity so he had an excuse to remain within earshot, then Geoffrey was the one who was blind, deaf, and dumb.

How like Caroline to totally misconstrue the situation. She saw the facts, but in her innocence, arrived at a completely erroneous conclusion. And now the woman wanted to investigate human carnal relations! It practically boggled the mind.

"Uh, yes," he said. "But we were speaking of your, um, new scientific interest."

She grinned, becoming more animated as she wrestled with her thoughts. "I have only just decided on it. It came to me only a moment ago, after Harry left."

"Harry?" What had that cow-handed youth gone and done now?

"Uh-hmm," she said into her tea cup, then she set it down with an audible click. "I wanted to kiss him. In fact, I arranged for my aunt to be out just so that I could see him again."

Geoffrey suppressed an irrational surge of jealousy at her comment. He wanted her to become leg-shackled, he reminded himself sternly. And as soon as possible. Then she would be someone else's problem. But if the ridiculous Harry could not manage to—

"He refused."

"What?"

"Exactly my thought'" she responded, thinking he was outraged rather than simply startled. "He told me his kiss had overwhelmed my maidenly modesty the first time, and he would not risk offending me." She spared a moment to glare at him. "He also said you told him not to do it again. Really, Geoffrey, of all the nonsensical folderol. You both should know I have no patience with maidenly airs." She lifted her chin, challenging him to agree with the absent Harry. "I am a scientist."

"So you have said," he commented, his voice dry.

She frowned at him, her steady gaze seeing much too clearly for a young lady, however intellectual. "Are you teasing me, my lord?"

"Yes," he finally confessed. "But only very badly. Please, continue."

She stared at him, apparently weighing his comment, then suddenly she shrugged it aside, launching into her new passion. "After he left, I realized nothing Harry could possibly say would sway me from my course."

Geoffrey narrowed his gaze, catching the note of defiance in her words. What had the dolt said to her?

"I intend to research exactly how the mind and heart and body interact to produce various sensations—"

"About Lord Berton—"

But she was too deep into her plans to allow him to distract her. She continued speaking as if he had not tried to interrupt. "For example, when Harry kissed me that first night, I was startled. He was too fast and too abrupt in his attentions, therefore I was unprepared and the sensations were something akin to revulsion."

She paused to take a fortifying sip of her tea before continuing. He was too amazed by her frank speech to interrupt her again.

"Your kiss, however, was a good deal slower." She glanced shyly up at him. "Do you recall touching my face?"

"Er, yes." Good God, did she think he could have forgotten?

"Well, the fact that you did not rush into…into a meeting of our lips allowed me time to relax, to anticipate the coming sensations. It made for…um, a quite pleasant experience." She pursed her lips, her fingers pressing against their delicate curve as she spoke. "Although I cannot help but wonder if you had not touched my face, would the situation have been equally pleasant? I was prepared. Perhaps if Harry and I had just stared at each other for a moment, his kiss might have been more amenable."

He blinked. Good Lord, how did he get into these conversations? "I can see you have given this a great deal of thought."

"Oh yes. I have even recorded my notes—"

"Notes?"

She looked slightly insulted. "Accurate records are essential in any scientific endeavor. My father always takes copious notes." Then she smiled slightly. "Or rather, I write them down as he tells them to me. Later I even organize them for him." She straightened with pride. "He finds my efforts invaluable, you know."

"I am absolutely certain of it," he responded truthfully. "But Caroline, about your research…"

"Yes, I have already catalogued my experiences so far." She gestured to a pile of foolscap on a nearby table. One glance showed him that her notes were neatly organized with tiny script and lengthy charts. "I cross referenced each," she continued, "by the speed of the kiss, physical sensation produced, other ancillary experiences—such as you touching my face—assigned a number to each, totaled the amount, and thereby rated each event." She leaned forward, her eyes sparkling with delight. "I must tell you, your kiss ranked most high. But I must warn you that a single kiss is hardly a statistical sampling."

"Er, I suppose not," he said, stunned by the sheer scope of thought that had already gone into her new passion. Then he cleared his throat and leaned forward, though his thoughts remained back on the bungling Harry. "You must tell me from beginning to end exactly what occurred to give you such thoughts. Did inspiration hit just today? From something Lord Berton said, perhaps?"

She sighed, waving away her childhood companion. "Harry was pompous as usual, but I have known him forever and have quite gotten used to it."

"But did he say something pertinent?"

Again, she waved his question aside. "Do you not understand, my lord? If I can decipher the formula, the exact connection between the heart and the body, then I would take all the guesswork out of marriage. Surely you can see how that would benefit the world over. Girls would no longer have to wonder if they were truly in love. They would merely have to consult a chart or table."

He shifted on the settee, intrigued by the concept despite the ridiculousness of her hypothesis. "That would be most valuable," he conceded honestly. "But Caroline, surely you realize that love and passion cannot be quantified."

"Well, of course there will always be a subjective nature to the study. Each individual must make a logical, unemotional evaluation of their physical responses. But there are commonalities. Literature talks of burning sensations. Of a fullness, sometimes even a wetness!"

Geoffrey swallowed, feeling the changes she mentioned in all too personal a way. "You have researched the literature?" he managed to ask, though his voice came out unnaturally high.

"Not in depth. And I believe there is a great deal more written that I have not been allowed to see."

He certainly prayed that was so. He had to make sure she never saw his friend Mavenford's library. There were at least two collections of poetry that she should never, ever discover.

He cleared his throat, doing his best to focus his thoughts. His first step, naturally, was to discover exactly how serious she was about her intended study. "You have set yourself quite an ambitious project," he began slowly. "How exactly do you hope to proceed?"

She took a long sip of her tea as she apparently considered his question. "That is exactly what I have been puzzling about. The topic does indeed feel quite enormous. I had hoped…" She glanced shyly at him. "Perhaps you could advise me on the best approach?"

He leaned back on the settee, pleased to be given such an opening. "Well, it is imperative that you start at the beginning."

She nodded, her gaze intent upon his face. "Of course."

"I have known women who claimed to tingle merely when a gentleman kissed their hand in greeting. Through their gloves!"

"Truly!" she gasped, clearly intrigued by the thought.

"Oh yes. I am absolutely certain that you should begin there. Take your time. And copious notes, of course."

"Of course!" She sounded almost insulted that he should suggest otherwise.

"You could spend the entire Season studying the effects of various gentlemen's kisses on your hand," he continued, making sure she understood.

"Through my glove?"

"Naturally. Then later, perhaps after the Season is over, you could progress further." By that time, he hoped she would be wedded and bedded, and most important, completely out of his circle of influence.

"Papa always says the beginning is crucial," she murmured to herself.

"Thoroughness is the key to any scientific endeavor," he said with a grin, amazed that she could be manipulated so easily. For whatever reason, Caroline clearly had a deep, abiding passion for science. That was unusual enough in a gently bred woman, but she apparently had not been taught to channel her scientific impulses into more appropriate areas. Given what he knew of her childhood, he was not particularly surprised. He, too, had been reared with little supervision or guidance. Fortunately for him, his passions had been curbed by his straightened finances. Gazing at Caroline now, he wondered what would have happened to him if he'd had even a modest income to indulge his more inappropriate interests.

Would he have spent a fortune designing impractical ships? More likely, he would have drowned while searching for underwater caverns or fantastical marine creatures. Whatever the case, he had come into adulthood with few people able to even guess at where his imagination took him.

So it was that when he gazed at Caroline, he felt a strange kinship to her. Not only did he admire her for continuing to pursue her passions despite what her Hadleigh neighbors must have thought, but he felt a reluctance to squash her interests despite their completely inappropriate nature. He did not wish her to feel the moments of regret or aching loss that sometimes assailed him. The goal, of course, was to keep her happily involved in the earliest stages of her study—on kisses through gloves or casual touches—and leave the rest for her to explore with her husband, whoever the lucky bastard might be.

Momentarily irritated by the thought of her future husband, Geoffrey downed the last of his tea wishing it were something stronger. But by the time he had returned his cup to its saucer, he had managed to regain control of his wayward thoughts. "Then it is settled," he said firmly. "You shall focus your research on kisses on your hand through your glove. When you feel you are ready, you can naturally proceed to dancing."

She shifted, clearly startled. "Dancing?"

"Oh, yes. Have you never felt that moment of alertness just before a dance begins?"

She frowned. "Perhaps…"

"You must absolutely explore that. It is the precursor to tingling. I am certain of it."

She nodded slowly. "If you think that would be best."

"I most certainly do." Then he leaned forward, abandoning his attitude as scientific mentor to reach out and touch her hand. "But you must not forget to sometimes simply relax and enjoy yourself. Not everything is about scientific study, you know."

She looked down at their joined hands, her expression wistful. "But a scientist must always be on the watch for disorderly thoughts. It is the bane of his existence."

He tightened his grip slightly, enjoying the feel of her delicate fingers beneath his. "Have you never simply tried to live, for a moment, without taking notes? Without thinking or analyzing?"

"Of course I have." She glanced up at him, her eyes wide open as she pondered his question. "But I invariably fall asleep."

It was fortunate for his composure that her aunt chose that moment to burst through the parlor door.

# CHAPTER 4

Caroline looked up to see her aunt burst through the doorway, her usual composure marred by the flush of embarrassment and hurry.

"Oh, my lord, I am terribly sorry. So terribly sorry."

"Aunt…" Caroline pushed out of her seat, wondering what her aunt could be apologizing for, but the lady continued without pause.

"I meant to be here. I was most meticulous in my plans, but then I had the oddest note from the modiste." She twisted and frowned at her niece. Caroline immediately discovered that his lordship's teacup was empty and set about refilling it. Unfortunately, neither her aunt nor his lordship seemed the least bit fooled by her maneuvering, so she silently settled back in her seat, doing her best to look completely innocent.

Her aunt pinned her with a look that promised future retribution. Meanwhile, his lordship did not help her out in the least by reaching for his tea. Instead, he narrowed his eyes and peered at her, his expression intense and…apologetic?

Was he contrite for something? Whatever could it be?

"In any event," continued her aunt after Caroline's continued silence, "I am here now, and Caroline…my, you look divine!" Her aunt's clear admiration startled Caroline. She was not used to such open amazement regarding her appearance. "Did you know his lordship was coming?"

Caroline shifted her gaze back to the earl, trying to make sense of her aunt's bizarre behavior. "Uh, no. Harry called and—"

"Pray do not tell me you have made up with him!" her aunt cried with her typical dramatic flair. "Not when his lordship has come just to introduce you to more eligible gentlemen."

Caroline blinked, finally feeling her thoughts settle into a clear order. But then she frowned. Her conclusion could not possibly be correct. Geoffrey had come to visit with her, not because of some nefarious social maneuvering with her aunt. "You must be mistaken," Caroline began.

"Nonsense," interrupted her aunt. "Hurry up now and get your hat. The earl is taking you for a drive in the park."

Never in her life had Caroline ever willfully denied reality. Not even when her mad mother ran out of her life to join the gypsies. But now, even seeing the truth in Geoffrey's downcast expression, she still had to ask, to hear the awful truth.

"Do you mean, my lord, that you came here today, not to see me, but because you arranged it with my aunt?"

Although she looked directly at Geoffrey, it was her aunt who responded, trying to bodily lift her niece off the couch as she spoke. "Pray do not climb into your high boughs, Caroline. His lordship's reputation is excellent, and his sponsorship will do wonders for your consequence." She glared at her niece. "I expect you to be properly grateful."

It was at that moment that Geoffrey intervened. Caroline had not even realized he'd risen from his chair, but suddenly he replaced her aunt. His touch was gentle as he helped her stand, and she found herself drawn to gaze into the murky gray of his eyes.

"I came to see you, Caroline. Yes, I arranged it with your aunt a few days ago, but I still would have called anyway. Perhaps not today, but someday soon. I would have come."

He pitched his voice low, soothing her with his words and the gentleness in his expression. Somehow both sunk into her bones, melting her resistance before she even had a chance to grow angry.

Still, she wanted to know exactly what he and her aunt planned. "So, you arranged with Aunt Win to visit today?"

He hesitated only a moment, his hands tightening slightly on her arm. Then he let them slip away, and the loss of his heat felt like an icy wind. "Yes," he said, his voice flat.

"And you intend to introduce me to other gentlemen?"

She saw him wince, but his voice remained even. "Yes."

"But why?" Caroline stared at him while Geoffrey frowned back at her, clearly baffled by her question. She couldn't understand his confusion. It was a logical thing to ask. "Why would you wish to squire me about?" As she repeated her question, panic flashed in his eyes—a moment of terror that he could not mask. Then it was gone, hidden under a cheeky grin and a too-casual shrug.

"Because I want to."

She folded her arms across her chest, her spine excruciatingly straight. "Not good enough, my lord."

"What?" He was clearly taken back by her response, but she had lived around Harry too long to miss the signs of a man avoiding something. So she took a step forward, keeping her eyes level, her posture uncompromising.

"By your own admission, you are a dandy who cares for nothing but the cut of his coat. Why would you exert yourself on my behalf?"

"Really, Caroline," interrupted her aunt in strident tones. "Could you not simply be grateful and leave it at that? Why must you always poke into the why of things?"

Although Geoffrey did not speak, Caroline could tell he heartily seconded her aunt's thoughts. She did not care.

"Why would you introduce me to other gentlemen?" she persisted.

The muscles on Geoffrey's chiseled jaw bunched in frustration. But when she did not react except to arch a single eyebrow, he finally answered her. His words were tight, as if he were being forced at gunpoint, each word a tiny explosion of anger. "Because I intend to bring you into fashion!"

Beside them, Aunt Win gasped in surprise, then began overflowing with gratitude. "Oh, my lord, you are too generous. How can we ever repay you? I had no idea you intended—"

Caroline shook her head, becoming angry in her own right. "But why?" she returned, more forcefully. And why, she added silently to herself, was this scene so painful to her? Geoffrey intended to bring her into fashion. She ought to be thrilled. Instead she felt an emptiness inside, as if the best part of her shriveled away. "Why are you doing this?"

He walked away from her, his movements uneven, almost jerky, then all too soon he spun back around, his casual dandy persona firmly replaced. "I do it, Caroline, because I choose to, and for no other reason than that." He arched an eyebrow, daring her to challenge him on it.

She did so without hesitation. "Then I do not accept."

"What?" Aunt Win gasped. "Of course you accept!"

But before the good woman could elaborate further, Caroline twisted enough to throw an angry glare at her favorite aunt. "Oh, do be quiet, Aunt Win. This does not involve you."

"Does not involve—"

"You are not the one to be paraded around like a stuffed goose at market. You are not the one who will be laughed at or pitied as a hopeless bluestocking."

"No one will say that." Geoffrey's voice had the tone of a vow, deep and heartfelt. But Caroline knew there were some things even he could not promise.

"They already have. And worse," she said softly, thinking of her last conversation with Harry. "I do not like the fashionable throng," she said firmly, lifting her chin in defiance of her own tears. The very tears she could feel building inside her, but she would not let fall.

Geoffrey stepped forward, reaching out to touch her arm, but she turned away from him. When he spoke, it was to her right shoulder. "They will not say it anymore. I swear."

Caroline lifted her chin, doing her best to look imperial, but knowing she appeared more like a stubborn child. "They will not do it because I will not do it." She turned back to her aunt. "I am done with the social whirl. I shall go back to Hadleigh."

"Hadleigh!" screamed her aunt in a panicked wail. "But whom will you marry?"

"No one!" She intended to march straight out of the room and pack her bags, but Geoffrey's voice stopped her midstep, his words freezing her in place.

"Ah, then I see you are not a true scientist."

She turned slowly to stare at him, fairly shaking at his insult. Each of her next words was a bullet: "I beg your pardon?"

He merely raised an eyebrow, his pose almost casual. "Can you indulge your new scientific interest in Hadleigh?"

She bit her lip. Hadleigh was a small village where one's every action might as well be posted on broadsides. She could not buy a book without its title being known by everyone from the vicar to the stable boy. It would not be possible for her to research human carnal relations without throwing the entire village into a bramble broth of scandal.

She sighed. "You have a point."

"Does that mean you will stay for the remainder of the Little Season?" he asked.

She could hear her aunt holding her breath, anxiously waiting for her decision, but Caroline was not ready to concede yet.

"You still have not answered my question, my lord. Why would you do this for me?" She focused on him, telling him without words she would not budge without an honest answer. She could see him grow more and more uncomfortable with her unwavering regard, but she remained adamant.

Finally, he sighed and stepped forward to take her hands. The gesture was clearly impulsive. She doubted he even realized what he was doing, but that did not stop her from relishing the warmth of his palms against hers or the tingling brush of his fingertips across the backs of her hands. Even before he spoke, she made a mental note to record all the details of his touch for her study. Clearly, he was correct that one could tingle from just a casual touch.

"You are right, Caroline. I am a dandy who cares for nothing except the cut of my coat. But I am also an earl who must marry an heiress." He glanced away, but then as if drawn to her, his gaze returned to face. "I was so close. I thought I had done it. But now." He shrugged and pulled backward, leaving her hands empty and bare. "Now I find myself surrounded by duty and obligations, besieged by responsibilities. And in all that, I find I have one joy, one thing that I do well."

"What?" The word came out as a whispered breath rather than a question.

"I am exceedingly good at bringing young ladies into fashion."

She frowned slightly. "You have done it before?"

His expression became wistful, and his voice distant. "Once. She…she married quite well."

Caroline experienced a flash of intense jealousy, as startling as it was uncharacteristic. The sheer strangeness of it all made her words unusually sharp. "And you want me to reach equally exalted heights of social consequence?"

He turned to her, his greenish-gray eyes the color of a silver maple in summer. "I want you to be happy. Do you honestly expect to find that with Lord Berton?"

Caroline shifted uneasily, the memory of her last humiliating conversation with Harry bitter in her mind. "I…I do not know," she hedged.

"Then stay the rest of the season. Let me introduce you to some of my friends. Who knows what you may find?"

She sighed, knowing she had been outflanked. She had, in fact, been outmaneuvered the moment he took her hands.

Her will seemed to disappear whenever he touched her, and she wanted nothing more than to do whatever he wished. Perhaps there was more of her mother in her than she thought. Obviously, she was easily distracted by her emotions, turned from her course by a handsome man.

That alone was a terrifying thought and enough to make her want to turn tail and run. But then her reason stepped in. Geoffrey had not appealed to her emotions today. He had not used pretty words or expressed abstract notions of joy and delight. He had, in fact, used very logical arguments. If she wanted to pursue her scientific interest, she would have to remain in London. And the only way to remain in London was to continue with the social whirl.

But to think he could bring her into fashion...The idea was absurd. Even she recognized that.

As if reading her thoughts, he frowned and pulled himself up to his fullest height. "You don't believe I can do it, do you?"

She flinched, unwilling to hurt his feelings, but certain no one could do what he proposed. "Some tasks are beyond even the most determined of wills," she said gently.

He laughed, the sound almost bitter. "Consider it my experiment, Caroline. After all, you cannot deny me my own scientific passion even as you have just discovered your own."

She could not. Indeed, she would never stand in the way of any person's scientific endeavor, however foolhardy. She tilted her head to one side, considering her options as she watched the sunlight touch the golden highlights in his brown locks.

"If you intend to bring me into fashion," she said slowly, "we shall be in each other's company a great deal."

He smiled, his expression a mixture of anticipation and fear. "I am afraid so."

"You shall have to squire me about to the most fashionable events."

"Do not forget driving," added her aunt from the sidelines. "You must be seen in the park at least two times a week."

"Of course," agreed the earl.

Meanwhile, Caroline's thoughts returned to her own research, finally accepting that this situation would be best all around. Not only would this plan allow Geoffrey to indulge his own scientific inquiry, but it would give her time to continue her own research. She could study Geoffrey's odd effect on her, discovering if her weakened will was the product of his kiss or her mother's mad blood. Staying in London would also give her plenty of opportunities to compare Geoffrey to other gentlemen. Now that she had experienced his and Harry's embrace, she knew kisses were perhaps as varied as the men who gave them. It was important for her to determine exactly what her reaction was to each of them.

With a little luck, she could have enough information for a preliminary hypothesis by the end of the month.

Suddenly, she was smiling, her heart and mind filled with the excitement of scientific zeal. "Very well, my lord. I gratefully accept your proposition to bring me into fashion. I shall go get my bonnet."

Then she practically floated out of the room, her aunt trailing behind her, spouting all sorts of nonsensical advice on ways to attract young gentlemen.

Geoffrey watched them go with something close to panic in his heart. What had he just done? She had been ready to go back to Hadleigh where she would be well and truly out of his hair. Where she could not do any of her damn experiments in human carnal relations. Where she would no doubt marry the cow-handed Lord Berton and live a life as exciting as…as sheep husbandry.

Geoffrey sighed and collapsed into a nearby chair. There was his answer, of course. Sheep husbandry—the mainstay of his family's finances. It clothed and fed them. It allowed his mother to live within the social whirl she adored. And mostly, it kept them out of debtor's prison.

And it was a fate worse than death.

He could not doom Caroline to that. Certainly not with the priggishly correct Harry as her life's companion. So he had promised to bring her into fashion, practically promised to find her a husband. Good lord, he was becoming as mutton-headed as the sheep he raised.

He scanned the room. When he did not find what he sought, he rang the bell and loudly ordered a decanter of brandy from Mrs. Winnifred Hibbert's shocked butler.

"My lord! What a pleasant surprise to see you in the park today."

Caroline turned toward the source of the shrill voice, smiling politely as Geoffrey greeted the woman and a young girl.

"Good afternoon, Lady Bradlow. Are you perhaps acquainted with Miss Caroline Woodley?"

Caroline nodded and smiled as she met the acid glare of the matron in the carriage beside them. "Yes, of course," the woman replied with a rapid dismissal. Then she turned to the young girl sitting next to her. "Let me present my daughter, Prudence."

"Delighted," Geoffrey said with a congenial smile.

Caroline barely had a moment to acknowledge the young female, clothed in an unfortunate shade of puce, before Geoffrey pushed the horses ahead.

They were driving in Hyde Park. The day was beautiful. The leaves on the trees created a fluttering mixture of fall colors that made Caroline yearn to be inside their boughs, surrounded by their kaleidoscope of color. Instead, she sat primly in the marginally comfortable seat of Geoffrey's landaulet, her ink-stained fingers hidden in the folds of her skirt. All around in carriages, on horseback, and on foot, the fashionable *ton* ogled them like visitors to the royal menagerie.

She felt a freak, and yet somehow she was surviving thanks to Geoffrey's warm presence beside her. His easy banter smoothed over any awkwardness. Twice now he had touched her hand, quietly reassuring her, calming her fluttering nerves. She almost felt comfortable. Even relaxed. Perhaps she could manage the social whirl after all.

"Lord Tallis," called another strident voice. "What a pleasant surprise. Have you met my niece, Miss Kimberly Carver?"

"Good afternoon, baroness," Geoffrey responded, his mellow voice sending silent shivers of delight up Caroline's spine. "Please allow me to introduce the vision that has brought me out of hiding: Miss Caroline Woodley."

Caroline started in shock, then blushed under Geoffrey's warm regard. Good lord, what was he doing practically declaring a romantic interest in her? And in front of the most fearsome gossip of the *ton*! Their names would be on every tongue within an hour.

"Miss Woodley?" From the baroness's tone, that woman felt equally shocked. "Oh, my word. Uh, you look quite elegant today."

"Thank you, baroness," she returned, amazed at her own steady voice. "You are very kind to notice. And your hat is most fetching."

"My dear, please forgive me," interrupted the baroness in an overly loud tone. "I fear I must point out that you should avoid wearing white." She leaned forward, her breath foul in Caroline's face. "It looks most odd on one of your years. One cannot help but compare you to…" Her voice faded as her gaze slid to her young niece, a dark-haired beauty in virginal white.

As insults went, it was a minor one. But it came at just the wrong moment. Caroline had begun to relax, to actually believe that she could be fashionable, beautiful, perhaps even sought after. With Geoffrey smiling at her, his easy manner relaxing her, she had thought perhaps he could indeed succeed in his experiment.

Until the baroness's spiteful comment. At that moment, Caroline recalled that some things could never happen. She felt the blood drain from her face as she became excruciatingly aware of her advanced age. Compared to the pubescent Kimberly, she no doubt looked like the ape leader she was. That she was a bluestocking as well made this whole charade seem totally hopeless.

What little courage she had gained rapidly failed her. Not even Geoffrey could bring her into fashion, she realized with disgust. Stifling her sigh, she managed a wan smile for the obnoxious gossip. She was on the verge of politely thanking the shrew for her advice, ill meant though it was, when Geoffrey spoke.

"If you will excuse us, baroness, we must be going on." His voice was clipped with anger, and Caroline was momentarily stunned. She had never imagined Geoffrey could be so cold.

The baroness must have felt the same way. Her face paled to a sick shade of gray, and her mouth flopped open in shock. "My lord!"

"Allow me to proffer my regrets regarding your niece's come-out ball. I am afraid I shall be unable to attend. My mother, sister, and Lord Wyclyff naturally send their apologies. Oh, and the Earl of Mavenford and his lovely wife will no doubt be otherwise occupied as well." His smile was everything that was polite, but Caroline could see the chilling cold in his eyes.

"My lord!" the baroness gasped. Her rigid spine now bowed as if from an enormous weight, and she braced herself with both hands.

"If you will excuse us." Geoffrey turned his back on the unfortunate lady and quickly maneuvered the carriage out of Hyde Park and the fashionable throng.

Caroline waited in silence, noting his clenched fists and tightened jaw. She did not speak until they were out of sight of the park, tooling along a less dense lane, well away from the debacle.

"Do not be concerned, my lord," she said softly. "Every scientist picks the wrong experiment sometimes. Why, my father has done it countless times. I do believe my aunt discussed father's cannon experiments with you." She glanced sideways at him, wondering if her attempt at humor had lightened his expression. What she saw drew her up short. He was frowning at her, his expression fierce.

"What the devil are you talking about?"

"Why, th—the baroness," she stammered. "The gossips will always say awful things, if not to my face, then behind my back."

His expression changed into a gentle smile. "On the contrary, Caroline, that shrew will now go fair out of her way to say lovely things about you."

"But why?"

"She hopes—in vain, I might add—that I will forgive her and attend her niece's come-out."

Caroline nodded, seeing that perhaps he had managed to manipulate the baroness to their side. Unfortunately, she knew many other queens of the *ton* would not be so easily swayed. And the more popular she became, the more venomous the gossip that would surround her. Especially since uglier words than bluestocking attached to her family tree.

"It will be harder than you think," she said softly.

"What?" He did not look at her as he spoke, keeping his attention focused on avoiding an upset applecart, but she knew he was more than aware of her presence. He was, in fact, probably regretting it.

"I know it is a hard thing, sponsoring a bluestocking," she said. He flinched but did not answer, not that she gave him much opportunity as she continued, "It is quite acceptable for you to back out of your promise, my lord. I find it equally arduous to be polite to empty-headed shrews and spiteful mamas. Let us just say your experiment had failed and proceed accordingly."

Suddenly she was jerked sideways in her seat as he hauled backward on the reins so hard his horses shied.

"Geoffrey!" she exclaimed as she grabbed for the edge of her seat.

Fortunately, he was a master with a whip, despite his angry gesture, and he quickly pulled his pair to a stop beside a nearly deserted park. Then he sat there, his hands clenched into fists, his breathing harsh.

She waited in silence, steadying her own nervous breathing before sneaking a sidelong glance at his set countenance.

"Do not ever do that again." His words were low and angry.

"What?"

"Do not ever speak of yourself as an experiment." She flinched at his hard tone. Even to the overweening baroness, he had retained some veneer of pleasantness. But with her now, it was as if she had threatened to kill his only child.

She bit her lip and frowned, trying to make sense of the odd reaction. "But I did not speak of myself as an experiment. I referred to this ridiculous attempt to bring me into fashion. It is tedious and humiliating to pander to them." She twisted and gave his profile a hard look. "I know you hate it as much as I do."

He turned to her, one dark brown eyebrow raised in cynical mockery. "On the contrary, I find particular satisfaction in throwing over the tabbies. They do not know whether they have misjudged my fortune or yours."

She shook her head, refusing to believe he enjoyed fighting the nastiness so prevalent among the women of the *ton*. "You are too cynical, my lord, for one so young."

His response was a brief, bitter laugh. Then his eyes softened to a gentleness that belied his attitude. "Tell me, Caroline. What were you about to say to the baroness? The one who gave you that snide advice on the color of your gown?"

Caroline shrugged, not wanting to remember the exchange. "I do not know. Something polite."

"A thank-you perhaps? Even though she meant to point out your age in the most insulting of ways?"

"I gain nothing by repaying her in kind, my lord."

"Exactly." He reached forward, absently touching a tendril of hair that had escaped the confines of her bonnet. "You are a true lady, Caroline. One who is polite and gracious no matter what the circumstances. Of course I enjoy squiring you about. Mostly because I like showing them exactly what a true lady is like." Then his finger slid across her cheek, trailing heat in its wake. When he finally stopped, he rubbed across her bottom lip, the smoky heat of his gaze holding her transfixed. "You were wonderful today."

Her mouth felt suddenly dry, and she unconsciously licked her lips, accidentally touching his thumb. She felt the texture of it, rough with callous but still infinitely fascinating. Curious, she extended her tongue again, tentatively stroking it back and forth, exploring the taste and feel of his thumb.

"Caroline," he growled, his voice dark with warning, but she was too intrigued to heed him. His eyes seemed to blaze into hers even as his pupils dilated, darkening his gaze until his irises appeared almost entirely black.

This morning, she had schemed and planned for a kiss from Harry. But at this moment, the thought of Geoffrey's kiss all but consumed her. She leaned forward, tilting her head up. He did not release her. Instead, his finger pressed harder against her lip, drawing her jaw down, her mouth open.

And then he descended. The moment he touched her lips, heat flooded her senses. His mouth pressed hard and hot against hers while his tongue swept inside. His hand shifted, cupping her cheek while his long fingers drew her ever closer to him. Her head fell back, and her mouth opened even wider. His tongue pushed deeper, then pulled back, then probed harder still, stoking a fire within her.

She mimicked his motions, learning from him even while trying to absorb the sensations that spread like a flash fire through her entire body. Then she felt his other hand, like a hot brand on her ribs, inching ever so slowly up her bodice. She whimpered, not even knowing why.

"'Ey now! Ain't no cause t' be doing that 'ere!"

She felt Geoffrey's entire body stiffen at the rude voice beside them. Then he abruptly drew away from her, his expression dark, his skin flushed red as he glared at the hackney driver beside them. For her part, Caroline could only gasp in alarm, realizing what they had been doing and in broad daylight no less! She hastily looked around, grateful that they were well away from the fashionable throng. She saw no one but a few street urchins and the other driver who was even now moving ahead.

Without a word, Geoffrey gathered the reins, clicking his horses into a brisk trot as soon as the road ahead was clear. Caroline also remained in silence, using the time to gather her scattered thoughts. She was so distracted, it took a good three minutes before she remembered to mentally catalogue her impressions of the kiss. And even then, her thoughts tended to very unscientific descriptions more appropriate to poetry than research.

"I am terribly sorry, Caroline. That was unforgivable."

She jumped, startled by the recrimination in his voice. And when she turned to look at him, Geoffrey appeared hunched, as if hiding—though from what she hadn't a clue. Worst of all, he chose that moment to turn to her, his gray eyes still dark, but this time with clear guilt.

"Why?" she asked.

She saw the muscles in his jaw clench, but he still managed to answer. "I may have just ruined you. Good God, we were completely exposed."

She smiled, reassured that she could easily calm his distress. "But no one saw us."

"We cannot be sure."

She reached out, touching the taut muscle in his forearm. "Of course we can. If someone did, there will be gossip."

"That is what—"

"And if there is, we shall simply explain that it was science. Research. I intend to write a treatise, you know."

His groan seemed to erupt from his entire body.

"I shall publish it under a pseudonym, of course. Ooh!" she suddenly gasped. "And you were just about to touch my bodice, too, weren't you? Oh, how wonderful you remembered." She squeezed his arm in appreciation.

"Caroline!" he cried, clearly exasperated, but she would have none of it. How like a man to be so concerned with silly notions of propriety when she was discussing science.

Unless, of course, she misunderstood the situation. She straightened, suddenly concerned. Perhaps he was upset for an entirely different reason. She studied his profile, trying to read his expression while he apparently concentrated on maneuvering through the streets. She could not guess at his thoughts except to know that they were very dark. How she wished he would smile.

"My lord," she began. "Geoffrey. It occurs to me that the woman plays a part in these kisses."

"Caroline—"

"No, do not cut me off. I wish to know." She swallowed. "Do not fear that you will hurt my feelings. I am a scientist, after all, and this is all part of my study." She straightened, disconcerted by her own question, but determined to have an answer nonetheless. "Did I do it wrong? Perhaps I am the one to blame for Harry's inability to make me tingle. For…" Her voice trailed away. Perhaps Geoffrey was angry now because she had somehow bungled his kiss. No man wished to appear the fool. And especially not in matters concerning kisses. "I am sure whatever went wrong was all my fault. If you would but explain to me what I need to do…" Her voice faded off on a hopeful note.

Meanwhile, Geoffrey slowed the horses, easing them into a sedate walk. To either side, tall trees shaded the lane, their leaves serenely beautiful in their fall colors. But Caroline could barely acknowledge them as her body coiled tight with anxiety while Geoffrey took much too long to answer.

"Caroline," he finally said, his voice infinitely sad. "You were perfect. Indeed, you shall set the standards by which I will choose my future wife."

She winced, and the glow that had begun inside her was eclipsed by surprise. "There are standards? In kissing?"

His expression lightened as his lips curved into a slight smile. "In all things, not just kissing. And you have set the bar very high. I fear there are few who will match you."

He was sincerely complimenting her. She could feel that he meant every word, could see the honesty in his still-smoldering gaze. And yet, for all that, she felt cold. "But your main criteria shall be money."

His gaze skittered away, and he turned back to the horses. "Yes. Unfortunately, that is all too true."

She leaned forward, resting her hand lightly on top of his. "Did the woman you sponsored before…Did she meet your standards? Was she a real lady?"

Caroline felt him stiffen beneath her fingertips, and she reluctantly withdrew her touch. When he answered, it was simple, the inflection in his voice curiously flat. "Yes. Gillian is a true lady."

She continued to study Geoffrey, seeing the stiffness in his shoulders, the slight clench in his hands as he held the reins. He felt pain when discussing this Gillian, she deduced. And she experienced an answering stab within her. "You must have loved her very much," she finally guessed.

She thought he would descend into another one of his bitter laughs, but he did not. He remained as still as if he were carved from granite, his jaw barely shifting as he spoke. "No, I did not love her. At least not nearly as much as Stephen did."

Caroline felt some surprise at that answer. "But how can you know that?"

He turned, and she was startled to see that the fire in his eyes had gone out. Now they seemed hard and cold as he spoke. "Because I was not willing to court social ruin to have her." He paused to make sure he had her complete attention. "Remember that, Caroline. There is a limit to what I will risk for anyone. Even you."

And with that, he eased them onto the lane in front of her aunt's house. Moments later, he bowed over her hand and left her at the door.

# CHAPTER 5

Geoffrey glared across his pocked and ancient desk at Mr. Jeremy Oltheton, his young solicitor. "You are certain?" he asked. "There are no others?" As he spoke, he toyed with a short stack of pages, each detailing a different young lady, her family, and her financial prospects.

It was a very short stack.

The young solicitor shook his head. "None, my lord. Your mother and I have worked most assiduously on this."

"Of course you have," Geoffrey returned, his heart sinking as he spread out the pages before him. Five pages. Five girls. And if all five combined their intellects together, they would still be unable to discover one original thought.

Obviously anxious to please, Mr. Oltheton leaned forward, his voice rising in pitch with his enthusiasm. "You may have noticed I ranked each of their fortunes as to how well their dowries will complement your own holdings. Naturally, I gave preference to properties that could be easily sold to generate ready cash."

"Naturally," murmured Geoffrey, his fingertip sliding over each girl's list of accomplishments. Each one sang and played an instrument. One painted as well. Another appeared quite fond of embroidery. "Can any of them read?" he wondered aloud.

"My lord?"

Geoffrey looked up. "Can they all read? Not just correspondence, but actual books."

"I am sure they are all well versed in the classics. I believe Miss Danes enjoys Minerva novels—"

"What about scientific papers? Academic studies?"

Mr. Oltheton shifted nervously. "My lord, that would be most unusual."

Geoffrey pushed away from his desk, his words curt. "And can any of them write?"

"Write?" squeaked the young man, becoming more distressed by the second. "I am sure their correspondence—"

"Not silly social letters," Geoffrey snapped as he paced about his desk, "but intelligent studies, biological and chemical experiments, or some other such thing."

Suddenly his solicitor's face brightened on a cry of delight. "Oh, my lord, I understand now. You wish to know if any of these ladies is involved in anything scandalous!" The young man bobbed his head. "You know your mother would be aware of the obvious social scandals. You wish to see if I have adequately searched for any more unusual peccadilloes. Well," he exclaimed with a gleeful clap of his hands, "let me set your mind at ease. None of those ladies have any unusual interests. Indeed, they are the epitome of what one would expect in a Tallis countess. Familiarity with the workings of society. Purity in mind and body, of course. Comely in their own particular ways. And not a hair or step out of place. Ever."

Geoffrey did not answer. His chest had constricted so much that he found it difficult to breathe. He simply stood there, his thumb toying with a hole in the seam of his pants, while his solicitor continued to babble.

"Indeed, I am quite certain that you shall be equally happy with any of the young ladies."

Geoffrey raised a single eyebrow, his sense of doom shifting into a hot rush of fury. "Do you mean to tell me that I could marry any one of them?"

"Of course, my lord."

"That it makes no difference who? Indeed, the ladies are similar enough as to be interchangeable?"

Mr. Oltheton beamed. "Exactly, my lord!"

"Get out!" he exploded.

The young man was so startled he practically jumped across the room, his only response a muffled shriek of alarm.

Geoffrey stared at his solicitor, then closed his eyes, mentally reining in his temper before he gave the chap a seizure. With a groan of disgust, he turned away, leaning against the window to allow the cool glass to leech heat from his side. "Leave, Jeremy. I am weary of this."

Geoffrey heard the unmistakable sounds of the young man hastily grabbing his papers. Worse still, he heard the boy begin to babble in his nervousness. "I am so sorry if I offended you, my lord. You did say you wanted me to be thorough. And your mother's requirements were most specific."

Geoffrey pressed his forehead against the glass, wondering if the cold would aid his headache. "You have done an excellent job, Jeremy. I am merely out of sorts."

"Of course, my lord. Of course. Should you wish to discuss this at a later time, perhaps when you are ready to make your choice, I am, of course, always available."

Geoffrey could not restrain a bitter laugh. "I assure you, even if all five ladies lined up before me, clergyman in hand, I would not discuss this one jot more." He turned to pin the solicitor with a heavy stare. "Now I suggest you leave before I find another reason to release my ill temper upon you."

The boy nodded quickly, his Adam's apple bobbing as he swallowed his anxiety. "Of course, my lord. As you wish. We will not discuss this again. I certainly won't. I would never. I am most discreet, I assure you. I—"

"Good-bye, Jeremy," he returned wearily. "Come back on Thursday with your thoughts on how best to sell the mines."

The boy's features flooded with relief. "Of course. I shall be here directly at nine. I shall work most assiduously—"

Geoffrey did not let him finish, shutting the library door with a ponderous thud, narrowly missing the boy's bowed head. With a loud curse, he threw himself back in his chair, then twisted around to stare out the dirty window.

Why was it the most brilliant minds had the most bizarre personalities? His young solicitor possessed the keenest brain Geoffrey had yet to find. Unfortunately, Jeremy's brilliance was nearly obscured by the boy's rabbit like nervousness. The slightest sign of intemperance from Geoffrey had the boy nearly prostrate with fear. Indeed, during the first year they worked together, Jeremy had been more prone to squeaks of alarm than actual conversation.

At least the tic was gone. Thank God for small favors.

Geoffrey wondered what poor Jeremy would do were he the one who had to woo an heiress. No doubt try to impress her with complex investment strategy analyses before running in terror should the lady ever be so bold as to try and kiss him. No, the lady destined to love his solicitor would have to be of a similar bent. She would need a mind equal to the young man's, a mind capable of being impressed by brilliant management of sheep stock and copper mines. Indeed, she would likely have to approach life from a similarly unique perspective, couching everything she did in scientific terms, for example. Why, even her kisses would have to be seen as an experiment!

In short, he decided, Miss Woodley would be a perfect mate for his young Mr. Oltheton, and he for her.

With a sudden curse, Geoffrey swept the pages off his desk, flinging them toward the hearth where they fluttered aimlessly before settling on the cold grate. Good God, what had happened to his life? Less than a week ago, his finances had been solid, or at least nearly so. His investments had been coming around. His life had finally found an even keel.

For a moment, he had even thought about buying a boat. Something small that he could learn to sail by himself on those rare days when there were no sheep to sheer, no mines to oversee. Nowhere in his secret thoughts had he ever said, "I want to be a matchmaker." Nowhere did he ever think he could possibly enjoy analyzing women according to their fortunes or evaluating men by their peccadilloes.

And yet here he sat: promised to introduce Miss Woodley to eligible young men and studying numbers that ranked eligible young heiresses. While all the time his thoughts centered somewhere else entirely. Somewhere scandalous.

On an illicit kiss.

Good lord, what would that last impulsive act cost him? It had already destroyed his equilibrium. From that first kiss during his mother's birthday ball, Caroline Woodley had occupied his thoughts. An odd creature, he called her in his mind. A beautiful woman intent on scientific discovery. The very thought was beguiling.

He should have realized he had no room in his life for such puzzles, beautiful or not. His life was comprised of sheep stock, mine shares, profit-and-loss columns neatly tabulated. And yet, he had gone to her home anyway. He'd only meant to return her fan, he remembered.

Except by the time he quit the Woodley household, he'd found himself embroiled in a plot to find the girl a husband! It suited his sense of challenge, he told himself, to bring the unique Caroline into fashion. Merely a game he enjoyed playing to lighten the burden of his real work: the getting of an heiress.

Naturally he had gone driving with her. Naturally she had shone like the diamond she was, the light of her sweet purity illuminating the spiteful reality that was the rest of the *ton*.

He had been captivated. He did not need to pretend warm, lingering looks in her direction. Indeed, he had found himself unable to tear his eyes from her. No societal maneuvering had prompted him to touch her. His fingers had found her cheek of their own accord, needed to stroke the sensuous line of her face. To caress the full lush curve of her lips. To draw open her mouth so he could plunder it.

He'd never thought about where they were. He'd forgotten they were sitting in broad daylight on the open seat of his carriage. No guardian angel had whispered into his ear about honor or propriety or, most base of all, that Caroline was not an heiress. In fact, were it not for that rude hackney driver, God only knows what he would have done.

Touching her bodice would have been the least of it. Sweet heaven, he was insane. What could have possessed him to toy with her like that? To play fast and loose with her reputation when he knew he could not marry her. She was not an heiress. He repeated the words out loud, just to make sure his poor brain would understand. "She is not an heiress."

His only hope was to find her a gentleman to wed immediately before he lost control once again.

"Miss Woodley, please allow me to introduce Lords Hillman and Powell. Gentlemen, this is Miss Woodley." Geoffrey tried not to grimace as he watched yet another pair of gentlemen bow over Caroline's hand.

His ploy had worked. Their excursion in Hyde Park five days ago and his attentive interest for the last several evenings had all combined to increase Caroline's consequence a hundredfold. Men were coming out of the woodwork to gain an introduction to society's newest mystery. What could there possibly be in the bluestocking, hitherto unnoticed wallflower Caroline Woodley that could attract the notable Earl of Tallis? They were practically tripping over themselves to find out.

And, better yet, not a breath of their illicit kiss had disturbed her growing popularity. Perversely, his temper soured even more while Caroline's circle of gentlemen grew larger. He found it disconcertingly easy to play the annoyed suitor. After all, he was the one who'd discovered the delectable mind beneath her quiet exterior, and yet here he was, decidedly outside her circle.

Still, he could not quarrel with the effects of his efforts. The attention seemed to give Caroline her own special glow that he, and every other male, found enchanting. She was dressed tonight in a simple white gown with an overnetting of gold. He could not decide if she appeared a princess or an angel. In either case, she was beautiful as her dark eyes laughed at some young buck's silliness.

Truly, Caroline had come into her element, he realized with almost paternal pride. Unfortunately, her element did not seem to include him. With an annoyed groan, he turned his attention elsewhere. He had better take himself off soon or his foul mood would start scaring off these obnoxious puppies.

Fortunately for him, the last few days had also done wonders for his own consequence. He let his gaze wander over the room, intercepting nearly a dozen flirtatious looks, hungry gazes, or frankly assessing stares. The female mind liked nothing better than a challenge, and his presence with one of society's leading bluestockings was a white glove thrown in the face of many of the reigning beauties. They were intrigued, they were shocked, they were doing anything in their power to speak with him. No one seemed to notice that he had worn the same clothing to the last three balls.

It made it so much easier to find an heiress if the ladies did most of the work.

Glancing back at Caroline, he found her in conversation with Perry Fairfax. From the snippets he could hear, they discussed sheep, of all things. Well, he thought with a shrug, Perry always had been a bit of a muttonhead. At least they were not speaking about Lord Whitley's latest paramour. In fact, he realized with a touch of surprise, Caroline had not behaved awkwardly at all. She did not stammer or blush or do any of the silly things she'd done in his presence.

Until now, he had only seen her so serene when elbow deep in science. Somewhere, somehow, Caroline had found her confidence.

He shifted uneasily, alarms ringing in his head at the thought. Could she be continuing with her experiments? Was that what she was doing now? And doing more than cataloguing kisses on her hand? He shook his head, convincing himself it was not possible. She was much too busy going to parties and routs to indulge in her shocking scientific inquiry. Her newfound poise was the natural result of having gentlemen practically hanging on her every word.

He looked behind her to Mrs. Hibbert. Caroline's poor aunt was clearly torn between pride at her niece's accomplishments and overwhelming anxiety about the girl's performance. He smiled reassuringly at her.

Caroline was fine. His work here was done. It was time he went on to his own task. Geoffrey sighed, fighting back the depression that suddenly engulfed his heart.

God, he hated the Marriage Mart.

With a strained smile, he turned, intending to take his leave of Caroline, but was unable to find a suitable opening. She was literally surrounded, and he had not the heart to force himself through. So he bowed discreetly to her aunt and took himself off to the nearest heiress.

What number had Jeremy assigned to this one? Ah yes, she was third on his recommended list of heiress. At least she was blonde. For some bizarre reason, he currently had a marked preference for light-colored hair.

Caroline watched Geoffrey leave with a mixture of dismay and relief. Her dismay was understandable. In the last few days, she had come to rely on his reassuring presence, his ability to make her smile even from across the room. Her relief came because she was finally out from under his watchful eye. She knew that deep down, he did not quite approve of her interest in studying human carnal relations, and so she had been scrupulously correct while he stood nearby. It had been a sore trial to her patience, but then she knew his mere presence would invalidate any of her new information anyway.

For some reason she had yet to understand, his very person seemed to cause the oddest sensations within her. His merest glance or slightest touch could heat her blood until she actually found it difficult to breathe. Then, odder still, his absence weighed upon her, the minutes creeping by until he next appeared.

One could not make accurate scientific investigations when in such a state. Indeed, she had nearly thirty pages of notes detailing the exact sensations the flooded her system whenever the merest thought of Geoffrey spun through her mind.

Unfortunately, accurate scientific research required comparisons. As she had told Geoffrey before, a single kiss—or rather two kisses now—simply were not adequate statistical samples. So, despite her great interest in further kisses with Geoffrey, logic demanded that she remain true to her scientific inquiry. And that meant further research. Except given Geoffrey's effect on her, she had to wait until he left her side.

So she sat, her emotions in turmoil, both regretting and anxiously waiting that moment when he finally took himself off to find his heiress. And now that it was here, she had trouble shaking off a deep feeling of melancholy. She watched him out of the corner of her eye as he sifted his way to a beautiful blonde, her hair so light as to be almost white. Within moments, the lucky girl was smiling, her laughter free and easy as Geoffrey bowed over her hand.

Caroline's stomach clenched tightly within her. She could not watch, could not bear the sight of him sacrificing himself on his family's financial altar. But she knew nothing she said would deter him from his course. He had too much pride in his family honor. It was best she let him go his way while she finally went on hers.

After all, she had a scientific inquiry to begin.

She tilted her head, scanning the young gentlemen around her until she decided on her most likely prospect.

"Perry," she exclaimed, waving her fan vigorously before her. "It is so desperately hot in here. Would you mind taking a stroll with me outside?"

As expected, Lord Derbarough leaped to her side, offering her his arm.

"Oh, thank you," she breathed. "But please, would you mind standing on the other side? I shall need you there when we begin our...uh, never mind. Yes, that is perfect."

Then she gave him her sweetest smile as she allowed him to escort her outside.

Geoffrey's next hours were boring, annoying, and absolutely necessary. He danced with young misses with dowries of varying sizes, but all were moderately wealthy. Sophia's wedding was less than three weeks away, and Geoffrey had to be married by then so he could pass on his own wife's dowry to his sister.

It soured his gut to think of what he did, but honor demanded nothing less, ironic though it seemed.

He was so occupied with the parade of potential brides that it was not until just after the supper buffet that he noticed something odd happening. Caroline kept disappearing. He was not positive, but a little time spent in careful observation revealed quite a disturbing pattern.

Caroline would dance with a gentleman, then decline a second turn, choosing instead to stroll out of the ballroom with the man. At first Geoffrey thought she simply was going in search of some lemonade. Once she and her companion wandered into the card room. But while she invariably returned in time for the next set, she would be gone again for the one after that.

Good Lord, what was the chit doing? She could not possibly be continuing her experimentation, could she? They had agreed that she would confine herself to kisses upon her hand. He'd most distinctly said her hand. And she might expand into dancing—if she felt it absolutely necessary.

Where was her aunt? As quickly as he possibly could, he disengaged himself from his current heiress-candidate and went in search of either Caroline or her aunt. He found the aunt first, sitting companionably with his own mother, of all people, chatting up a storm. He wasted no time on niceties.

"Where is Caroline?" he demanded, rudely cutting into their comfortable coze.

"Geoffrey!" admonished his mother. "Yorkshire seems to have badly damaged your manners."

He barely spared his parent a glance, focusing instead on Mrs. Hibbert. She turned, her eyes widening in shock at his abrupt behavior. "W-Well, I am not entirely sure, my lord," she stammered. "Is she dancing?"

"No, she is not." He scowled down at the woman. "You do not know where she has gone?"

Mrs. Hibbert scanned the crowd, her forehead wrinkling as she peered at the dance floor. "Well, she is definitely not dancing."

"I already told you that," he ground out, wondering what had happened to him that his temper was so short.

"Then she is no doubt getting some lemonade or taking a tour of the card room."

"I think," he said tersely, "that she may be luring young men into the gardens."

"Geoffrey, please," cut in his mother. "Your implication is simply appalling."

Mrs. Hibbert frowned, her expression frosty as she spoke in stiff tones. "You have been most gracious in your attentions to Caroline, but I would remind you she is a sensible girl. You know she dislikes the frivolity of dancing. Perhaps she wanted a few moments of private conversation with one of her young gentlemen, but she would hardly lure anyone anywhere."

"But—" he began.

"Your concerns are most unnecessary, my lord," Mrs. Hibbert said coldly.

Geoffrey glared down at the two ladies, each staring back at him with a mixture of confusion and censure. They had no idea, he realized with sudden shock. They did not in the least bit suspect the deviousness of Caroline's mind. Or if they did, they had not the tiniest suspicion of her latest scientific inquisition.

With a muttered oath, he spun on his heel. Clearly, it was up to him. Since he could not bring himself to tell the sweet Mrs. Hibbert that her niece was not the angel she believed, it fell to him to try to somehow moderate the willful Caroline's behavior.

And that meant searching her out in the garden. But where? Lady Bedford's backyard was almost as bad as Vauxhall Garden's Dark Way for hidey holes and quiet places for lovers' trysts. It was, in fact, why he had chosen this particular evening's entertainment just outside of London. He'd hoped to lure some sweet heiress out into the moonlight. The thought that Caroline did the very same thing with other gentlemen set his blood to a slow boil of anger.

After five minutes of searching in the back greenery, he had seen so many couples and scrutinized so many gentlemen engaged in less-than-gentlemanly pursuits, he was in a towering rage.

Where was she?

"Really, sir! You are not doing this in the prescribed manne—umph!"

He'd found her! He knew it. No other lady would protest unseemly advances in so...erudite a manner. Geoffrey paused only a moment to focus in on the sound before crashing through a row of bushes.

What he saw was something out of a nightmare. Caroline was in the grips of some huge, thick-set man with wayward hands. Even as Geoffrey watched, the so-called gentleman worked on unfastening her bodice as he pushed her roughly toward the ground.

"Really, sir, this is not at all—*umph*."

Geoffrey did not hesitate. With one swift movement he lifted the man off Caroline, sending him reeling backward into a nearby tree.

"Wha—?"

Geoffrey caught a glimpse of thick lips and a red face before he planted his fist dead center in the man's leer.

The boor went down like a stone.

Geoffrey turned quickly, searching for Caroline. She sat flat on the ground, her mouth slightly ajar, staring at his still-clenched fist.

"Good show," she breathed, clearly awed by the power of his punch. "But hardly necessary."

"Hardly necessary?" he sputtered. "In another moment, he would have had you spread out beneath him like a damned tart." The very thought made his stomach clench painfully in his gut.

"Nonsense, my lord," she returned as she nimbly gained her feet. "I am not completely defenseless. I was just loath to use such drastic measures against one of my father's dearest friends."

He gaped at her. "Drastic measures?"

She lifted her gaze from where she brushed off her skirt. "A blow to the groin can cause permanent damage to one's ability to produce offspring."

He blinked, a part of him dazed that she was not falling on him in gratitude for her rescue. "I had not realized your pugilistic education was so thorough," he said dryly.

"Oh yes. Harry's lessons were most extensive. He did not wish anyone to take advantage of my innocent nature."

"Of your…" he repeated, his thoughts reeling. He grabbed her by the arm, trying to pull her away from the odious scene. "Then what in the name of Heaven were you waiting for? You should have hit him immediately."

She blinked at him, her head tilted to one side. "I had not yet completed my study of the subject."

He ground his teeth in frustration, realizing all his fears were indeed correct. "You *are* continuing with your wretched experiment."

She lifted her chin, clearly stung that he could possibly think otherwise. "Well, of course I am."

"I thought we agreed you would study the effects of a kiss on your *hand*."

She nodded. "I did that."

"Impossible," he retorted as he clenched his hands. "You could not have gotten a...a..." What were the blasted words she'd used?

"A statistical sampling?"

"Yes!"

"I did." She tilted her head, looking at him through her wide blue eyes. "A great many gentleman have kissed my hand lately, my lord. Indeed, it was growing quite tedious."

He could not argue with that. He had certainly found it alarmingly irksome. "But then you were going to study dancing...that moment before the set began?"

She sighed, looking a bit apologetic as she spoke. "Yes, well, I know you found that moment particularly appealing, but I must confess that I don't find it at all interesting. Perhaps," she added on a hopeful note, "you should begin a study. I would be delighted to hear your conclusions once you've completed your work."

He gaped at her. Did she honestly expect him to perform a study of dancing? Pushing aside the ludicrous thought, he focused on the subject at hand. "When did you decide to compare kisses?" Then his heart seemed to leap into his throat as a horrifying thought occurred to him. "You are just comparing kisses, aren't you? Nothing else?" He did not want to speculate where else her bizarre mind had taken her.

"Just kisses, my lord." She drew a sheet of foolscap out of her gown pocket with a mischievous grin. "And I have made a great deal of progress just this evening!"

He grabbed at the thin piece of paper, snatching it out of her hand. "Not while I am sponsoring you," he growled as he took hold of her arm and tried to forcibly draw her away. She looked longingly at the foolscap, then resisted.

Her eyes traveled back to the prone figure of her latest "subject."

"Should we move Mr. Loots? He looks most uncomfortable."

Geoffrey turned, pausing long enough to make sure the blackguard was merely unconscious and not dead. As soon as he saw the telltale lift of Loots's chest as the man breathed, he lost all interest in the man's comfort. "Leave him," he said, his voice clipped as he tugged on Caroline's arm.

She dug in her feet and twisted around. "But he is one of my father's friends. They are in the Chemical Society together."

Geoffrey froze, his eyes suddenly narrowing on her. "You are not enamored of him, are you?"

Her response was gratifyingly quick. "Mr. Loots? Of course not, and certainly not after that display." She frowned down at the big man. "He was most unwilling to take the simplest direction."

"What?"

"I was using him for comparative purposes," she continued as if he had not spoken. "Except for my aunt's footman, Loots is the only non-titled gentleman who fit the parameters of my research. But as he is much older and an eligible suitor, I decided it would be best if I included him, too, in my experiment."

Geoffrey's grip tightened on her arm, but he kept his voice low. He knew if he allowed himself a full breath, he would end up shouting. "You kissed the footman? On the mouth?"

"Oh yes." She grinned impishly up at him. "He was quite the youngest man of my acquaintance. I thought perhaps youth was all that was required for certain necessary physical effects. They seem to be more enthusiastic in their efforts, and enthusiasm does seem to help. Of course," she noted with a frown, "Mr. Loots was also enthusiastic, and he is quite old. Almost forty, I believe."

"Bloody hell." Had she immediately upon leaving him flouted his suggestion to stick to kissing hands?

She lifted her gaze, suddenly focusing on him. "You are also one of my older gentlemen, though not quite as aged as Mr. Loots. But I would not describe your kiss as enthusiastic, as much as..." Her voice trailed away as she searched for the appropriate word. "*Practiced.* You are quite practiced in kissing, are you not?"

His spine stiffened uncomfortably. "My practice, as you put it, is absolutely none of your concern."

She pouted, her full red bottom lip drawing a reaction from his body even as his mind was still in the grip of a towering rage. "Oh, very well," she said on a resigned sigh. "If you no longer wish to assist me in my investigation, that is certainly your right. But I will thank you next time," she said, directing a telling glance at the unconscious Mr. Loots, "to delay your interference until a more appropriate time. As it is, I shall have to invalidate this entire experience with Mr. Loots." And with that, she deftly snatched her piece of foolscap back, meticulously smoothing out the creases before returning it to her gown pocket.

He rounded on her, shocked at her outrageousness. "Delay my interference! Good God, woman—"

"I keep telling you I had the situation under control. Mr. Loots was simply overly enthusiastic. I am sure after a sharper rebuke on my part, he would have settled down, and we could have completed the experiment in better form. But I can hardly have him kiss me now. Even if he were awake, constant dread of your hard fives would undermine the entire process." She sighed. "It was most vexing of you, you know."

"My most abject apologies for standing in the way of medical science," he ground out. Then he grabbed her arm and hauled her away, down a darker garden path to a more private location where he could pound some sense into the woman once and for all.

He brought her to a quiet spot and set her against the wall beneath a looming locust tree. They seemed very removed from the evening's activities there. The moonlight barely filtered through the dazzling fall colors that surrounded them, and the bright yellow leaves of the tree kept a steady rainfall of gold onto her hair.

She looked beautiful. The moonlight touched her dark eyes with silver, and with a leafy bower beneath her and the crisp scent of autumn in the air, he would be hard put to find a more idyllic location. But he was much too furious to do more than note the flush of color on her cheeks and the dreamy look in her eyes.

"This is the very spot I have been taking my gentlemen," she commented. "It is so delightfully romantic." Then she frowned slightly. "Although gentlemen seem to take much less notice of the environment than I do."

Her mention of her "gentlemen" quickly recalled him to his purpose. Stepping back from her tantalizing body, he straightened his coat and took a deep breath. "You cannot continue this nonsense, Caroline."

"But—"

"No," he cut her off. "You cannot go around kissing every man you meet on the mouth."

"But I do not!"

"You just pick the fashionable, eligible ones," he said grimly.

"Absolutely not!" she responded, clearly insulted. "I choose the ones that fit the area I am particularly interested in researching at the moment."

He shuddered to think exactly what interested her in the heavyset Mr. Loots. He teetered on the verge of demanding a detailed explanation of her idiocy when a golden leaf spun from the tree above them to land right on the soft curve of her breast. He reached out instinctively, brushing it away with the lightest of touches, but his hand lingered, tingling and hot. She gasped at his touch, and he felt as much as saw the hot blush that burned just beneath his fingertips.

He whipped his hand back, startled by the fierce reaction of his body, angry at his sudden loss of control. "You cannot continue!" he ordered brusquely, wondering exactly whom he spoke to. "It is immoral, unseemly, and cruel."

She flinched away from his tone, but refused to give way before his anger. "Immoral? Unseemly and cruel?" she asked.

He nodded, sure that was exactly what he meant.

"As opposed to your behavior flirting with heiresses so you can give their money to your sister."

He blanched. She had scored a true hit. His actions were no more honorable than her own. Just more socially acceptable. Somehow it made him all the more determined to prevent her from continuing. He had to make her understand.

"Very well, then," he finally said, his tone resigned. "It is dangerous. Forget your reputation, Caroline, and your aunt's reaction if she were to discover your actions." She paled at his words, but he continued, pushing his advantage. "How long until you meet a man you cannot control with a well-placed kick?"

She thought about that, her focus turning inward as she worried at her lower lip. "No line of inquiry is without its dangers, my lord." He groaned aloud, wondering if there was no end to her outrageousness. Then she placed her gloved fingertips across his lips, stopping his retort. "But I will agree the situation is markedly inefficient. I had meant to discuss this very problem with you."

He shook his head, finally succeeding in dislodging her tantalizing press against his lips. "Caroline," he said through clenched teeth, "what the devil are you talking about?"

"Your mistress, my lord."

It was like being abruptly submerged in arctic waters. He felt completely shocked to the point of numbness. "What?"

"Your mistress, my lord. I assume you have one."

"Well, there is…" He blinked. Why was he talking to her about this? "What—"

"You are correct that my current line of inquiry is decidedly awkward. Although I certainly feel capable of handling most situations, I am willing to grant there are perhaps some rather large gentlemen I might have difficulty controlling. Especially if they are rather, um, enthusiastic."

"As with Mr. Loots."

She paled, and he instantly regretted bringing up the oaf. "I must confess, kissing him was like being taken for shearing."

"I beg your pardon?"

"Imagine how the poor lambs must feel. Grabbed by someone twice their size and deftly removed of all their protective clothing. Except, thank heavens, Mr. Loots was not nearly as deft as the men I employ to shear my sheep."

"Thank God," Geoffrey responded. The entire image was filling him with an excruciating sense of horror. He could only pray she was more affected than she seemed.

"Well, yes," she commented, a blush staining her cheeks. "That and the fact I am no doubt repeating someone else's exact line of inquiry."

"I assure you, Caroline, no one else has your same scientific interest."

She smiled at him, apparently relieved. "Probably true. But I cannot go about kissing every gentleman I meet. It would take years to get a significant statistical sampling."

He released his pent-up breath. At last he was making headway.

"Therefore, I must interview other ladies who have already dedicated their lives to kissing gentlemen."

He narrowed his gaze, following her comment to its logical conclusion. "You are not going to speak to my mistress."

She sighed, the tone resigned as if she had already anticipated his response. "Very well. It appears I must visit a bawdy house."

"Absolutely not!" he roared. She winced at his loud tone, and he moderated his volume if not his temper. "Good

Lord, Caroline, you are highly intelligent. Surely you can grasp the dangers here. You are playing fast and loose with your reputation."

"Well, of course I am aware—"

"How many men have you kissed tonight?"

She drew out her notes, consulting them before answering. "Four, but that—"

"Four! Good God. Your reputation will be in tatters by morning!"

"Nonsense. I have sworn each of them to secrecy. Except for Mr. Loots, of course, but I cannot see that he would wish to speak of our unfortunate incident." He did not miss the reproachful glare she threw at him.

"You cannot possibly be that naive," he snapped, his expression grim.

"You do not mean they will talk to one another anyway?" Her eyes widened in shock. "But they swore on their honor!"

He sighed, seeing it was hopeless. She would never understand the need of a young buck to prove himself to his cronies. "Whom have you kissed, Caroline? I will speak with them each."

She swatted irritably at another leaf that drifted toward her face. "Oh, very well. But this only increases my determination to speak to your mistress, you know. It is suddenly quite apparent you gentlemen are not to be trusted with a lady's honor."

He suddenly grinned. Two concessions in one night. Perhaps he was learning how to handle the irrepressible lady. "Give me the names, Caroline," he said softly.

She gave them to him, quietly but firmly reading them off her list. And as he stored each name in his memory, he was relieved to note that except for Mr. Loots, she had chosen her victims wisely. Most of them were good men who would have no desire to harm her.

Her reputation was safe. At least for tonight.

Which left her unsavory request to meet his mistress. On no account would she ever be allowed to come within a half mile of his former mistress. There was no telling what damage the forthright Louise would cause. Despite Caroline's scientific and logical mind, there were just some things she was not ready to learn about human carnal relations.

"Very well," he said after she had once again tucked away her notes. "I will speak to these gentlemen tonight. In the meantime, I suggest you wait here while I get your aunt." He smiled as he carefully pulled half a dozen leaves from her hair. "You look as if you have been rolling about in a bower."

She smiled as she brushed several golden leaves from his hair, her touch gentle and soothing, even as it set his senses on fire. "That is the one drawback to locust trees and romantic atmospheres. They can be quite messy."

He caught her hand, knowing there was a limit to his self-restraint. But instead of releasing her fingers, he pulled them close to his lips, dropping a kiss onto them even as he spoke. "Caroline, did those other gentlemen kiss you too roughly…" He paused, unsure how to phrase his question. "Were they careful in their attentions?"

She was watching her hand, seemingly transfixed by his lips upon it. And he, too, took an inordinate amount of pleasure in not only the feel of her gloved hand against his lips, but the way her eyes widened as he began to unbutton her glove, tugging it downward away from her hand.

"Caroline," he called softly. "What exactly happened with the other gentlemen?"

She frowned, a look of intense concentration on her face. "Why, nothing," she sighed mournfully. "No tingling at all."

He succeeded in removing her glove, smiling as he stroked the smooth skin of her forearm, feeling her slight gasp turn his blood to fire. "And are you tingling now?"

"Oh yes," she whispered. Suddenly her eyes flew upward, meeting his gaze with an innocent hunger. "Will you touch my bodice again?" she asked.

He had not meant to. Indeed, he was absolutely certain he should leave now to find her aunt. Caroline in a secluded bower was too dangerous for any man. And yet, his right hand had already begun stroking her forearm, trailing slowly up her arm, feeling the heat from her body sear his fingers even as he continued the movement, curving past her elbow. Her breast brushed the back of his hand, her tremulous breath making it quiver against him. Then, to his amazement, he found he had turned his hand to cup her breast, stroking his fingers around the sweet mound while his thumb tumbled across its taut peak.

He felt her breath catch, her breast lifting slightly, as if seeking more. He did not deny the unspoken request. Indeed, his other hand answered her call, and he heard himself groan as he molded and teased her nipples through the fabric of her gown.

She arched into him, her eyes slipping closed. The fire had caught his brain now, burning through the objections clamoring through his thoughts until they slipped away like so much smoke.

He bent his head, needing to taste the pulse point in her throat, kissing her neck, drawing long, wet lines with his tongue under the curve of her chin, teasing her earlobe, glorying in the shiver of delight that ran through her body into his.

Lower down, he ground against her, pressing her against the tree even as his mouth at last found hers. He kissed her. Deeply. Thoroughly. Boldly invading her mouth as he longed to do below.

And all the while, he held her breasts with both hands, pulling, tweaking, grasping, doing all the things he dreamed of doing while she writhed in response, her soft cries of delight telling him exactly what she liked. Exactly what he wanted to do to her.

"I do apologize for Geoffrey's behavior. The stress of the season, you know. It makes men do the strangest things."

Geoffrey froze, unable to reconcile his mother's voice with Caroline's passionate moans. Some sounds were never meant to coincide.

"I completely understand," returned Mrs. Hibbert's voice. "Why, even my own dear Alastair was wont to say the strangest things during balls. He simply could not abide society functions, you know. Would make up the most ridiculous things just to escape them."

Pressed as she was against him, Geoffrey could feel Caroline's every muscle tense as her aunt's voice carried over the hedges.

"Well," continued his mother from what must be a scant few feet away. "At least we have assured ourselves that Geoffrey is completely wrong. Your Caroline is much too innocent to be out here." Her last word was filled with contempt for their surroundings, and Geoffrey caught Caroline's panicked expression as she looked to the right. If their voices were anything to judge by, his mother and her aunt were within seconds of rounding the corner and coming upon them.

Geoffrey looked down, seeing her breasts still in his hands. Caroline's mouth was dark red and kiss-swollen. Even though her clothing remained completely in place, except for her glove, there would be no doubt as to what they had just been doing.

He hastily backed away, cursing himself for the slow reluctance with which he released her. His body felt thick and sluggish, and his heart beat a heavy tempo that urged him back to Caroline and the bliss he could find there.

For her part, Caroline, too, seemed to realize exactly how she appeared. With shaking hands, she snatched up her glove from the ground, drawing it on with jerky movements. And all the while, their relatives stood on the opposite side of the hedge, continuing to chat as if they were sitting down to tea.

"Men are such contrary creatures under the most normal of circumstances," his mother commented. "One moment hot, the next cold, and all over the most trivial of matters. Why, I recall when Geoffrey was a child…"

Geoffrey closed his eyes, silently calling on the Almighty to open up the earth to swallow him whole. Just when he thought things could not get worse, it now appeared that he would not only be caught making unseemly advances on a young innocent, but would be subjected to a minute dissection of his youthful foibles as well. He glanced sideways at Caroline. Except for the leaves that still sprinkled her hair and clothing with every breeze, she appeared to be completely restored to order, her attention well and truly caught by the coming tale.

He was on the verge of storming around the corner, screaming in a fit, or simply running madly in the other direction—anything to stop the coming conversation—when Providence did indeed rescue him.

The midnight dinner bell sounded.

Never had he been more grateful for the stroke of midnight. His mother ceased her discussion practically midword. "Oh," she gasped. "I am simply famished. Shall we?"

Mrs. Hibbert apparently agreed, because Geoffrey could hear the rustle of fabric and shrubbery as they turned. "Never fear, we shall find Caroline sitting to dine just like the sensible girl she is."

His mother's laugher echoed in the night air, fading as she walked away. "I have always known sheep herding would drive Geoffrey insane one day. I pray night and day that he finds his heiress soon." Then her words were lost in the general noise of couples strolling back toward the dinner buffet.

Taking his first deep breath in what felt like years, Geoffrey turned back to Caroline. Though she appeared perfectly at ease, he could still see the echo of passion in her eyes—a dark hunger when her gaze traveled to his face, lingering on his mouth, before rising to meet his dark challenge. She never said a word, and yet his blood seemed molten, still hot and heavy with a need that nearly pushed him back into her arms.

But that way lay madness. "Caroline," he said, his voice hoarse, "this must end."

He did not even know to what he referred—her insane experiment or their frequent kisses. Whatever he meant, she appeared to understand, nodding with a slow dip of her chin.

"Good," he said softly as he willed his body to move away from her. "I will find your aunt and tell her you do not feel well and need to go home. There is a bench back the way we came. Will you wait there while I find her?"

Again, she nodded and as he watched, she seemed to rally, gathering her thoughts and her dignity. Her shoulders straightened and a spark of keen intelligence flashed through her eyes. "It will give me time to record my notes."

He stifled a sigh. At least she would come to no harm. Most of the guests would be headed for the buffet, so she was unlikely to be seen. And even if she was, he would make it clear that she had gone into the garden to escape the heat.

Her reputation was safe. Still, there remained one last item to make clear. "Oh, and Caroline, my mistress died last winter. Of the pox." He shrugged. "That happens sometimes when you kiss too many gentlemen."

He lingered long enough to hear her soft sigh of dismay. "Very well, Geoffrey."

He grinned, congratulating himself on such a clever bit of perjury and started to walk away, cutting through the hedge in the opposite direction from Caroline.

"I suppose I shall just have to content myself with observing the couples in the gardens tonight."

He spun around too late. She was already gone. With a muttered oath, he pushed through the gardens toward the ballroom and her aunt. He had better get her married off fast or he would check himself into Bedlam just to escape her.

It was not until he saw her safely closed in her carriage and the ponderous vehicle slowly wending its way back toward London that he recalled her words.

*It appears I must visit a bawdy house.*

A bawdy house? Surely she would not try that? But the throb in his temple told him Caroline never joked about scientific matters.

# CHAPTER 6

Caroline toyed with her quill, twirling it around and around in her fingers, neither dipping it into the inkwell nor using it to write.

Geoffrey had touched her bodice. Indeed, he had touched her so much that the resulting tingles nearly lit her on fire. She could hardly credit that the leaves around them had not burst into flame. In fact, the memory was potent enough to set her tingling all over again.

This definitely warranted further research.

If she were honest with herself, she truly did not need another of Geoffrey's kisses for her initial study. She already remembered every single detail, every nuance of his touch from his first two kisses. She relived them constantly in her mind, dreamed about them at night, fantasized about them in twilight.

She remembered everything about him. Even when they fought and his anger made his eyes flash, she still remembered more of their conversation, more of the feelings and sensations that permeated their harsh discourse, than any other experience with any other man. Even their kisses.

It was as if, compared to him, all others faded into nothingness.

It was a coil, to be sure. She had set out to discover the link between the mind and the heart only to learn that there really was not any.

Take Perry Fairfax, for example. She found him amiable, charming, and surprisingly astute regarding sheep. She liked him quite well, and therefore had expected to like his kiss quite well. Unfortunately, it had been a dry sort of fumbling affair that tried her patience more than set her body to tingling.

Then there was Lord Hillman's kiss. He was by far the oldest of her suitors, nearly into his dotage. But he had a mischievous twinkle in his eyes and a firm grasp on human peccadilloes. She'd found an almost scientific keenness in his observations regarding his fellow man and expected a somewhat scientific kiss, a cool and detached event composed of necessary movements performed to precision. Except his kiss was nothing like that. It was fervent, enthusiastic, and very much like the footman's. It left her warm, in a youthful sort of way, but not in the least bit tingly.

The other gentlemen were equally confusing, up to and including Mr. Loots. As a dear friend of her father's with interest in chemicals, Mr. Loots's kiss should have been tender, scientific, or at least pleasant. Instead it was even worse than Harry's. All hurried movement that seemed to have no regard for her own wishes whatsoever. And he was always so pleasant whenever they chanced to meet, which seemed to occur more and more frequently these days.

In short, there was no hope for it. She simply had to speak with a woman who had more knowledge of this business. And that meant finding Geoffrey's mistress. Why she fixated on his mistress was rather convoluted even to her own mind. She decided that since Geoffrey's attentions produced the most physical and mental response within her, his was the kiss she needed to investigate further. That meant speaking with a woman who had kissed not only Geoffrey, but a good deal of other men.

She could, of course, wander through members of the *ton* looking for women who had kissed Geoffrey, but it was much easier, much more practical to find his mistress.

She completely dismissed Geoffrey's statement that the woman had died of the pox. Caroline was well aware of the lengths men went to deny the existence of their women of leisure. The pox, though possible, was probably a fabrication. All she needed to do was locate the woman. And for that, all she needed to do is approach her aunt, for Aunt Win knew everything about everybody.

Caroline would just have to do it very, very carefully.

"Aunt Win," began Caroline, as she sauntered into her aunt's sitting room.

"Goodness, Caroline!" exclaimed her aunt, dropping her embroidery into her lap. "I thought you were going riding with Lord Powell."

Caroline shook her head as she settled down onto a chaise next to her aunt. "I am feeling a trifle weary of the social whirl, so I sent round a note asking if he would not mind delaying until tomorrow."

Her aunt frowned, as Caroline knew she would, but it could not be helped. She would have cancelled even without the added necessity of finding Geoffrey's mistress. Sometimes all that chatting and smiling gave her a headache. "He was most solicitous in his response, Aunt Win. I have not frightened him off."

"Well, good. I cannot help but think you should be applying yourself a bit more."

Caroline let the comment go, not wanting to be drawn into another one of the woman's lectures. Instead, she leaned over and picked up a corner of her aunt's embroidery, toying with the threads even as she admired the exquisite design. "I quite like this. Is it your garden in Hadleigh?"

"Come now, Caroline. You have not searched me out just to comment on my stitching. What is it that bothers you?"

Despite the sharpness of her words, Aunt Win's tone was gentle, almost motherly.

Still, Caroline blushed that she could be found out so easily. "It is nothing of significance," she hedged. "I just wondered if all gentlemen have mistresses."

"Goodness! That is not a proper topic for conversation."

Caroline shrugged, looking everywhere but at her aunt. "I know, but I was just curious. Does Lord Tallis, for example, keep a mistress?"

The older woman did not answer at first, just directed a long measuring look at her niece. Finally, she sighed. "You are not developing a tendre for the man, are you?"

Caroline sighed, not answering except to look forlorn. There was only one way her aunt would give her the information she sought. Only if she thought Caroline was on the verge of falling into some romantic passion. Information, her aunt had often said, was the only way to disillusion the naive.

"You know he is looking for an heiress. He—"

"Will not marry me. Yes, I know." She released another sigh, very reminiscent of a girl in the grip of a desperate passion. "But what if he truly loves me?"

"Then he would not have a mistress," her aunt returned tartly.

Caroline tried not to smile. Her plan was working brilliantly. "Then he does have a mistress?"

"Of course he does. All gentlemen do, although I heard he gave her his conge."

"Conge?"

"Taken leave of her, dear, no doubt for financial reasons. A mistress can be frightfully expensive."

Caroline brightened considerably, letting her expression linger in the dreamy. "Then he could truly love me."

"I heard he still visits the woman on occasion," her aunt said repressively.

"But maybe just as old friends…"

Her aunt stabbed herself in the thumb with her needle and cursed softly. When she finished dabbing at the wound and set aside her stitching, she turned fully toward her niece with a firm expression. "I thought you had more sense, Caroline. Louise Fletcher and Lord Tallis are not friends. Women such as she do not have friends. They have protectors."

"Oh," sighed Caroline. "Maybe Louise Fletcher is under someone else's protection now. Maybe Geoffrey never visits her at all."

"Nonsense," her aunt snapped. "She is a dancer." Her tone was sharp with disgust. "Believe me, Caroline, Lord Tallis frequents her lodgings and has no budding tendre for you." Then she softened her voice, her expression worried. "I am only telling you this so you will understand you can never bring him up to scratch. He is looking for an heiress."

Caroline nodded, wondering why she was not practically jumping with delight. She had learned what she needed to know, but for some strange reason, her aunt's words had her disgustingly cast down.

"Are you feeling quite the thing, my dear?"

Caroline shook herself out of her confusing thoughts. "Of course, Aunt Win."

"You know, dear, Geoffrey made the oddest comment to me last evening at the Bedfords' rout." Aunt Win paused for emphasis. "He said you were luring young men into the gardens for kisses. And now all these questions about his mistress. You are not doing anything scandalous, are you?"

Caroline fidgeted under her aunt's too-perceptive gaze. What could she say? "Of course not," she lied. She thought she did a rather credible job of it too. She made her eyes wide and assumed the most innocent of expressions. Apparently her aunt was not deceived. The lady folded her arms across her chest and frowned while Caroline bit her lip in consternation.

"You are being overly curious again, aren't you?" Aunt Win demanded.

Caroline stiffened. "Papa says curiosity is the most wonderful of attributes for a scientist."

"And Heaven knows your father is considered an expert on the social graces," Aunt Win snapped in return. Then she released a heavy sigh. "Very well, Caroline, what is it you wish to know?"

"I beg your pardon?"

"You want to understand something, but you fear I shall be upset by your line of inquiry or some other such nonsense. Well, I promise you, I shall not. Ask your questions. I shall do my best to answer."

Caroline felt herself flush bright red. Whereas she had no difficulty confessing her scientific passion to Lord Tallis, she felt daunted by the task of explaining it to her aunt. Though highly open-minded in many matters, Caroline could not imagine Aunt Win allowing her to visit Geoffrey's mistress in order to ask about such things as human carnal relations. Therefore, she had to think of another line of inquiry, before her aunt began to suspect anything. "Well," she began slowly. "It is about Lord Tallis. I just wondered about...about the woman he sponsored."

Aunt Win did not move. She did not start or jump or even freeze. She simply seemed to tense with a sudden wariness that intrigued Caroline to no end. Clearly this topic was worth pursuing. "Surely," her aunt said on a breathy laugh, "you do not think Amanda Wyndham was Geoffrey's mistress."

Caroline started. Amanda? She was sure Geoffrey had called her Gillian. "Are you sure—"

"Of course, I am certain," her aunt snapped. A sure sign that Aunt Win was not in the least bit certain.

Caroline sighed and decided to take the most reasonable approach to this most unreasonable situation. "You might as well tell me it all. I am bound to find out sooner or later."

"You mean you are *determined* to find out."

Caroline shrugged, no doubt confirming her aunt's worst suspicions. "Whom did the lady marry? What happened to her?"

Aunt Win shrugged, picking up her stitching as she spoke, but not the needle or thread. "That is just it. No one knows."

Caroline frowned. "What do you mean 'no one knows?'"

"Just that. One minute Miss Wyndham was the toast of the town. The next, she had disappeared. Gone. Her family said she married some gentleman from Scotland and the two emigrated to Canada."

Caroline shook her head. "Are you sure you have the right lady, Aunt Win? If...Amanda...was all the rage, then why would Geoffrey need to squire her about?"

"Because she was not at all popular before he began." Aunt Win lifted her silver threads, separating them one by one. "Thanks to Lord Tallis, she became an Original. Everyone expected an announcement. It was supposed to be the match of the season."

"What happened?" Caroline was barely breathing. Had Geoffrey nearly married the girl? He had claimed that he would not court social ruin for the woman, but had he wished to?

Aunt Win twisted the thread back and forth between her fingers, her gaze distracted. "*Nothing* happened. She disappeared. So did Lord Tallis. We all assumed they eloped, except he returned to London still a bachelor, and she was gone. Her family said she eloped with some other gentleman no one had ever heard of. Then, to top it off, her guardian, the Earl of Mavenford, also found a new wife." Aunt Win leaned forward, her voice dropping to a scant whisper. "A woman rumored to be a bastard. The two of them left for the Continent for an extensive honeymoon, and no one has ever learned exactly what happened." She lifted her chin, pinning her niece with a warning glare. "They have only recently returned. Indeed, in five years only the family has met her. Mavenford, of course, countenances no scandalous talk. He is most protective of his bride."

Caroline looked at her hands, frowning as she sorted through the various pieces, trying to fit them together. She kept her voice almost casual as she continued to probe for information. "Could it not have happened just the way they said? This Amanda, she probably met a man who literally swept her off her feet, and the two went to Canada."

Aunt Win shook her head, clearly disgusted with her niece's naiveté. "She was the toast of the season—an earl's ward with a dowry to match. Why would she run off with some nobody Scot when she could have her pick here in London?"

Caroline shrugged, her thoughts wandering the same direction. Why would anyone give up Geoffrey? "Perhaps the Scotsman was her true love."

Aunt Win snorted as she began sifting through the rest of her thread. "I suppose when you are an heiress, you can indulge yourself. But the rest of us…" She sighed, dropping the colorful strings. "We make do."

Caroline felt her jaw go slack at the woman's casual comment. "But Aunt Win, I thought you wanted me to find true love."

Her relative lifted her eyebrows in surprise. "Of course I do, Caroline. Well, I want you to be as happy as you possibly can given the circumstances."

"But Harry—"

"Will not make you happy, I think. He is an acceptable second choice, perhaps." She gave her niece a hard glance. "But only a second choice. At least wait until the season is over."

Caroline nodded, the move mechanical and not in the least bit related to her thoughts. She had expected a wealth of answers from her aunt, but what she found instead were contradictions and more questions. "Aunt Win?"

"Hmmm?" the lady responded as she threaded her needle.

"You did not wish to tell me about Amanda Wyndham. Why?"

The lady sighed, dropping her hands back into her lap. "Because I do not know all, and I know you cannot abide mysteries."

"But—"

"You are liable to plague his lordship to death, asking him what and why, and believe me, this will not be something Lord Tallis wants to discuss. If he did elope with Miss Wyndham, then something went terribly wrong during the nuptials. What man would want to explain that? If he did not elope with her, then plaguing him about it can only serve to dredge up old unfounded rumors. I would not want him to think we listen to ridiculous gossip."

Caroline remained silent. She already knew it was a forbidden subject. While Geoffrey had not explicitly refused to speak about Amanda, or Gillian, or whomever, clearly it was a struggle for him to discuss her—and Caroline was loath to press about something so obviously painful for him.

"I shan't plague him about it, Aunt Win."

"Good. Because he is doing you an enormous favor by bringing you into fashion. Do not jeopardize it with your insatiable curiosity."

"No, Aunt Win."

They lapsed into silence as Aunt Win rang for tea, each woman absorbed in her own thoughts as the tray was served with excruciating slowness by the aged Thompson. When the man finally left, Caroline once again turned to her aunt.

"You mentioned Stephen Conley—"

"The Earl of Mavenford."

"Yes…" Caroline let her voice trail away as she picked up a scone. "What is his wife's name?"

"Gillian. Why?"

"No reason." Caroline looked away, praying her expression did not reveal her excitement at unraveling her first mystery regarding Lord Tallis. One woman suddenly disappearing. Another just as abruptly appearing married to Stephen Conley.

She had the answer. It was crazy, but…Amanda and Gillian had to be the same woman. Yet, why? And why had she—whatever her name was—thrown over Geoffrey?

Questions, questions, questions, Caroline thought with a small tremor of excitement. She had found a whole other direction of inquiry, and a whole new source of information for her research.

"Caroline? What are you thinking?"

"Hmmm? Oh, nothing. Just that I would like to meet the countess."

Aunt Win narrowed her eyes, apparently not in the least bit fooled by Caroline's show of innocence. "As would everyone, but Caro—"

"I wonder where Father is. He is usually home by now from the Chemical Society. You do not think he and Mr. Loots went to that awful club again, do you?" She thought her transition away from the topic of Lord Tallis rather smooth. Aunt Win constantly worried about Father and his new friend, Mr. Loots. And after her experiences in the Bedford garden with the hateful man, Caroline could not help but be equally concerned. She herself certainly did not wish to associate with Mr. Loots on a regular basis, though Papa seemed to be bringing him by disconcertingly often. Unfortunately, this most interesting topic did not appear to interest her aunt.

"What are you doing, Caroline?"

Caroline blinked, startled by the odd question. "What?"

"I know how much you hate being on display, as you call it. You are not interested in frivolous chatter or dancing or even cards. Why are you letting Lord Tallis squire you about? And all these questions! Are you falling in love with him?"

Caroline felt the blood drain from her face. Her aunt was the last person she'd expected to question her actions. After all, Aunt Win wanted her to go through this torture of dancing and socializing. "I, uh, I thought you wished it."

Aunt Win frowned. "Of course I do, but I expected more of a fight. My wishes never influenced you before. Out with it, Caro. Are you falling in love with Lord Tallis?"

Caroline felt her breath freeze in her throat. In love? With Geoffrey? His kisses certainly made her tingle, not to mention the inferno he created whenever he touched her anywhere else. Indeed, she felt herself heat at the very thought. But she had a good deal more research to do before she would come to the conclusion of love. She pointedly disregarded the tremors of excitement building at the thought. "No, aunt," she responded evenly. "I have not fallen in love with him."

Her aunt nodded, but her expression was still grim. "That is all to the good, because he will not marry you. He needs an heiress."

"Yes," Caroline responded dryly. "So you and he have said. Repeatedly."

"So that still leaves the question: Why do you allow him to squire you about?"

Caroline sighed. Her aunt was nothing if not tenacious. She could see that unless given a satisfactory answer, Aunt Win would pick at her until she had the whole unvarnished truth—kissing experiments and all. Caroline opted for giving half the truth and prayed it would suffice.

It was an awkward thing to confess, so she glanced away, toying with her teacup as she spoke. "If you must know, I have decided to make an experiment of him."

"What!" The tea service rattled from the force of her aunt's explosion.

Caroline dropped her teacup on the table and glared. "He intrigues me. He pretends to be nothing but a frivolous ne'er-do-well, and yet I know he has worked hard, very, very hard in his lifetime. He claims he needs an heiress, yet he spends his time squiring me about, not sweetening up any of the eligible girls presented to him. It is odd, and I want to know more."

"My goodness, Caroline, why can you not just say you like the man? That perhaps he makes you laugh, and you enjoy his company?"

Caroline frowned, frustration making her reach for, then tear apart, her delicate tea pastry. "Because," she said with false composure, "that is entirely beside the point. Yes, I like him. But more he is a puzzle, and I like studying puzzles."

Aunt Win sighed, the sound coming from deep within her. She reached out and stroked Caroline's cheek, the gesture tender and very motherly. "Caro, dear. Life is not an experiment. It is meant to be lived and enjoyed, not dissected."

"I am living—"

"You are studying. Just as your father does. Your mother used to love life. Can you not remember what it was like—"

"Before she went insane?" Caroline interrupted. "No, Aunt Win, I do not remember." She saw her aunt's eyes widen at her terse reply, but she did not stay to belabor the point. She pushed up from her seat, intent on escaping, but her aunt was quicker than she expected. The older lady grabbed her arm, effectively holding her in place.

"Your mother was not insane." The stem words echoed in the small parlor.

Caroline simply arched her brow in disbelief. "You would prefer I call her heartless? Cruel? Or perhaps unnatural, to abandon a family who adored her."

Caroline felt her aunt's grip loosen, then slip away. "Can you not remember her as lonely? She did not mean to hurt you, you know."

"She was insane, Aunt Win. And in her madness, she ran off with the gypsies."

"You could be so like her, you know. There is much of her in you." Her aunt sounded sentimental.

Caroline did not flinch, barely even breathed. She would not let her aunt know how those words turned her soul to ice. Instead, she simply shook her head. "I have nothing of my mother in me. Nothing." And with that she carefully, calmly, gathered the tea service and quietly quit the room.

Winnifred Hibbert watched her niece leave like a queen dismissing her subjects. The girl's spine was stiff as a rod, her head lifted almost to the sky for all that she carried the tea tray.

Things were becoming decidedly awkward, she realized as the door slipped shut behind the girl. But for the life of her, Winnifred could not decide if it was good or bad. Caroline had become happier in these last few weeks. Her smile was more apparent, her laugh less forced. But if it was all because she had fallen in love with Lord Tallis, what would happen when the man finally found his heiress?

Yes, the situation was definitely becoming uncomfortable. The question now was what to do about it.

With sudden resolve, she rang the bell. As expected, Thompson appeared immediately. No doubt he had been eavesdropping from the hallway as was his wont. Winnifred did not mind in the least. It was the only way she found out about many of Caroline's bizarre actions. But even he had not been able to discover her niece's current obsession.

She shook her head. There was only one person who might know what was going on, and she was determined to speak to him immediately. She wanted answers, and she wanted them now.

"Thompson," she said, as she moved swiftly to her writing table. "I want a footman to send a note to Lord Tallis. He is to be direct and insistent. Do you have someone who can accomplish such a task?"

The old man bowed, his bones creaking with every movement. "Yes, mum. It shall be accomplished forthwith."

"I certainly hope so," she grumbled in response. She would talk to Geoffrey this instant. Whatever Caroline was doing, he would know the truth of it.


Caroline climbed the stairs of Miss Fletcher's building with trepidation. Finding the dancer's apartments had been easy; once Caroline had the lady's name and profession, obtaining her address was child's play. But now that she was there, less than a half hour after her talk with Aunt

Win, Caroline found herself strangely reluctant to face the woman.

What would Geoffrey's mistress be like? Probably petite with long legs and a radiant smile. She played a grecian maid in the ballet, which suggested long blond tresses and a willowy body. In short, everything that her own gangly, full-breasted frame was not. The thought of Geoffrey kissing Miss Fletcher the way he had kissed her was almost more than she could stand. Even in the name of science.

Still, she had traveled all this way and gone to great lengths to get there. It was only logical that she continue. Besides, there was a good deal she wanted to know about kissing that only Miss Fletcher could tell her.

So with a steady hand, if not a steady heart, Caroline rapped on the door.

It was answered almost immediately, not by a butler or servant or even a maid, but by an elfin girl with freckles on her cheeks, a riot of red curls trailing down her back, and full bouncing breasts.

"Oh, la!" the girl trilled. "You ain't wot I expected."

"I am terribly sorry," returned Caroline, her face flushing with embarrassment. "I am looking for Miss Louise Fletcher."

"That be me," the girl chirped, then skipped away from the door.

Caroline followed her inside, shutting the door behind her as she studied her strange hostess. The woman wore a pale green dress that wisped just below her hips, revealing muscular legs that seemed to bounce whenever she moved. She did not walk so much as jump and hop and dance. In fact, the girl never seemed to be at rest. She moved constantly, and the sight was both exhausting and charming.

"I am just finishing me breakfast, ducky, as I slept rather late. Care t' join me?"

"Um, no, thank you." Caroline followed the woman into the main room, a rich green salon with bright yellow and blue and red furnishings that dotted the area like flowers. It was like stepping into a wild patch of meadow flowers except it was compressed into a small area. And it fit Miss Fletcher perfectly. "What a beautiful room," Caroline said truthfully, already drawn to the girl's free and easy manner.

"I do likes color. Don't you?"

"Oh yes. And you get to dance too. Every night. Whatever you want."

"Lawks, no, ducky," she returned with a trilling laugh. "I dances what they tell me. It's in 'ere that I do wot I like." Then the girl stopped moving long enough to eye Caroline, her gaze quick yet thorough. "You be quality," she finally said. "You're Geoffrey's bluestocking, ain'tcha?"

Caroline looked away. Had Geoffrey talked about her? She was not sure what she thought about that. What had he said? "I…How…"

"Aw, don't be shy. I know about all the quality. And you, ducky, are quite the news these days." She gave Caroline a broad wink.

Caroline managed a weak smile. "Does, um, does Geoffrey talk about me?"

"Sweetings, *everybody* talks about you."

"But—"

"But Geoffrey keeps wot 'e think close to 'is chest."

Caroline could not control the sinking of her heart. Right down into her toes. "Then you are his mistress," she said sadly.

"Lord, ducky! Geoffrey ain't been round 'ere for years. I was a gift," she confided in an undertone. "From 'is friends for one month after 'e reached his majority. 'E ain't never 'ad the blunt to keep me proper, but I likes 'im so much, I let 'im visit whenever 'e wants. But that ain't been for a long, long time."

"But you were his mistress? For a short while?" Caroline didn't know why it was so important for her to know, but it was, and so she pressed for details.

Louise leaned forward and her hair tumbled off her shoulders, giving the illusion of movement even when the girl was still. "The gentleman likes me 'cause I got boundless energy. That's wot Geoffrey told me. Boundless energy. Christened me Lady Boundiful." She started laughing, a merry tinkling of bells that seemed to fill the air. "Ain't that enough to toast yer toes!" The girl stepped forward, tugging on Caroline's hand, urging her toward a bright yellow settee. "Now, sweetings, does that ease yer heart? That 'e ain't been here in years?"

Caroline smiled. It did, though she didn't want to examine exactly why. She simply enjoyed her release from her nervousness, relaxed as she decided to begin her research. "Truthfully, Miss Fletcher—"

"Louise, ducks."

"Very well, Louise; I shall get directly to the point. I am conducting a scientific study." She lifted her chin. "Regarding kissing."

Louise had been standing, one leg extended upon the back of the settee as she stretched her legs. But at Caroline's comment, she lifted her head in shock. "Kissing!"

"Yes. I am interested in the link between the body and the mind as regards to certain, um, well, tingling effects."

Louise frowned, her elfin body stilled for the first time. "Blimey," was all she said.

"Can you remember anything of Geoffrey's kisses?"

"'Course I can!" She pulled her leg down from the settee, raising up as she twirled about the room. "He has ever the sweetest touch."

Caroline felt her face heat as she looked down at her hands. "And, um, did you tingle? I mean, compared to other gentlemen. Did he…I mean, did you like…"

Suddenly Louise stopped, turning back to Caroline with a gleeful expression as she released a squeal of laughter that abruptly cut off Caroline's words. "Sakes alive, ducky, you want t' know wot 'e likes in bed!"

Caroline felt the blood drain from her face. "Uh, no…I…"

But her words were cut off as Louise leaped over the coffee table to land directly before her guest. "Glory be, but

I wish other ladies thought t' do the same. Would be a mite fewer gents coming 'round 'ere, I'd say."

"But—"

"Now don't be shy," interrupted the girl with another musical laugh. "I suppose it takes a bluestocking t' see wot she has to learn. Come along, ducks." Somehow this tiny girl, perhaps a stone lighter than Caroline, was pulling her out of the settee. "Come into my boudoir, and I will tell you all you need t' know about pleasing 'is lordship. I knows all the tricks."

"Tricks?" Caroline had meant to refuse. Indeed, she could tell that this conversation was rapidly spiraling out of control. But with Louise's last comment, Caroline's curiosity became fully engaged. "Are there many tricks? And have you tried them on many gentlemen? I mean, have you kissed many gentlemen?"

"Only 'alf the gents in London. And as for tricks," she continued with a wink. "There be all these wonderful devices!"

"Devices! I had no idea," Caroline cried, suddenly delighted with her decision to come here. She genuinely liked this exuberant girl who somehow seemed a good deal older than Caroline's own twenty-one years. But better yet, the girl was a delight to be with—cheerful, warm, and most of all, she had a wealth of information that she seemed only too willing to share.

Caroline immediately decided to spend the entire afternoon with the girl, learning everything she could. And if there was more to learn after that, then she would come back as often as possible.

With that happy thought, Caroline followed the girl into a velvet boudoir and all the secrets contained within.

# CHAPTER 7

"You told her what?" Geoffrey shot out of his chair.

Mrs. Hibbert merely stared at him, her eyes cold. "Of course I told her about your mistress. It was the only thing I could think of to dissuade her from you. Good lord, Geoffrey, she said she is making a study of you. Now, I want to know what you are doing to turn her head so."

"Me!"

"You know"—Mrs. Hibbert lifted her chin—"very soon I will be forced to demand you do the honorable thing by her."

"I will kill her, is what I will do. Where is the confounded woman?"

Mrs. Hibbert pushed out of her chair, rising to her own regal height, her tone imperious. "Calm yourself, young man. She has only gone to the lending library."

"The lending library? Of course, that is where she is," he muttered, the irony thick in his tone. "If you will excuse me."

"I most certainly will not!"

Geoffrey spun on his heel, crossing the room with large, angry strides. "Then, I am afraid I shall have to be ruder than I would normally dare. Good day."

"Tallis!"

But he was already gone, heading with all due speed toward his carriage, Mayfair, Louise, and certain disaster.

Good lord, but he should have known this would be a horrible day. It was bad enough being summoned out of his club by Mrs. Hibbert's huge bear of a footman. Though excruciatingly polite, the man made it clear it was either come willingly to Caroline's aunt's house or be carried there. Geoffrey had no choice but to comply.

Then to arrive and immediately be subjected to a dressing down by the formidable woman, a demand as to what it was he thought he was doing with Caroline. For a few moments, he'd felt like a boy of five, still in short coats, as his mother scolded him for playing soldier in her wardrobe.

He had only just managed to gain control of the situation when her aunt said she'd told Caroline about Louise. Good God, he lambasted himself for perhaps the thousandth time, he should have known Caroline would not give up so easily. Lending library indeed!

The chit was in Mayfair. With Louise. Learning God only knew what.

He spurred his horses faster.

He arrived after three lifetimes' worth of anxiety and worry. Bursting inside, he found a sight worthy of any man's worst nightmare.

He found Caroline and Louise stretched upon his onetime mistress's bed, eating bonbons and exchanging confidences with the ease of longtime friends.

*Good God*, he thought with horror, *I'm doomed*.

"Good afternoon, yer lordship," Louise called from her position on her bed. She did not even bother to get up, but waved him in from where she was, stretched out in a flimsy negligee. "I 'ave kept 'er right entertained, 'aven't I, ducky?"

Caroline grinned and nodded. "Oh, Geoffrey, I have had the most fascinating time." She waved at an array of sexual aids scattered across the bedsheets, including a tiny nightgown of flimsy material that she lifted up toward her face. He had no trouble envisioning her in such an outfit, and his body responded with mortifying thoroughness to the image. Heedless of his state, Caroline continued, picking up first one object then another. "Louise has been most informative. I never realized there was so much to the business."

"Bloody hell."

"Aw, don't worry." Louise fell backward and stretched one long leg luxuriously over her head. Flexibility had always been one of her greatest assets. Right now, it set Geoffrey's teeth on edge, especially when she peeked out from just behind her knee and winked at him. "She only wanted t' know wot would please you most."

"That is not true!" exclaimed Caroline, her face beet red. "I merely wanted Louise to compare your kiss with other gentlemen's. And that of course led to other comparisons..." Her voice trailed away, an analytical expression on her face. He had the most disturbing sensation that he was being studied and catalogued in her prodigious intellect. And he was not exactly sure of his classification.

With a sudden surge of anger, spurred on by mortification, Geoffrey strode across the room and pulled Caroline out of the bed. "That is enough. I am taking you home this instant where, if your aunt has a lick of sense, she will pack you off to Antarctica immediately!"

"Geoffrey!" Twin exclamations of outrage assaulted his ears. He did not care in the least, but continued to pull Caroline to her feet.

"Geoffrey," she repeated, her voice low and angry. "You will release me this instant."

"I will release you when you are safely in your aunt's household and I can, with honor, wash my hands of you. Good God, do you know what risks you took coming here? Your reputation will be in tatters!"

"Oh no," Louise stuck in. "Ain't nobody saw 'er, and she was covered from 'ead t' toe when she got 'ere."

Geoffrey glared the woman into silence. Then he turned his attention back to Caroline. "There are things a lady never does. And spending an afternoon with a dancer is certainly one of them."

He had finally managed to wrest Caroline to her feet, but once there, she dug in her heels, pinning him with a fury that would have burned him to a crisp if he had not matched it heat for heat. "I am not a lady," she declared to his face. "I am a bluestocking. And if I want to spend an afternoon talking with a new friend, then I bloody well will!"

"You bloody well will *not*!" he bellowed right back.

"Good God! You are just like Harry!" Caroline gasped. Then suddenly she twisted in his grip, turning to address Louise. "In your experience, Louise, are there any men who ever try to reason with a woman? Or do they all bluster and threaten and use their superior strength to bully us into submission?"

"Coo, miss. Ten minutes ago I woulda said 'is lordship was different." She shot Geoffrey an arched look. "But it appears I was mistaken." He did not miss the look of pure delight sparkling in her eyes. One could not buy this good a show at the theater.

"Caroline, I have had my fill of this nonsense," he snapped, his voice as commanding and authoritative as he could make it. It was the voice he used to bring the most stubborn sheep to ground, and the one that made men jump to do his bidding. It had even been known to make his mother quail.

Caroline was having none of it. She spun back to him. "Then leave, for I have a good deal more to ask Louise."

"Caroline!" Her name was a growl of frustration. His left hand fisted, and he knew his grip was bruisingly painful on her arm. He would not hit her, but his emotion was like molten fire in his blood, needing some release, even if it were one of Louise's blindingly bright chairs.

But when he looked at Caroline, he saw challenge in her eyes. Good God, her own fists were bunched, ready to give back as good as she got despite his larger size and the fact that he could probably snap her in two. She would not give in to him, even if he were to beat her bloody.

God, what a woman! He did not know whether to kiss her or strangle her.

Into this confusion stepped Louise, with her forthright ways and blunt words. "Blimey, she just wanted t' know 'ow it was done. Why don't you show 'er?"

Geoffrey blinked. Show her! Of all the scandalous, irresponsible, dishonorable suggestions. Show her?

"Go on," pressed Louise. "It's the only way t' quiet 'er questions."

Quiet her questions…In his fuddled state, the thought actually made sense to him. They were standing practically nose to nose, a mere two inches separating their lips. In less than a heartbeat, he closed the distance.

Caroline was innocence and sensuality spread like hot toffee against him. Her lips opened to him, her body melted, and she was sweet willingness and chocolate bonbons heated to a burning flame. One of his hands trailed across her cheek, from the burning heat of her skin to her silken curls. The other hand shifted lower, across the curve of her spine, pressing Caroline closer.

She sighed, and he caught the sound, tasted it, felt it echo through his soul. Never had he felt such desire, such hunger, such…

Tingling.

Oh, God, he groaned, and then he kissed her again.

*Bang! Bang!*

"Louise!" came a singsongy, very drunk male voice from the hallway, following the rapping at the door.

"Blimey. It be Ralph."

Chills arced up Geoffrey's back. Tearing himself from Caroline's lips, he clutched her very close, gazing over her beautiful blond curls toward Louise. "Ralph? As in Baron Ralph Aldin?"

Louise nodded, her dark eyes huge. "'E's been the best. Lots o' blunt, an' in town only a few days a month."

"Bloody hell."

"Too right. 'E's got a mouth like a street hawker. 'E'll never keep mum."

The last thing Geoffrey wanted to hear was confirmation of his own fears coming from Louise. Shaking himself out of his aroused state, he frowned at the girl on the bed. "Stall him. We shall go out the back way."

"This isn't bleeding Buckingham Palace! There ain't no back way."

"Louise!" called the drunken baron from outside. "Open up, honey, it's yer sergeant-at-arms calling!"

"Oh, blimey," groaned Louise. Then she called louder to the door. "I'm coming, luv. Just let me get everything set t' rights."

Geoffrey's curses were more colorful but equally unproductive. Caroline said nothing at all, just leaned against him, her body a sweet temptation that was a constant drag on his thoughts. Still, he refused to set her aside.

"Where is your cloak?" he asked, trying not to inhale the gentle lavender scent of her hair.

Louise scrambled through her bedroom door into the sitting room. "I'll get it."

Geoffrey nodded, then looked back down at Caroline. Her expression was vague, as though she were deep in thought, but her lips were curved in the sweetest smile. Her skin held a delicate blush of rose on cream and whenever he inhaled, he smelled clean innocence.

"Caroline?"

"Hmmm?"

"I shall have to pretend you are a…a tart to get you out of here. It has to appear so ordinary, you will not stand out and he will not remember you at all."

"Very well, Geoffrey."

He frowned, searching Caroline's face. She looked calm. Actually, she looked beautiful. Her eyes were dazzlingly bright, as if filled with the stars above. She gazed at him with absolute trust, as though he were her knight in shining armor, and she was sure of his rescue. "Good God, but you are ravishing."

"Truly?" she asked, her eyes pulled wide with surprise and delight.

"Truly," he answered, dropping a chaste kiss on her nose, Then, with their mouths so close, hers tilting up to him, it was no surprise that before long he found himself again drowning in her kiss.

"Blimey," Louise said, sighing. "You two are worse than his nibs the Baron out there, and he's drunker than a pig wots caught the rum."

From outside, loud off-key singing shook the rafters. Inside, Caroline gazed up at Geoffrey with a mischievous twinkle in her eye. "Geoffrey? Do you think you can touch my bodice again? I believe I require more experience with that to fully comprehend everything Louise has told me."

He groaned, not sure he wanted to know exactly what she had learned. But his body was already tightening with hungry interest.

"Come on, luv," Louise coaxed. "Into the cloak and wrap it up tight."

Caroline did not seem in the least bit interested in covering up, but for the sake of his own sanity, as well as her reputation, Geoffrey quickly set her aside and bundled her up until naught but her nose appeared from beneath the gray wool.

"Go on, Geoffrey. I know wot t' do," Louise said, pushing them toward the door. Then she gave him a lusty wink. "But you got t' make it look good."

From deep within the folds of gray fabric, he heard a slightly strained sound. At first he was alarmed. Could Caroline be overset? Perhaps it had just dawned on her what sort of predicament they were in. Was she becoming hysterical? That was the last thing he needed. Quickly, with fumbling fingers, he pushed open the hood to see Caroline deep in the midst of a near-silent fit of laughter.

She must have seen his worried expression, for she stretched up on her toes to whisper into his ear, "Louise says there is so much more than simply touching my bodice. You will do it, won't you? After all, we must make things look correct."

He blinked. He could not tell if she was serious. It did not matter. The whole situation was beyond ludicrous, and the best option was to play along. So he said, with absolute seriousness, "Excellent suggestion, my dear. I am so glad you reminded me."

She flowed against him again, fitting her body with erotic ease to his. "I have never had so much fun with science before," she whispered.

"Is it better than your cannon experiments?" he asked, his voice hoarse.

"Oh, much!" came her enthusiastic response. And then they had no more time for conversation as he bent to claim her lips again, except that she was near shaking with laughter. That, of course, brought on his own fit, until all too soon, they were gasping for breath, their giggles rolling out while Louise stood over them shaking her head.

"Quality!" she said with a mixture of disgust and awe. "Bleeding soft in the 'ead, all of you."

Then she tugged Caroline's hood back in place before shooing them out the door. Simultaneously, she dragged in the boisterous baron. If he noticed who they were, both Geoffrey and Caroline were too busy laughing to see.


The ride back to her aunt's house was too quiet for Caroline. The laughter had died away, leaving her alone with her thoughts as the London streets passed unseen all around her.

She had tingled. Straight down to her toes, she had tingled and burned and hungered as never before. She had also laughed, and it was the most wonderful feeling in the world. It would take at least a page of notes to adequately describe these incredible sensations.

Why, she was tingling even now. They were sitting in Geoffrey's landaulet, her thigh pressed intimately against his, and she could barely think of anything except that he was right here with her. And she still tingled.

Which meant she was in love with Geoffrey. And probably had been for a while.

It was a wonderful thought. It was so delightful, in fact, that she wanted to sing aloud, to dance on the rooftops, to throw caution to the wind and declare herself right then and there.

Except he could not marry her. She knew that. He was looking for an heiress and nothing would sway him from that goal. Because for him, marriage was a matter of honor.

Caroline sighed, and into her murky, confused, unscientific thoughts, Geoffrey broke with a most unsettling question.

"Was what Louise said true? Did you really go there to find out how to...how to please me?"

Caroline swallowed, not sure how to answer. "N-no," she stammered. "I went there to gain another woman's perspective on your kisses. For my research, of course."

"Of course," he responded dryly as he clicked the horses into a faster trot.

"Louise merely got the wrong idea," Caroline continued. *Or the right one*, she told herself. After all, in light of her new knowledge of her own feelings, it was possible Louise had understood things better than Caroline could ever have guessed. She would have to discuss it with Louise next visit.

"You know you cannot go back to see Louise. Ever again."

Caroline jumped, startled by his perceptive comment. It was almost as if he had read her thoughts. "I...I like her. She has been very helpful."

"I do not doubt it." She could not miss the irony in his voice. "But it simply is not done. If anyone saw you, if the baron recognized you, it would be disastrous. You would be ruined. I would have to ma—" He stopped speaking abruptly, his words cut off by some tightly-reined emotion.

"Marry me?" she finished for him, her voice deadpan. "Surely you know that is not true. There could be any number of reasons for me to visit Louise."

"Do not be ridiculous. She is…She is not appropriate company for a gently bred woman." He spoke sternly, as if he did not wish to view the thing logically.

"But I am a bluestocking engaged in scientific research," she returned hotly. When he began to groan, she cut him off. "Very well, then. If you do not wish to reveal the truth to others, could we not simply say that I was engaged in charitable works? Aunt Win often visits the poor and wretched souls near Hadleigh. She brings them food and clothing and all manner of helpful things. Why could I not be doing that with Louise?"

He slanted a wry glance at her. "And what could you possibly bring Louise? Given her current protector, I vow she had more ready blunt than you do." Then he began shaking his head. "It won't fadge, Caroline. If you are discovered, if someone saw you, then I would be responsible. I would have to marry you."

"Your sense of honor requires nothing less," she said slowly, studying the words, wondering if indeed it were true. Not his sense of honor. She knew he had that in spades. But could they truly not find a way out? Even assuming she were caught in association with Louise? Or was Geoffrey somehow hoping to be forced to marry her?

Suddenly her heart leapt in her breast as she simultaneously wondered and prayed and wished it were so.

She saw his hands tighten on the reins, and when she looked up at him, she saw the harsh lines of pain etch deeper into his face. "I cannot marry you, Caroline," he said, his voice thick and rough. "I have my family to think of. Do not ask me to choose between you, my honor, and my family…" He cut his words off again, clearly in the grip of powerful emotions he refused to explain.

But she could not allow him to hide from her. Not when it was so important, to him as well as to her. She had to understand what he was thinking. "What, Geoffrey?" she pressed. "Explain this to me. I am not poor. I have a reasonable marriage portion. Are things so awful for you?"

"I have no dowry for my sister. I used it"

She blinked. Never in a thousand years would she have guessed Geoffrey would do something so questionable. Surely he'd had a good reason. He was not the sort of man to do things he himself thought so obviously immoral.

He did not look at her as he spoke. It was as if he explained to his horses, except each of his words seemed to tear at him like an open wound he exposed for her sake. "Our finances were recovering, but it was going slowly. With all my father's debts and the mortgage, everything was precarious. All I needed was a little ready cash, enough to replenish the stock and make some vital repairs. Perhaps a couple of investments."

"So you used her dowry?" That still did not seem like the Geoffrey she knew.

He nodded. "My sister swore she would not marry. She insisted I use it, said that she never liked the property anyway."

"You sold it."

"With an option to buy back anytime in the next five years. I was not going to lose her inheritance. It is her money, her property. But she insisted. Mother too. And with no suitor in sight, I…"

"You gave in."

"Except she has fallen in love. And they will be married in less than three weeks." He sighed. "Actually, they married in secret a few weeks ago, but I will not have to hand over her dowry until the formal event."

Caroline leaned forward, the financial side of her nature pushing to the fore. "What if you sold the new stock?"

"I overextended, Caro." He spoke softly, and she knew his confession cost him dearly. "If only I had a few more months. Time, at least, for prices to recover. I had not expected them to drop so fast."

"It will be shearing time soon," she offered. "The profits from that…"

"Not enough," he cut in. "Not unless I wish to starve the people who depend upon me. And not soon enough either. Three weeks, Caro. And with the mortgage due as well…" His voice trailed away as he shook his head. "If I had known, I would not have put in the mine improvements. I would not have bought so much stock. I would not have done this."

Caroline bit her lip, knowing he would not like her suggestion, but forced to voice it nonetheless. "Does your sister need her dowry?"

"It is *her* money!" Geoffrey exploded. Then he took a deep breath, though the movement seemed to press him deeper into his seat. "And yes, she needs it. The Major cannot support her as she is accustomed. They intend to travel, which is frightfully expensive. And she is…" He paused as he adjusted the reins in his hands. "She is in delicate health. They need the money to travel safely."

Caroline did not comment. Indeed, it seemed he needed her to listen to him, to hear his misery without judgment.

"I worked so hard, Caro. I never thought I would be here again. Back where I was five years ago when I had to find an heiress immediately."

"When you eloped with Gillian Ames."

Geoffrey stiffened, as Caroline knew he would. But she did not expect him to stop the horses dead in the road and turn to stare at her. "Who told you that?" he demanded harshly.

"No one. I reasoned it out."

"Of course." His words were dry and his expression grim as he turned his attention back to his horses.

She knew he did not want to discuss it further, but she could not let it go. She needed to understand. "How far did you go before Lord Mavenford stopped you?"

She was not sure he would answer. Then, when he did, she wished he had not. "We were married for ten minutes when Stephen arrived."

Caroline nearly fainted right then and there. He had married the woman? "But—"

"We had enough time to walk from the chapel to the dining room. Long enough for both of us to have second and third and fourth thoughts."

"But, if you were married—"

"Two earls together can accomplish many things, Caroline. And Stephen and Gillian were so in love." He sounded almost bitter. She was not sure why she was surprised. After all, he had plenty of reason to be angry. If he had married Gillian, he would not be in this predicament—still looking for an heiress, afraid of being exposed as a thief of his sister's dowry, and, worst of all, saddled with a woman who conducted kissing experiments and talked in detail with his mistress.

Geoffrey had become a ray of sunlight for her, the carefree man of society who never failed to make Caroline laugh, but somehow this pained side of him was even more endearing. Seeing his vulnerability made her want to comfort him as only a woman could.

But they were in the middle of a London street, so all she could do was reach forward and touch his gloved hand. It was a soft touch, a light caress meant to comfort him, but she felt the effects of it reverberate through her entire body.

Her blood heated as if a bonfire burned within her. Breathing became difficult, and all she could think of was where they could find a secluded location where she could kiss him again. And one look at his burning expression, the banked hunger that heated his gaze, told her his thoughts traveled along the exact same lines.

"Geoffrey—"

"This must stop, Caroline. This...this line of inquiry, as you put it, will destroy you."

"But—"

"No arguments! I cannot be forever snatching you out of disaster."

Caroline looked at Geoffrey's stem profile, read the clear determination on his face, the absolute belief that he had the right to dictate to her in such a way. But he did not.

*He did not*, she reaffirmed silently. So she folded her arms across her chest while the passion in her blood shifted to anger. "You sound very much like Harry when you speak like that." She saw him flinch and felt a measure of pleasure from it. "And I shall tell you exactly what I told him. I intend to continue whatever research I deem fit, and there will be no more discussion."

She meant to look away then, giving him her back as best as she could in the confines of his landaulet. But at that very moment, Geoffrey pulled hard on the reins, swerving them around a corner in the most alarming fashion.

"Geoffrey!" she cried out in true fear.

He did not even spare a moment to glance at her. Instead, he focused his entire attention on maneuvering his horses through the congested streets, never slowing his pace no matter what the risk.

"What are you doing?" she demanded.

"I am taking you somewhere private where I intend to pound some sense into you."

# CHAPTER 8

T hey arrived in short order at a small house in a respectable but rather poor area of town. Still, the residence appeared cheerful and well kept. Much more cheerful, in fact, than her companion.

"Is this your home?" Caroline asked quietly.

He did not speak, but nodded at her with a hard jerk of his chin. Indeed, beyond his last cryptic threat to pound some sense into her, Geoffrey had steadfastly refused to speak at all. He continued his silence as he drove the horses away from the house, around the back, and into the mews, and he did not help her down as he jumped from the landaulet and donned a protective apron before unhitching and storing the vehicle himself. Caroline could do no more than stand nearby, watching the play of his powerful muscles as he moved the conveyance into its proper place.

After nearly ten minutes, she stepped forward to speak with him, but his glare stopped her. "Not a word," he growled. "Not until we are inside and in private."

She nodded as she pressed her lips together. Then she watched as he went to work on the first of the two horses, grooming the animal and seeing to its feed. He had barely started when Caroline spied another apron. Without a moment's hesitation, she put it around her own clothing and began to care for the other horse. She thought at first that he would object, but this time her own steely determination won out. He returned to his task in silence.

As she worked, she could not help but shed a few tears. It broke her heart that he had to do such things himself. Many of the aristocracy would consider driving their own carriage and caring for their own horses beneath them. That Geoffrey did it without even a grumble underscored exactly how close to ruin the Tallis family teetered. Geoffrey obviously could not even afford a stable boy. Which meant his situation was more dire than she had ever guessed.

He finished his task before she did, coming up beside her and taking the brush from her hand. "You are getting your clothes dirty," was all he said.

Knowing better than to argue, Caroline stepped away, once again relegated to the position of observer while he quickly completed the task. Then, still without speaking, he grabbed her arm at the elbow and steered her toward the house.

He opened the rear door with his key, ushering her inside and forward into a sparse parlor. No butler offered to take her cloak. Indeed, no footman, maid, or other servant appeared at all. The house seemed deserted.

As if sensing her thoughts, he glanced toward the empty hallway. "Though no one knows, Mother and her maid have gone to Staffordshire to help Sophia. We have no other servants."

Caroline nodded, accepting this further proof of his poverty as she pulled off her cloak. "Is Sophia ill?"

Geoffrey's lips twisted into a rueful expression. "Not ill. Just delicate. And overwhelmed with planning for both a wedding and a move to India. For some female reason I cannot understand, Mother thought it less suspicious if she claimed an illness and supposedly took to her bed. Since Sophia has always been so independent, Mother thought it might seem strange if she ran to her daughter's side now."

Caroline frowned, trying to absorb his enigmatic comment, studying Geoffrey's expression as much as his words. Then her eyes widened as she at last understood. "Sophia is in a *delicate* condition. She's pregnant. That is why her wedding cannot be delayed."

He nodded, his expression grim. "My point is that you are, right now, visiting my ill mother. Your reputation is safe."

She sighed. "You know I don't in the least bit care—"

"I know you don't!" he exploded before she could finish. "And that is entirely the problem! No experiment, science or otherwise, is worth your reputation. Caroline, don't you understand? You could be ruined. For life. Then what will you do? How will you survive?"

She threw her arms up in the air, amazed that he could be so stupid. "I am a scientist. And scientists perform scientific experiments."

"In human carnal relations?" he scoffed.

She glared at him, her anger making her heart pound within her chest. "I want to know," she said loudly. Firmly. "I have always wanted to know…"

"Why your mother left?"

She stilled, her breath caught within her as she stared at him. When she could finally force herself to inhale, it came as a loud gasp.

"Caroline?"

"This has nothing to do with her," she finally managed.

"Truly?" he challenged. "Then you don't wish to know why she would abandon you and your father for a gypsy? This…" He gestured vaguely out the door toward Mayfair. "This research of yours doesn't have anything to do with finding out why passion could so overwhelm a woman that she leaves her home and family?"

She flinched away from him, feeling his words cut into her. But he would not let her go. Before she could do more than turn her head, he was in front of her, holding her shoulders steady, his gaze uncompromising. "Caroline—"

"You don't know anything about my mother!" she cried before he could say anything more.

"*I* would want to know," he returned evenly. "If I were you, I would pursue it like a dog after a bone. I would dig everywhere, ask everyone, read everything just to find out. What could so entice a parent away from his family?"

She frowned at him, catching the pronoun switch from "her family" to "his family." And suddenly she understood. "Your father. You wanted to know why he stayed away."

Geoffrey released a bitter laugh as his hands dropped. "Oh, I know why. Wenching and gambling and town life is much more exciting than sheep husbandry." He slanted her an arch look. "I believe you, too, are beginning to understand that."

She felt her face heat with a blush. Yes, London was much more exciting than Hadleigh. And yet...She looked at Geoffrey, her pulse speeding up just by seeing him, by knowing he was within reach, that all she need do is take a single step, and she could touch him.

But her mind would not let her take that step. It was still focused on Geoffrey's past. On how he was so different from his father. "You have stayed away from London. You have raised sheep and watched your coffers. You have not been..." She struggled to find the word. "You are not tempted to..." She leaned toward him. "Why?"

His expression softened, and he reached out, extending one finger to stroke her cheek. She felt his caress like a brand, burning her skin as he trailed it across her cheek until he tugged at her lower lip. "I am tempted," he said, his voice rough. "But I already know."

"What?" Her word was barely more than a breath, but he heard it anyway.

He stepped closer, and his finger dropped away from her lip. She drew a small breath, mourning the loss of his heat. But then she felt him cup her left breast, his touch casual even as he lifted it, rubbing his thumb across her tightened nipple. "That this is fleeting."

She shook her head, her eyes closing of their own accord. "No," she whispered. "It is wonderful."

"Yes," he murmured, as his other hand took hold of her right breast, squeezing her until she moaned out loud. "Wonderful. Exciting." His voice held a note of awe, and then suddenly, he pulled away. "But over in an instant."

The loss of his support nearly overbalanced her, but she caught herself on him, grabbing his arms as she gazed up into his dark gray-green eyes. In them, she saw a hunger to match her own, and despite his impassive expression, she felt a shudder run through his body into hers. "It is not over," she whispered, wondering if her words were a command or a plea.

Either way, he denied her, setting her away from him with a firmness belied by the way his fingers still lingered over her own. "It is," he said softly.

"I don't believe you," she returned, amazed by her own certainty. Her pulse beat through her thoughts like a drum, urging her forward into his arms and giving strength to her words. "I have kissed many men, Geoffrey. I have pages of notes." Indeed, she tugged the pages out of her reticule, dropping them on the floor by his feet. "Each kiss felt sweet in its own way—"

"Caroline," he groaned. "You cannot—"

"Each kiss except yours," she interrupted. Then she stepped into his arms, raising up on her toes to lightly brush her lips against his. He stood stock still, even when she stroked the outside of his hands, fisted by his thighs. "Their kisses were sweet, then over. But yours..." She tentatively extended her tongue, licking and teasing his closed mouth as he had once done to her. "I dream about your kisses. I sit at my desk during the day and remember them. I lie in bed at night and pretend you are with me." Taking his clenched hands in hers, she raised them up, kissing his fingers, gently tugging at them until they relaxed, opening up. Then she drew his hands back to her bodice, molding them against her. "Your touch is different, Geoffrey. And I want to know why."

"No." His word came as a groan—a denial and a plea. But his hands never left her breasts, and even if he tried to release her, she was pressing against him, reaching up to draw his mouth more firmly against hers.

"Show me, Geoffrey. Please."

He was resisting, holding himself apart from her, but at her words she felt his will melt away. He made no sound as he claimed her lips, and the power of his touch spoke more eloquently than any words.

Her lips were already open, waiting for possession. He took them with a ferocity that stole her breath. Always before, she had felt a slight distance in his touch. As if part of him objected to their union. But she felt none of that now. He invaded her mouth, stroking, taking, owning all of it. And she gave herself to him completely.

His fingers pinched at her nipples, sending shocking tingles straight to her belly, making her arch against him, press her lips against the thick brand within his trousers. She had never felt one before, and even through the separation of their clothing she was amazed at the size.

Then she lost all thought as his mouth left hers to nibble along her jaw, her neck, and down across her collarbone. Her dress loosened about her before she even realized that his hands had left her bodice. And then he used his teeth to draw the gown from her shoulders, pinning her arms against her as he tugged at it.

"Don't move," he said, his voice a low rumble that seemed to sink into her blood and set her limbs trembling.

Her gown settled on her hips, the shoulder caps trapping her wrists. Pressing her backwards, Geoffrey guided her to the settee, helping her sit, even as his fingers settled beneath her chemise, lifting it off of her. Soon, she was naked from the waist up, exposed to his hungry gaze.

"You are truly beautiful, Caroline," he whispered reverently against her dun. "Don't let anyone tell you differently."

She would have answered him, would have told him his judgment of beauty was clouded. But the way he looked at her, the raw desire she saw in his eyes and felt in his touch, all combined to keep her silent. They told her, without words, that she was indeed beautiful to him.

"Thank you," she finally whispered. And then he began again.

She thought she understood. She thought from a few strokes and kisses that she could extrapolate what it would feel like to have a man touch her naked skin. She was wrong. The brush of his palm against her distended nipple shot enough fire through her body that she nearly leaped off the settee. But he held her still. He pressed down against her, settling himself between her knees as he kissed first her quivering belly, then higher, beneath her left breast, across its mound, before capturing the peak.

*Glorious.* The word shot through her mind on a current of electricity. Even as she cried out at the sensation, part of her mind catalogued it all: the rough scratch of his afternoon beard across her skin, the cool whisper of air across the places he had wet with his lips, and the pull and tumble of his tongue as he suckled. Those were the external sensations.

Of much more power was the explosion of feelings within her. Her heart pounded, seeming to pulse wherever he touched. Her limbs trembled with weakness, allowing her legs to go slack, opening further as he pressed between them. And her womb, the area low in her belly which had never before occupied her thoughts, now seemed to grow liquid, softening, perhaps melting from his attention.

She wanted to touch him, but her hands remained manacled by her gown. "Take off your shirt," she whispered.

He did not seem to hear her, even when she began to squirm, desperately trying to free her hands from her sides. Finally, she succeeded, ripping her dress as she freed herself. She reached forward without hesitation, tugging at his clothing, fumbling with his buttons as much as her awkward fingers allowed.

He helped her, shedding his coat, cravat, and shirt with efficient movements. Caroline took the time to push her gown to the floor, kicking it away as she tugged at her stockings. But before she could finish, his fingers replaced hers, drawing the fabric down her legs, opening her wider as he stroked her sensitive skin.

She looked at him then, his golden skin outlining the corded muscles of his upper body. She saw no softening in the hard planes of his chest, but when she reached out to touch him, the muscles flexed and rippled, like waves on a pond.

"Adonis," she whispered.

He glanced up at her, and she saw surprise in his dark gaze. "I once saw a picture of Adonis," she explained. "Harry said no man really looked like that, but he was wrong." She smiled, continuing to stroke him, glorying in the hot silk of his skin. "You do."

He pressed a kiss against her inner thigh, and she looked down, suddenly realizing her position. She sat completely naked before him. He kneeled between her legs, exposing her as she had never been before, even in private. But she felt no shame, only a glorious wonder as his kisses continued.

"I am going to show you," he said against her skin. "You will feel what women feel. And then you will know."

She knew what came next. Louise had been most explicit, so she reached down, tugging at his trousers, ripping two buttons free before he grabbed her wrist, firmly drawing her away. "I will not take your virginity, Caroline. I will not ruin you."

She drew back, startled by his statement. Until he had spoken the words, she had not realized what they were about to do. What she wanted him to do. "I want this," she said softly, speaking more to herself than to him. "I want to know." Then she looked directly at him, showing him the determination in her mind and body. "I want to feel. All of it." Then she felt a sudden wave of self-consciousness, of awareness. Perhaps…"Don't you? Don't you want…me?"

She had not expected pain to flash through his expression, not with the raw, open desire that blazed in his eyes. "I want you," he said, his voice low and guttural. Then he placed his hands on her knees, abruptly pushing them apart. "I want to bury myself so deeply inside you that we shall never be parted again." He looked up, and she saw that his jaw was clenched with the effort of his restraint. "But I will not. I will not dishonor you."

"But…" She started to straighten off the settee, but he did not allow her. Instead, he pressed his face to her in the most intimate of kisses, and the explosion of sensation that shot through her body had her screaming his name.

Moments before, she had tried to catalogue what she felt, storing the sensations in her memory for later analysis. This time, no part of her remained distant. Her entire mind, body, and soul participated, reeling from the myriad impressions, quivering with the tension he created. She felt his fingers opening her wider while his tongue swirled over some incredible place, some amazing spot she had never dreamed existed.

Then he twisted her sideways on the settee, lifting her leg, trapping her as much with her precarious balance on the settee as with his own body pressed against her. She felt an invasion, the press of his finger pushing into her, but not deeply enough. Not fully enough. She arched, wanting more, crying out in need as she began to tremble. Her legs tightened around him, even as she felt another finger join his first.

Yes. Deeper. Fuller.

More.

Then, abruptly, she shattered. Her body convulsed, and she screamed. The tremors shook her whole body, overcoming her precarious balance until she tumbled off the narrow settee. Fortunately, Geoffrey caught her and they fell together. She barely knew what was happening, except that, when at last her consciousness reassembled, she lay in his arms on the floor, her naked body at last touching his bare skin.

"Geoffrey," she whispered with awe, but he stopped her.

"Shhhh," he said as he kissed her forehead. "Rest a moment."

She complied, closing her eyes as she perceived a strange languor throughout her body. And yet, it did not seem enough. Even as her fingers began stroking across Geoffrey's chest, her mind began to work, thinking and wondering.

"I think I understand now," she said.

"Good," he returned. But she noticed his voice was tight, and even more, that his muscles beneath her fingers still quivered and jerked beneath her stroke.

"This is why my mother left," she said. "For this feeling."

"Yes," he answered quietly.

Except as wonderful as she felt, the sensation had a hollow feeling, an empty echo that whispered a discordant note through her mind. It took a while for her to identify it. She was lying, languid and content, her legs intertwined with Geoffrey's, but somewhere in her thoughts something was wrong.

She tried to analyze it, to scientifically move through the sensations, but her mind was still too fuzzy to focus. And besides, she suddenly realized, this was not about thinking. It was about feeling.

And that was the moment she understood.

Geoffrey. Geoffrey was not as content, as relaxed, as open as she was. Whereas she had been completely exposed to him, her feelings and thoughts, indeed her entire body unveiled, he had remained distant from her. That was why he remained tense now. That was why he called the experience fleeting. Because despite his assistance in this most glorious event, she had gone through the experience alone. He had kept himself apart from her.

Thinking back to her mother, to her parents, she suddenly understood the parallel. As much as she adored her father, he too was completely absorbed in his own world. In his science. In his research. In himself. When her parents had shared this most special time, most likely, her mother had gone through it alone.

Aunt Win had said her mother was lonely. Looking at Geoffrey now, Caroline realized it must have been true. Mama had no one to share her life with, and so she had left. Just as Geoffrey now spent his life alone, using his honor, his lack of finances, his duty to his family to keep himself apart. He had given her a gift of this moment, but he had refused to share it with her, and so ultimately it had been unfulfilling.

She shifted, turning to study his face. "Geoffrey..." she began.

"Yes?" He was still tense, his face and his body closed to her even as she lay in his arms.

"Is this how all your liaisons have gone? Is it always like this?"

He paused, they nodded. "Essentially. Yes."

She knew why he hedged. But she was focused on something else entirely. "Do you share your feelings with Louise? Do you talk to her?"

He turned to look at her, his brows pushed down in confusion. "I have not talked with Louise in years."

"And there has been no one else, has there? No one at your estate?"

She watched his lips curl slightly in a self-mocking expression. "Only you, Caroline. I have not touched anything but ledgers, livestock, and mine improvements for many years." He dropped a gentle kiss upon her forehead. "Does that make you feel better?"

She shook her head, reaching out to stroke his chiseled jaw. "No, Geoffrey. It does not. It makes me sad. It reminds me of my mother."

She watched surprise spark in his eyes. "I assure you," he drawled. "I am not insane."

Caroline ignored the small hurt that welled up inside her and said, "And perhaps neither was my mother." She shifted against him, lifting up onto one elbow so she could see him more clearly. "I saw her once, you know. With her gypsy. They were walking in a field together."

"And they were laughing? Completely happy?" His voice was dry with cynicism.

She shook her head, and her hair brushed across his shoulder. "No. Actually, I think they were discussing something quite serious. Or perhaps not, I don't know. But I do recall the way he looked at her. He listened when she spoke, holding her hand and looking directly at her. And then when he said something, she became equally still, sharing in his words. They were completely in tune with one another, completely open without barriers."

She shook her head, struggling to find a way to express herself. "I do not know how to explain it, except that I had never seen two people like that before. My father, Harry, even Aunt Win, they say things then hurry away. Even when we are all at the table, it is as if each of us sits there alone. Looking at my mother and her..." She swallowed, able for the first time to say it aloud. "Seeing Mama with her gypsy lover, I knew that when they ate together, they would not be alone. They were with each other. Indeed, I believe that even when they were apart, before she left us, even then her thoughts were with him."

She focused back on Geoffrey, wondering if he understood what she was trying to say. What she saw startled her. He wore an expression of longing. It was an intense expression quickly covered by a wistful shrug. "No," he whispered, "I don't suppose your mother was mad. Indeed, if what you say is true, she may very well have been the most sane person in your entire household."

Caroline nodded. "I am beginning to think so, too."

Then Geoffrey reached up, caressing her cheek before absently coiling a lock of her hair around his finger. "And do you think that I am equally besotted with you?"

She shook her head, feeling her eyes tear with the movement. She knew now the truth of it. That as much as she loved him, Geoffrey had not opened himself up to her nearly that much. And that as long as he remained closed off, as long as he remained in his honor-bound prison, he would never be able to love anyone.

And it was at that moment that she came to a decision. It was not a fleeting thought nor a lust-based desire, but a full blown decision appearing completely whole in her mind. As long as Geoffrey clung to his honor, using it to isolate himself from his family, his friends, from those like herself who loved him, he would never find a love of his own. He would never be able to express that love or open himself up to it.

Therefore, step by tiny step, she had to convince him to abandon his honor. Except she had no words to do that. Indeed, words could easily be ignored. But actions...

She looked down at him, seeing his drawn features and clenched jaw. Farther down his body, past his bare chest, she noticed the bulge pushing through his trousers and knew what it meant. He still wanted her. Physically. But he was holding himself apart because of his honor.

She trembled slightly, understanding the risk she was about to take. By forcing the issue, by making him abandon his honor, she would be betraying him. Not only would she lose her virginity, but she might very well lose him to his anger.

But he was worth the risk. For Geoffrey, she would risk everything, including her virginity.

If she could show him, just once, what it was like to truly share with a person, to allow himself to feel as she had just done, then perhaps he would be able to love. Certainly she prayed that he would love her, but even if he did not...

She swallowed, forcing herself to continue, even in the silence of her own thoughts. Even if he did not come to love her, then he would at least be able to find love somewhere else. Was that not worth everything she had to offer? Even her virginity?

"You are remarkably quiet," he said softly.

"I am thinking," she returned.

She watched his lips quirk into a half smile. "Oh pray, not that. Whenever you begin to think, I end up—"

"Doing something you regret?"

He smiled, and again he stroked her cheek, his expression hauntingly vulnerable. "No," he whispered. "No, I shall never regret the moments I have spent with you."

If she had not fully decided before, his words laid her last doubts to rest. He did not regret his time rescuing her, watching over her, or even showing her what he understood of love. Therefore, how could she regret showing him what she had learned? The answer was simple. She could not.

And so, with her decision firmly in place, she shifted up to her knees.

"Caroline?"

"I want to see it," she said firmly as she began to trail her hand down his chest.

"What?" He grabbed for her hand, holding his still against his belly.

She looked directly into his horrified eyes. "Louise said there were things I could do that would not endanger my virginity."

He released a bitter laugh, part humor, part groan. "Caroline, my sweet, there are limits to even my self-restraint."

"Trust me," she returned as she reached forward to kiss his clenched jaw. "Close your eyes. I know what to do."

As she moved, her breasts rolled across his chest, igniting the fire in her blood once again. They seemed to do even more for Geoffrey; his body jerked in reaction, his hand coming off the floor to touch her. He was resisting. She could tell by the uneven movements with which he claimed her breasts. A hard grasp one moment, a reluctant release the next. All the while, his eyes were clenched tight, and he groaned her name. "I will not dishonor you," he gasped.

"I am not dishonored," she soothed as she gently tugged her hand out of his restraining grasp. "You could never do that." She kissed him again, tiny bites along his lips while her hand trailed down his chest, moving slowly until she at last reached the barrier of his clothing.

She was pleased when he finally gave in to the inevitable. His touch gentled, became teasing as it had been earlier.

And, as she finished undoing the buttons of his trousers, he released her long enough to help her tug them free.

Then she could look at him. Openly. Scientifically.

Hungrily.

She was stunned by the heat in the area. Even before his clothing had been completely removed, the backs of her fingers felt seared. And now there was his size. He was large. Amazingly so.

"Caroline, don't…"

She turned back to look at his face, a grin pulling at her lips. "I absolutely will," she said firmly. "Now close your eyes. I cannot do this with you looking at me."

He slowly complied, reluctance in every line of his face. She did not care. Instead, she reached out, touching him first gently, then more firmly. She felt his textures, his ripples and bulges. She noted his veins and how tight his skin seemed stretched.

Indeed, the entire area was fascinating to her. But what she found most interesting was the noises he made. He told her so much of what he enjoyed merely by the catch of his breath or an occasional low moan. She watched in delight as the muscles in his belly contracted with her movements. She felt his thighs bunch, pushing him forward against her hand.

Mindful of what Louise had told her, Caroline shifted into a better position, closer to where she explored. She changed her touch from gentle to firm, then back again to gentle, establishing a rhythm that seemed to beat in her own blood as well as Geoffrey's.

Indeed, she seemed to have grown as excited as he was. Her own breath had accelerated. Her nipples were tight, and she released her own small cry as he reached down and caught one tight bud in his hand, holding and tweaking it even as she shifted to again firmly stroke him.

He moaned her name and she closed her eyes, relishing the sound. She knew it was time. If Louise were to be believed, his moment of triumph was near. Already, he was moving hard against her hand, the slide and feel of him a strange and delightful thing.

She was ready as well. Her body liquid with fire as he tweaked and pulled at her breast. Lower down, she felt open, womanly, and oh, so hungry for him.

So with a single quick motion, she did it. She straddled him, pressing herself downward onto him before he could do more than open his eyes. He slid in so perfectly, and nothing could have felt better.

It was sharp. Hard. And full.

It was smoother than she expected. And the bite of pain as her virginity broke less intense than she had been told.

*Wonderful.*

"Caroline!" He jerked upward, reaching for her, grabbing her arms as he tried to pull her off. But she would not release him. Instead, she let her head drop back, pressing deeper onto him, feeling herself stretch around him.

"Share this with me," she said. She felt so full, her heart and her body swelled with love for him. He was inside her now, and she could not be more content. She looked at him, opening her heart and soul to him, silently willing him to feel as vulnerable with her as she was with him.

"Oh, my God," he groaned, but she did not know whether he spoke in horror or ecstasy.

Louise had not told her what to do at this point, but she seemed to know anyway. She rolled her hips, relishing the feel of him inside of her. Then she raised up slightly before settling back down.

She heard his breath catch and felt his hands grip her arms spasmodically. She continued to move; could not seem to stay still, wanting to feel every sensation, every movement of his body within hers.

"You should not have done this," he said between gasps.

She grinned and leaned down to kiss him. "I had to."

He seized her breasts with his hands at the same moment she captured his mouth. His kiss was frenzied, demanding, and oh so hot. And even better, he began to move of his own accord. Not fighting her, but surging into her, hard and deep.

*Look at me*, she cried silently as he built the wave again. *Be with me*. She matched his rhythm, crashing against him as he rose up toward her. Her body began to quiver, and her mind began to expand.

This was true fullness. Together. One inside the other.

The wave was part of her now, drawing her upward then pulling her downward in a crashing ecstasy.

She looked down at Geoffrey, seeing the tension in his body, the hunger in his movements as he, too, became engulfed in sensation. Then he opened his eyes. Their gazes caught and held. She saw it then, saw his eyes widen as he realized what had happened. He saw directly into her soul, saw the love there, saw the ecstasy he built inside her.

And she saw it within him. Love was within them both. It surrounded them. It was them.

And then, at the final thrust of his hips, she felt herself shatter again. Her consciousness splintered, but this time he was with her. Their cries mingled. Their bodies fused.

And for the first time, her heart felt truly whole. With Geoffrey.

"At last," she whispered as she collapsed onto him. "I understand."

But did he?

Geoffrey stirred, a myriad of contradictory sensations assaulting his mind. First and foremost, he realized he was smiling. In fact, a bone-deep feeling of contentment seemed to have sunk into him—body and soul. The attitude was so rare that it felt odd, and yet it seemed so perfect he couldn't imagine why he'd ever stopped searching for just this feeling.

Other sensations crowded forward, clouding his rosy aura of bliss. A warm, naked body curled against his side, her silky hair spread across his arm and shoulder like a wonderful cocoon.

*Caroline*. As her name whispered through his mind, his smile grew to a grin, and he turned his head to drop a kiss on her forehead. Unfortunately, that movement brought with it a host of realizations.

They were lying on the floor, he noticed. The parlor floor, as a matter of fact, and frankly, his body was not used to resting on such a hard surface. Then, as he bestowed another kiss, his left hip shifted painfully over a new bruise, and he released a muffled groan.

At that awful moment, everything came flooding back. The bruise brought to mind exactly what they had been doing to cause the injury. Caroline had straddled him, and the resulting scenario…

She had straddled him!

He had taken her virginity.

Dishonored her!

"Geoffrey? Are you all right?"

He shifted to look into her beautiful blue eyes. He saw the flushed look of a well-loved woman and felt the sensuous slide of her long, satiny legs across his. More than that, he felt himself grow heavy with desire again.

"Oh, God!" he exclaimed as he scrambled to his feet. He was not delicate. In fact, if she had not already lifted her head from his shoulder, she likely would have bounced it on the floor as she tumbled away from him.

"Geoffrey?" Her eyes were wide with shock, and he saw fear skate through her expression as she bit her lower lip.

He looked at her mouth now, memories flooding his mind. He had kissed those lips. And if he let his sight drift lower…The things they had done! "Oh, God," he groaned. Then he tore his gaze away from her luscious body, forcing himself to focus on something else. Anything else.

His clothes. He snatched them up, more interested in hiding his obvious interest in her than in donning the restrictive fabric. And all the while, his mind whirled while he babbled out loud. "I shouldn't have…We shouldn't have. But…You…I…But, I can't!"

"We did, Geoffrey," she interrupted. Then her face lit with pleasure. "And I understand now. All my life, I have wondered. Why did she go? How could she have left me? Left us, my father and me." She grinned as she looked at him. "It was for this."

"No!" He lowered his head as he tried to think.

"Yes. For love. Oh, Geoffrey, what we did, what we shared; it was love. I am in love with you."

His head jerked up. "Caroline," he began, though he hadn't the foggiest idea what he meant to say.

"Just as my mother was in love with her gypsy, I am in love with you. Just like her, I would risk everything." She suddenly shifted, raising to her knees as she spoke. "I would leave everything I know for you."

He moaned. It was not an intentional sound, but a feeling that surged from deep within him. "You cannot…"

She grinned. "Of course not. There is no need. But my mother had to. And now I see why." She hopped up onto her feet. "Oh, thank you, Geoffrey."

He threw his arms up to his face, pressing his palms to his eyes as he tried to contain the pain he felt, to hold in the anguish. "No!" he cried. "You cannot, because I cannot!"

"Of course, I can, silly," she giggled. "I love you."

Then when he moaned in agony, she came to him. He felt her tug at his arms, pulling them away from his face. He let her do it. He allowed his arms to drop back down, then forced himself to look at her when he crushed her hopes. "Don't you understand?" he said. "I cannot throw everything away for you. It would destroy everyone to no purpose." He gripped her hands as he pressed his point. "Caroline, you cannot love me!"

"But I do," she responded happily. Then, before he could speak, she freed her hand and pressed her fingers to his lips. "I do not expect you to marry me. You have made your position quite clear. I just wanted you to know that I do love you. Which I never expected. But you are the only one since my mother who can make me laugh, who can make me forget that I am an old bluestocking with nothing but chemical experiments and sheep husbandry in my future." She lifted her fingers, then pressed a sweet kiss to his lips. "I know you did not intend to take my virginity. That was entirely my doing." She twirled away from him, raising her arms in happiness. "But I understand everything now!" she cried. "Thanks to you."

He watched her spin, seeing joy surround her like a glowing aura. Indeed, her entire body seemed to sparkle in the fading sunlight, and his heart twisted painfully in his chest. Guilt, shame, dishonor, all those emotions knotted within him, coiling like snakes in his soul.

And yet, he had brought her such an odd but unquestionable happiness that part of him could not regret his actions. She was giggling. The sweet beautiful girl was actually giggling.

"I do not understand," he moaned.

"But of course you do!" she exclaimed as she spun back to him, reaching for his hands. "You felt it, too. I know you did. You shared it with me. You loved me!" She meant to kiss him then. She, the most incredible, amazing woman he had ever known, was going to kiss him, the man who had just ruined her.

It was too much for him. Reaching out, Geoffrey pulled her into his embrace, circling her body with his as he once again breathed in the heady scent that was her. "Oh, God, Caroline, I cannot think. I don't know what to do."

He felt her smile. He knew without looking that it was a mischievous expression, a secret womanly smile filled with some special plan. He was not even sure he wanted to know, but she told him anyway. "I know you cannot marry me," she said happily. "Not until I have a fortune."

He sighed, feeling the weight of his name like an anvil around his neck. It dragged at his shoulders, and he curled even more protectively around her. "You have scores of men throwing themselves at you. Even now. After today…" He swallowed painfully around the constriction in his throat. "After how I have dishonored you—"

"But you haven't!"

He shook his head, continuing despite her denial. "I shall find you a husband. One who will give you more than chemical experiments and sheep. I swear it."

She lifted her head, beaming a golden smile at him, and he saw love shining through her eyes like a beacon. "But I have found someone," she said. "Now I must find a fortune so I can marry him—or rather you."

He felt his body still. His whirling thoughts shuddered to a stop, and he looked down at her. "Find a fortune?"

"Yes, you silly goose," she returned, her smile still blindingly bright. "How else can we marry?"

He stared at her, his mind too numb to grapple with what she'd said. Find a fortune? She could not be serious, could she? He took in her calm demeanor, the absolute certainty shining in her eyes, and he knew that she was indeed serious. She intended to find a fortune.

# CHAPTER 9

Geoffrey was reeling. First she said she loved him. He probably should have expected that. Their…encounter…this afternoon had been the best experience of his life. He could not even find the words to describe their lovemaking. And it had been her first time.

Of course, she would think she loved him. It was the natural conclusion any gently reared female would make. But it was an illusion. One that even he, with all his experience, felt dangerously tempted to believe.

But it was not love, and she had to understand that.

"Caroline, I know what we shared was—"

"Wonderful?"

He smiled. "Oh yes."

She grinned, her dimple winking mischievously at him. "I thought so as well. And now I know why."

"Because it was your first time." He leaned over, grasping her chemise off the settee and offering it to her. He could not think rationally with her standing naked before him. It was too tempting a sight. As it was, he barely restrained himself from extending to caress her full breasts as they bounced with her movements. "Please, could you not get dressed? Your aunt will be wondering where you are."

She looked out the window where, through the gauze curtains, the last rays of sunlight were fast losing ground to the dark buildings of London. "Oh…of course." She quickly pulled on her chemise, her muffled voice coming through the fabric. "But you know, first times are not always wonderful. Why, Louise told me—"

"Please, do not bring Louise into it."

Caroline looked over at him, watching as he gathered the various articles of her clothing. "But she was most specific. She said the first time is usually quite painful unless the girl is in love." She grinned. "I can barely recall the moment, Geoffrey. All of it was so exceptionally perfect. The pain was nothing!"

He groaned, at last seeing the source of her misconception. "An experienced gentleman—"

"Such as yourself," she put in, though from her expression, she did not like that particular fact.

"Er, yes. An experienced gentleman can make the first time extremely pleasurable for both parties."

She shook her head, her curls spilling across her shoulders in the most erotic fashion. "But you did nothing, Geoffrey. If you recall, I was the one—"

"I remember," he said. Indeed, how could he forget? "But you were quite, um, prepared beforehand. And that, my dear, was entirely my doing."

She did not comment at first, simply busying herself with the necessities of dressing. He assisted, of course. She could not have buttoned her dress otherwise, though the heat from her body, the smooth play of fabric across her back, nearly had him undoing the very work she had just completed.

Nevertheless he remained firm, and soon she was appropriately clad, allowing him to breathe freely for the first time in several moments.

"You do not think we are in love?" she challenged as she began pinning up her hair.

His heart lurched, but he forced the word out nonetheless. "No."

"You do not believe our kisses are different because we adore each other?"

"No." This time, he had to push the word out between clenched teeth.

"You do not think—"

"No!" He did not know where his anger came from. It was certainly not the appropriate response of a man who had just taken a naive girl's virginity, but it burned through his system nonetheless. He jerked on his shirt, glaring at the buttons as he fastened them. "I would marry you, Caroline," he said harshly.

Out of the corner of his eye, he saw her shoulders lift as a dreamy look came over her expression. "Oh, Geoffrey—"

"I would, but I *cannot*. I told you that from the very beginning. Without a fortune, Mother and I will end up in debtor's prison. And whereas I might be able to survive, she is too old. Too fragile."

He watched her expression slide from dreamy joy to a steely determination that terrified him. "I understand that," she said. "Which is why I have to go make my fortune."

He groaned, dropping his head back as he contemplated the cracked plaster ceiling. "No one just goes out and finds a fortune."

"I do," she returned happily. He ground his teeth, but she was quick to forestall his comments. "I do not expect to search for it under the cabbage roses like some buried treasure. Be sensible, Geoffrey." Her eyes danced with merriment, and he could do little more than gawk at her.

She was teasing him! Caroline Woodley, the most serious-minded woman he had ever met, was teasing him. The question was just how much of this was a joke?

"Caroline—"

"I have investments, Geoffrey. I have been working on them for a while, here and there as time permitted. Only now I intend to devote my efforts exclusively to making enough money so I can become your heiress."

Geoffrey ran his hand over her face, frowning as he tried to grapple with her intentions. "It is not as easy as it sounds,

Caroline. You cannot just invest in something and have your money double overnight."

"I know that. I expect it will take at least a couple of weeks—"

"A couple of weeks!" he sputtered, struggling to maintain control of his sanity. But before he could get the words out, he felt her hand warm on his. A surge of lust washed over him, reminding him that a bare hour ago, she had been soft and pliant in his arms, her delectable body open and hungry for him. "Caroline…"

"Do not worry. I have managed my father's estate since I was twelve. I know what I am doing."

He twisted away from her, wanting to draw her back into his arms, to press her beneath him, lose himself in her until they both forgot everything, including this latest bizarre scheme of Caroline's. But he could not. Touching was exactly what had landed them in this muddle in the first place. He had to use reason, appeal to her scientific side, convince her with straightforward, honest logic that she was being foolish.

"Caroline." He began slowly, planning each word before he spoke. "Managing an estate is far different than choosing appropriate investments. You could lose everything in an incredibly rapid amount of time. It all depends upon spotting the difference between a sound investment and one that will go bankrupt in a fortnight— something that even the most brilliant investors sometimes muddle."

She smiled at him, her nose wrinkling in the most adorable way. "I know all that. I am not a child."

"But—"

"Besides, I will have you to assist me. By all accounts, you are a brilliant investor."

He groaned. "If that were true, I would not be in need of an heiress."

"Nonsense. You have paid off all your father's debts, you have begun buying back your family lands, and you may even realize some profits soon from that mining enterprise.

If you weren't trying to replace your sister's dowry right now, you would be in a relatively healthy position. The timing is wrong; that's all."

Geoffrey felt his eyes widen in surprise. "How do you know all that?"

Caroline shrugged. "I asked Aunt Win who asked your mother who spoke at length with your man of affairs. We had tea together last Thursday."

"Spies," Geoffrey muttered. "Spies in my own household."

"Nonsense," returned Caroline. "Oh, and I quite agree with your mother. You should not feel such obligation regarding your sister's dowry."

"My obligations are none of your affair!" he snapped.

"Well, of course they are. You have invested her dowry and that's why you need to find an heiress. Though, why you do not just give them a portion of the investment—"

"They will be living in India, Caroline. It shall be rather difficult for them to get a few hundred head of sheep onto the boat."

"Oh. True." She frowned, her gaze growing abstract. "And now is not the time to sell your stock?"

"No."

She looked up at him, her forehead furrowed as she concentrated. "What about giving them equivalent shares in the mine?"

He shook his head. "The agreement I made with my financers was that I alone control the investment. I cannot sell out."

"Hmmm. Which leads us back to my first conclusion. I must find a fortune."

Geoffrey shook his head. "Caroline—"

"Oh, hush. You are worse than Aunt Win. You do not think I can do it."

"That is not true." He was firm as he touched her, holding her arms so she could see how very serious he was. "If anyone could do it, I think you could. But Caroline, the risk is too great. You could lose everything."

"Oh, pooh."

"Oh, pooh? That is it?" He cut his words off, taking deep breaths to calm himself. "All right. Listen. I can give you the name of a good accountant, a solicitor, maybe a man of affairs who specializes—"

"But you are going to help me."

"This *is* helping," he began.

"I mean *you.*"

Geoffrey swallowed. This would be difficult, but he had no choice. The girl thought she was in love with him when any fool could see that she…that she what? That she was not old enough to know her own mind? He of all people knew that Caroline understood exactly what she wanted. And would set about getting it in the most bizarre fashion.

He looked at her, seeing the rosy sunset burnish her hair through the window. Then she smiled at him in a way that made him want to forget everyone and everything. Yet she was still young, just now learning what passion meant.

She was not in love with him, he told himself firmly. She was in love with how he'd made her feel. He looked away, his mouth dry, his heart constricting painfully in his chest. "I…I think I should concentrate on my own affairs."

"Oh." She looked down, her gaze shifting away from him.

"Caroline, I had not meant to phrase it like that. It is just—"

"I understand," she said softly. "You are not ready to accept that you love me. And you are not ready to open yourself up to love. So now you are running away."

"I am not running away!" he bellowed. Then he shut his mouth abruptly as he pressed his fingers against his temples, wondering what was wrong with him. This was a simple thing. Dashing a woman's hopes was never easy, but he had done it a dozen times already with perfect calm. This time, he felt completely out of control. "Caroline," he began, making his words deliberately harsh, "your aunt asked that I help you become fashionable. I have begun that. But I must also concentrate on—"

"My aunt asked you to do that? I thought it was your idea."

Geoffrey frowned, his thoughts spinning backward. Caroline knew this already. She had to. But one look at her stricken expression, and he knew it was not true. "It was my idea. Though she asked—"

"I thought you wanted to help me," she said, more to herself than to him.

"I did." He took a step forward. "I do."

"No, you did it because your mother and my aunt are bosom friends. No doubt they both appealed to your sense of duty and responsibility, not to mention your chivalrous instincts. Oh, Geoffrey." Her eyes shimmered with an odd sort of misty softness. "It is fast becoming hard to see you as anything but my own personal knight errant."

"Good God, Caroline," he said with a sigh. "I am no hero. I am certainly not some medieval knight."

"That's true," she said with a smile. "You are too pompous, overbearing, and arrogant to be a perfect hero. But I love you just the same. And if you will only wait a few weeks, I shall be an heiress and we can get married."

Geoffrey sputtered, unable to articulate any of the thousands of things he had to say to this impertinent, willful, wholly distracting woman. Finally he landed on the one thing he had no intention of ever saying, expressing himself in the most blunt and coarse way possible.

"I will not marry you!"

Caroline blinked, hurt making her eyes wide and vulnerable. "But why ever not? If I am wealthy enough—"

"You are *not*!" He pushed away from her, choosing to stand by the fireplace, staring into the cold grate instead. "And it is impossible to become one quickly enough." He paused, trying to sort through his jumbled thoughts. Never before had he had such a feeling of doom. It was almost overwhelming, choking the words before he had a chance to express them. But he had to explain to her, had to make her understand. "I cannot marry you, Caroline."

"Do you love me?"

Geoffrey sighed, not knowing what to say, not even knowing what to think, so he decided to duck the issue. "It does not matter—"

"Of course it does."

"It does not!" He spun again to face her, hardening his heart against the sight of her soft lips, her wide blue eyes, and the sweet lure of her lavender perfume. "I cannot marry you. I can, however, give your name to an excellent man of affairs, perhaps an accountant—"

"No."

"What?"

"No." She lifted her chin in that stubborn motion he had come both to know and dread. "They will only want to moderate my plans, and I am not in the mood to tread softly. I am in love."

"Caroline!" Good Lord, would nothing get through to this woman?

"The only one I will ever allow to dictate to me— occasionally—is you."

"That is ridiculous," he sputtered.

"That is love. Now if you do not mind, I must get home. I have much to do. Creating a fortune is not an easy thing, you know."

What could he say to that? It was clear she would not listen. Not now, maybe not ever. All he could do was take her home and stay clear. Perhaps she would become distracted or find someone else. Or perhaps, if he absented himself from the scene, she might truly fall in love with someone else.

That is what he would do, he decided, trembling at the thought. He would have to make himself absent from her life forever. Firmly. And without mercy.

He kicked idly at an ash mark on the floor. He was done with her. He ought to feel relieved. Instead he was consumed with an overwhelming sense of emptiness. But it was for the best. He had to be firm. She still had the chance for a happy life, if only he stayed out of the way. "I shall not change my mind, Caroline. No matter what happens, I will not come to your rescue."

"You will not need to. I promise," she said.

Geoffrey waited one more moment before turning back toward her, catching her gaze, then holding it with an absolute, unwavering will. "I will stay away from now on. I will not dance with you, I will not speak with you. I may not even stay at the same rout with you. You must understand. It is the only way for you to get over this silly infatuation with me."

He expected her to be hurt. Expected perhaps a scene. Not a large one, just a tiny one to show she not only understood his intentions but objected.

He should have known she never did what he expected.

She actually smiled. "You likely will not see me, Geoffrey. I will be too busy."

He gaped at her, then shut his mouth with a snap. There was nothing else to say. So with a heavy sigh, he gestured toward the door. "I shall hitch up the horses, then I will take you back to your aunt."

She nodded silently, her own firm will evident in every line of her body. But before he could quit the room, she leaned down, picking up her discarded notes on her kissing experiment. She smoothed out the pages, then slowly, significantly pressed them into his hand.

If only he knew what she meant by the gesture. "Caroline?"

"Will you discard these for me please?"

"Your notes? Caro—"

"I have learned that life is meant to be experienced, Geoffrey. Not analyzed or held at a distance. And certainly not for something as silly as science." She paused, catching his gaze with heavy import. "Or honor."

He felt his throat close down, not knowing how to react. His emotions felt knotted within him, threatening to escape the bounds of his control. And yet, he could not release them for fear of what he would lose if he allowed even one thought, one feeling to escape. Emotions had led her to straddle him, throwing everything away for what she thought was love. Thinking had set him to borrowing his sister's dowry, urging him to risk everything in order to recoup the Tallis fortune quickly. And feeling had set him to kiss Caroline in the first place, that first evening when she climbed into the music room at his mother's ball. That one kiss had brought her into his life and created the chaos he now faced.

He could not let his control slip again for fear of what disaster awaited him around the next corner, and so he turned away. He did not even take her notes, but allowed them to slip from his fingertips to flutter like so much wasted time to the floor.

But as he left the room, he began to think. She was the strangest creature he had ever met. One minute she set him on fire with a natural sensuality so intense it nearly drove him mad. The next minute, she was all business with her odd experiments and even odder financial plans.

There was no understanding such a woman. All he could do was throw up his hands and admit she was too much for him. He could no longer control the runaway disaster that was Caroline, and thank God, he no longer had an obligation to try.

He had washed his hands of her. He told her their marriage would never be. And what had she done? Smiled at him and toddled off to make her fortune.

Good God, he almost thought she could do it. But then if she did, he would be obliged to marry her, and that was the last thing he wanted.

Wasn't it?

He didn't know. And that infuriated him all the more. Madness. That's what she drove him to: pure madness. Suddenly he was possessed by an overpowering urge to get himself to Brooks'—his father's favorite club. Once he dropped Caroline at her aunt's home, he would head straight for Brooks', settle down into his father's favorite chair, and call for a deck of cards.

\* \* \*

Caroline arrived home filled with zeal. She had no doubt she could create a fortune in the next few weeks. After all, men won and lost thousands in their gaming clubs every night. How much harder could it be to make money on the Exchange or on some other investment? It was just a form of gambling, only with more predictable variables than the random chance of a deck of cards.

All she needed was the appropriate investment.

As for Geoffrey's claim that he would not marry her even if she were rich, she dismissed it as nothing more than male pride. Men hated it when a woman realized something before they did. Geoffrey she knew, for all his heroic qualities, had an overabundance of male pride.

She intended to coax him out of it that night at Lady Kistler's ball.

Except that he did not attend the ball.

Nor did he attend Baroness Schulz's rout the next evening. And he bowed out of Lady Shimmon's card party just after Caroline arrived.

It was maddening, the lengths to which men would go simply to protect their pride, Caroline thought. Could he not see that she loved him? Of course he did, she admonished herself.

But he had not said that he loved her.

It was at that moment, standing at Lady Shimmon's window watching Geoffrey drive away, that the first seeds of doubt entered her mind.

He *did* love her, didn't he?

Of course he did. How could she doubt it when he looked at her with such hunger in his eyes? He was simply being noble, acting chivalrous by stepping aside so she could find happiness with someone else. He loved her but would not give up his familial obligations to make himself happy.

Caroline squared her shoulders. That thought only redoubled her drive to succeed in her financial endeavors.

The following days, Caroline practically locked herself into her library with Mr. Ross. There was no use attending parties if Geoffrey would not be there. Instead she chose to devote herself entirely to making her fortune.

At last came the day, nearly three weeks later, when she stared across her desk at a beleaguered Mr. Ross. For the first time in her entire life, she admitted that perhaps she had overestimated her abilities.

"They destroyed it all?" she asked, not even bothering to hide the quaver in her voice. "But I put everything I had into those weaving machines. It should have quadrupled their output."

Mr. Ross's eyes were downcast as he explained, "Yes, miss. That was exactly the problem. When we could convince the workers to use them at all, the machines worked so well the men feared for their jobs."

"But it would have quadrupled their output. Look at these figures, Mr. Ross." She pushed forward a page of her own neatly tabulated columns. "According to my figures, I should realize my first profits—"

Her nervous man of affairs pushed his glasses farther up on his nose. "They feared for their jobs, miss. Too many people were out of work to begin with. There simply was not enough raw material to continue production at such a rate. They knew that."

Caroline shook her head, wishing she could deny his statements. Wishing more fervently that she had anticipated her workers' fears. "I intended to import additional wool."

"It did not matter, miss. The Luddites would not take that chance."

She stared at the young man across from her, her thoughts in chaos, her body numb from shock. "They destroyed everything?"

"Yes." He swallowed nervously.

Caroline blinked, hearing the words but not the meaning. "But I sunk my last guinea into those machines," she repeated for perhaps the hundredth time that afternoon.

"Yes, miss."

"And now the estate mortgage is due. Do I have any—"

"No, miss."

"What about my other investments?"

"None have realized any profit as yet." He lifted his hands in an uncertain gesture. "For most, it is simply too early for any return. I am sorry, miss, but you must think about selling."

Caroline felt a knot of panic clutch at her heart. "Sell what? The sheep? Woodley Manor? I have nothing else except smashed machinery and an empty factory."

Mr. Ross had been wringing his hands, twisting one over the other, over and over. It had become so common a sight that she never even bothered serving him tea. He never stopped long enough to drink.

Now, for the first time in weeks, his hands stopped. They did not move, did not twitch, and their very stillness was like another knife twisting in her gut.

"I have detailed various options," he began. "None of them pleasant." He pushed forward another page, this one covered with his neatly tabulated figures. Then he glanced up. "I did try to warn you about such short-term notes."

"Do you think the moneylender would extend his loan?" she asked hopefully.

She heard rather than saw him shake his head. "I have already asked. He, um, is not the most forgiving of people. You should not have taken out that loan. Certainly not for so much…" His voice trailed away.

Caroline nodded, not wanting to think about might-have-beens had she listened to her man of affairs. What a fool she'd been. She'd been so intent on gaining her fortune that she'd bet and lost everything.

She looked down at Mr. Ross's figures, then quickly looked away. She could not bear it. Not yet. So she transferred her gaze to the library window where a gray fall day seemed too cheery for her mood. "They were new machines, new designs. They should have wanted to try them, to be the first to work on such things. To touch the future."

He remained silent, waiting for her to adjust. She let her thoughts travel to the towering elm just behind the house. If she craned her neck far enough, she could see it out the window. She closed her eyes, pretending she was deep within the branches, the leaves whispering their soothing…

"Ahem."

Caroline tried not to flinch at the grating sound of her man of affairs clearing his throat. She knew the sound well; he always made it just before saying something unpleasant. She bit her lip in consternation. She was not sure she was ready to hear whatever it was, but then again, wishing she were in the boughs of a tree would not accomplish anything.

She opened her eyes, fixing the man with her steady regard.

"Go ahead, Mr. Ross, you might as well give me the whole."

"You understand that if you cannot find the money to make the loan payment, the moneylender will seize Woodley Manor and all the assets contained within."

Caroline blinked away her tears. She and her father would be homeless. They would have nowhere to go, no way to live. Aunt Win could not support them. She was already paying for Caroline's Season and that alone had severely strained the dear woman's savings.

"Have you thought about your dower property?" Mr. Ross asked, his voice unnaturally high. "If you had access to the property, you could sell it or at least borrow against it."

She shook her head. "*I* cannot touch the dower property, Mr. Ross. It is entailed. Only my husband can sell it."

His leaned forward, his expression earnest. "Is there a gentleman who wishes to marry you?"

Her thoughts immediately flew to Geoffrey. She had intended to be well on her way to a fortune by now. "I—"

"Because if you could marry before the notes come due," he interrupted. "The dower property is worth almost enough to cover three loan payments."

"Three payments," she echoed weakly. She had meant to approach Geoffrey with a fortune, not another pile of debts.

She could not go to him now. "No, Mr. Ross, that particular solution is not available."

"You have not set your heart on any particular gentleman?"

She nearly broke at that question, but she kept her pain inside, not wishing to cry before her man of affairs. "No. There is no one."

"Well...perhaps, um, a solution will present itself soon."

Caroline frowned at his odd statement and for the first time that afternoon, she studied her young man of affairs. He seemed pale, embarrassment warring with guilt as he sweated and twisted in his seat. For perhaps the fifth time in two minutes, he glanced at his pocket watch.

Then, in the silence of the library on a sulky gray day, she heard the distinct sound of the door knocker. Immediately after that sound came Mr. Ross's relieved sigh. She looked at the young man, her eyes narrowing.

"What have you done, Mr. Ross?" Her tone was cold, her stomach clenching tight with dread.

He glanced away, then back, his movements becoming almost birdlike. "Perhaps you were unaware that one of your dearest family friends has also retained my services."

Caroline raised a single eyebrow but refused to comment.

"He, er, he is a most generous man with his brandy." Mr. Ross's face was now turning a blotchy shade of purple. "I realize it is highly unethical for a man of my position to reveal the financial details of another—"

Caroline closed her eyes, far too afraid to guess what disaster lay before her now. "Whom, Mr. Ross? To whom have you told the intimate details of my fiasco?"

"Only Mr. Loots, miss. And he was most sympathetic. Really, it was a most fortunate stroke, as he insisted on coming. This afternoon even, although I begged him to wait until three." In the hallway, she heard the ponderous strokes of their grandfather clock chiming three times. "I needed to acquaint you with the situation first."

Caroline did not know where to begin. The idea was simply too preposterous. The awful Mr. Loots aware of her disaster and somehow come to…

Her thoughts careened to a numbing halt. Good God, what could he be here to do?

"Dearest Caroline!" boomed a voice. The deafening sound was immediately followed by a massive body bursting through the library door. Behind him glided her aunt, statuesque, cool, but with eyes flashing green fire of irritation.

"Caroline!" she exclaimed. "Mr. Loots! This is not the place or the manner for afternoon visits. Now I must insist—"

"Hush your twittering, Mrs. Hibbert," Mr. Loots said with an arrogant wave of dismissal. "Caroline knows the reason for my visit, and I dare say it is a relief for her to know I am here to take the burden off her delicate shoulders."

"Mr. Loots, I beg you," Mr. Ross began, his voice creeping higher with each word. "I have not had time to fully broach the subject—"

"Oh, do be quiet, Ross. We don't need you here now. You have already acquainted me with the generalities. We can go over particulars of the marriage portion later."

"Marriage!" Aunt Win exclaimed. "Caroline, explain the meaning of this immediately!"

But Caroline was in no state to explain anything. Her world was spinning out of control beneath her feet, and she felt herself flounder for purchase. Marriage? To Mr. Loots? How could this come to pass?

Both Aunt Win and Mr. Loots were speaking to her, alternately demanding or blustering in their own particular ways. She could not make sense of it all, and the sounds rushed past her like debris on a swift river.

She needed to think. She needed an anchor in a world suddenly at sea.

*Geoffrey.*

She latched on to the image of him, holding it close. But she could not keep it there. Not with the certain knowledge that her financial fiasco would keep them apart forever. Though she longed to be with him, it would be too painful and too awkward to send for him right now, especially after he'd told her he would not rescue her. No matter what.

She had to see if she could correct the situation before she spoke with him. But before that, she needed a moment of peace.

So she stood, knowing immediately where she would go. "Excuse me, Aunt Win, sirs, but I am going to step outside."

"But Miss Woodley," Mr. Ross began. "There is a great deal that still must be…"

"Listen here, gel," Mr. Loots boomed. "I have come to propose to you. You cannot just walk out like…"

"Really, Caroline," her aunt chastised, "you cannot just abandon…"

The sentences continued, but she blocked them out, barely hearing their tones much less their words. She went to the back door and to their tall, stately elm tree. At the last moment before she achieved her escape, she overheard one last order, this one at least giving her a profound sense of relief.

"Thompson," her aunt commanded, "send a note around to Lord Tallis requesting his presence. Immediately."

# CHAPTER 10

Geoffrey reined in behind an overburdened, too-wide dray, and cursed softly. Twice now. Twice, he had been summoned to the Hibbert household by that huge brute of a footman. Twice he had been ordered to appear like some lackey brought before the king or some knight errant to save the day.

It never occurred to him this might be a social call. No, this was surely a summons to a tragedy.

For the last few weeks, he'd had a growing feeling of imminent disaster. It had begun the moment Caroline announced her intention to acquire a fortune.

He'd tried to distract her. He'd ducked in and out of doorways like some silly turtle so she would not see him. He'd even steered every eligible young man in England in her direction. He'd made the young ones dance with her, got the older ones to chat with her, even convinced Derbarough to bring her posies daily.

Nothing had worked.

In fact, after the first week she'd become a recluse.

He ought to be pleased she was not continuing her kissing experiment. Nor had she returned to see Louise. He'd made his former mistress promise to send for him immediately should Caroline appear, and even paid the energetic dancer money he could ill afford to ensure her compliance.

He'd gotten nothing.

Except the certain knowledge that Caroline was headed straight for catastrophe, and nothing he did would make any difference.

Now the waiting was over. Now, clutched in his fist, was her aunt's politely phrased disaster notice demanding his immediate presence at the Hibbert household. He swore under his breath and pulled into a side alley, hoping to pass the ridiculous dray that was slowing him up.

He arrived at the Hibbert household no less than twenty-five minutes after receiving the message. Good time, considering where he had come from and what he'd had to go through to get there. Nevertheless, Mrs. Hibbert met him in the hallway, seeming less than pleased as he handed his hat and gloves to her crotchety butler.

"High time, Lord Tallis. I have done my level best in your absence, but I must say I cannot bear the burden of this much longer."

The woman was in high dudgeon as he had never seen her before. He felt the first flutters of alarm as he bowed over her hand. "I came as soon as I could. How can I be of—"

She did not let him finish, but gestured up at the staircase almost before he released her hand. "I tried to make him go away, but he refused. Thompson managed to get rid of him all those other times, but this time he simply will not leave. Said it was imperative he inspect some of her documents first."

"Who?"

"Thank God, Albert returned," the woman continued, ignoring him. "They are upstairs discussing his latest experiment."

Geoffrey frowned, alarm making him grind his teeth. "Who is upstairs and where is Caroline?"

"Mr. Loots, of course—and a more boorish, impertinent mushroom I have never met."

Geoffrey had no trouble remembering the obnoxious Mr. Loots as the man he'd knocked flat in the gardens for accosting Caroline, "Where is Caroline? What has he done?"

But Mrs. Hibbert was not listening. She was still pacing in the hallway in full view of Thompson as she continued her diatribe. "I hold you directly responsible, you know. If you had been more attentive, none of this would have happened." She paused long enough to glare at him. "Marriage, indeed! But I do not know how to stop it. He says it is necessary. I have sent round to Harry, too, but sweet God in Heaven, Geoffrey, I do not understand a word of any of it'"

Panic was clearly written on the woman's face. She was beside herself with it, gesticulating and mumbling with increasing agitation. That sight alone frightened him enough that Geoffrey did something he had never done before. He grabbed hold of a woman and shook her. Not hard, but enough to jolt her out of her ramblings.

"Where is Caroline? Has he hurt her?"

Mrs. Hibbert blinked, stared hard at him, then nodded, as if reassured by what she saw in Geoffrey's eyes. When she spoke again, she was more in control. "Caroline is outside in her tree. I do not know what happened except that Mr. Ross is wringing his hands in the library and that obnoxious Mr. Loots is behind it all."

Geoffrey glanced upstairs, wishing he had the time to beat the truth out of Mr. Loots, but the urge to find Caroline was overpowering. "Which tree?"

"In the garden."

He pushed past Mrs. Hibbert, but she grabbed his arm. "Do you wish me to detain Mr. Loots for you?"

He shook his head. "I can find him later. But do not let Mr. Ross out of your sight."

She nodded, but he had not waited for her response. He was already out the rear entrance. The "garden" was a small strip of grass that one could cross in two steps. There were a few straggly flowers and one huge, towering elm tree, its leaves in glorious full color. A sturdy rope ladder dangled before its trunk, the top lost in the depths of the branches.

Geoffrey went straight for it, tilting his head upward as he tried to peer through the boughs. He saw nothing, except the colors of fall and the dark bottom of some platform.

"Caroline?"

"Here," came the muffled response.

"It is Geoffrey."

"I know."

"I would like to speak with you, if it is convenient."

He waited, his concern doubling every second she remained silent. Finally, she answered.

"I would be happy to converse with you," came the polite response.

Geoffrey sighed. "Caroline, could you please come down? My neck is beginning to hurt."

Another long silence. "I would rather not. You could join me. It is beautiful up here. Quite peaceful."

Geoffrey contemplated his options. He had none. He could leave, of course, but he had no intention of departing until he actually saw Caroline and assured himself she was in good health. He could wait out here until she came down of her own accord, but knowing her, he might be out here until the end of the week.

That left only one choice.

With a sigh, he stripped off his coat. Then Geoffrey Rathburn—Earl of Tallis, tulip of the *ton* and mature man—climbed a large and rather dirty elm tree. He did not even spare a sigh for his expensive Hessians, though he did try to keep the worst of the dirt from his buff trousers. Another tear and they would be fit only for the rag pile.

Given the ladder, it was an easy climb, but he did not want to think about how she managed it in a dress. He angled his shoulders through a small hole in the platform and looked quickly around. The first thing he saw was a large expanse of creamy skin exposed by a rip in Caroline's formerly white dress. It was quite a distracting sight and one he thoroughly enjoyed as he climbed the rest of the way up. She had such slim ankles and shapely calves, not to mention creamy white thighs.

God, she was a beautiful woman. Her body was slim, not bony as he'd once thought. Her waist was tiny, almost infinitesimal, especially juxtaposed with her full breasts. It was the kind of body a man dreamed of, all soft and shapely in just the right ways, for all that it was out of fashion right now. He could not deny it had haunted his dreams every night since they first met.

Pushing aside that thought, Geoffrey stepped onto the sturdy wood platform, then immediately cracked his head on a branch.

"Oh! Pray sit down," gasped Caroline. "I am afraid Aunt Win built this for me as a rather small child. She had no idea I might come out here as an adult."

"Clearly an error in judgment," he mumbled as he sat down, bracing his back against the tree's trunk. He took a moment to catch his breath as he admired the sunshine filtering through the multicolored foliage. The light painted her dress in brilliant colors, making Caroline seem a wood sprite or autumn fairy. Her skin was pale, her hair a rich gold, and her face…

His thoughts trailed away as he saw the thin line traced in a dirt smudge on her cheek. She had been crying. "Caroline?"

"Hmmm?"

"Are you all right?"

"It is beautiful here, is it not? I often sneak up here on the bright days when Aunt Win is not watching. I have the most amazing tree house in Hadleigh."

He nodded, letting her ramble while he watched her from his perch. He usually thought of Caroline as a mixture of energy and intellect, always moving, always planning—always looking for ways to get into difficulty. Now for the first time, he saw her when she was still. Her body did not move except to breathe. Her eyes were open, but their focus was abstract, not from intense thought, but from relaxation and an absence of anything but the simple elements of tree, sunshine, and blue sky.

He had never found her more beautiful or more compelling. He had never wanted her more. So to distract himself from drawing her into his arms, he forced her to speak. "What happened, Caroline?" he asked. His voice was low, but the sound still filled the leafy bower.

She glanced away, clearly not wanting to discuss it. He insisted.

"You must tell me, you know. Your aunt blames everything on me."

She jerked slightly against a branch, twisting to face him. "She cannot mean that."

"Oh, but she does," he countered. "She said so not more than five minutes ago. She said if I had been more attentive, then this would not have happened. So you see," he added, trying to tease a smile out of her, "I must understand what has occurred if I am to defend myself. Truly, I fear for my life."

Caroline shook her head, tears making her eyes shimmer. "But she is wrong. This all is my fault. I have ruined everything, and no one could have stopped me."

She looked so tragic with tears spiking her lashes that he could not resist. He pulled her into his arms, wanting to feel her against him. It was awkward given the restrictions of branch and tree, but he needed to touch her almost as much as she seemed to need him.

He braced his legs and pulled her close, letting her slide against him in a move that set his blood on fire. Then she settled into the V of his legs, her head resting against his chest. He knew she would cry. All women did, and at the most awkward moments. Oddly enough, he looked forward to comforting her, to being the man who held her as she poured out her sorrows.

"Geoffrey?"

He let his cheek settle onto her hair, feeling its silky texture, smelling the sweet lavender that surrounded her. "It is all right to cry, Caroline. I do not mind."

Suddenly she tilted her head, her eyes wide with surprise. "Cry? I was going to ask if you wanted to buy a factory. Or rather, if you knew anyone who wanted one."

He lifted his head, frowning as he peered down at her. "What?"

"I have a factory. Do you know anyone who wants it?"

"Of course," he said stiffly, wondering at his sudden surge of anger. "Derbarough was just saying yesterday that what he needed was a new factory. The perfect accessory for a fashionably tied cravat."

She blinked at him, then her gaze dropped down to where her hands pressed warmly against his chest. "You are angry."

"Caroline, what have you done?"

She remained silent, settling deeper against him. He had to stifle his groan of tortured delight as she shifted again, her gaze slipping down to his boots. "Apparently," she sidestepped, "I have caused you to ruin your Hessians."

She was changing the topic, and for the moment, he decided to let her. So he followed the direction she pointed, lifting his leg so that he could inspect the gash in his boot. "Disgraceful."

"Why did you not just take them off?"

He chuckled, the sound feeling good as it rumbled out. "For fear of what my mother would say. Or your aunt. Or any of the servants and neighbors lining this street. An earl must maintain some standards, no matter what the sacrifice." He pretended to a lofty tone, but she was not the least bit fooled. He felt her giggle reverberate through his body.

"That is why I love you, Geoffrey. You make me laugh."

He smiled and could not resist dropping a light kiss on the top of her hair. She seemed happier now, more able to face her problems. "What happened, Caroline?"

"I bought a factory that weaves cloth."

"So I gathered."

He felt her entire body stiffen. "And I took out a loan. A huge loan with Woodley Manor as collateral."

He felt his blood freeze at the thought. She couldn't possibly have lost her home. Not so quickly. "What happened, Caroline?"

Her sigh seemed to deflate her entire body. "I used the money to buy the factory and a lot of machines. Wonderful machines that would help the workers weave cloth at four times the rate of before."

"Oh God," he groaned, already guessing where this was leading.

"The Luddites destroyed them all. Mr. Ross says they were afraid for their jobs, and with so many out of work already…"

"They panicked."

"Yes."

He could not believe what she was saying. She could not possibly have been so reckless. But then he remembered he was speaking of Caroline. The woman did not believe in half-measures, in caution, in plain common sense.

"How much did you lose?" he asked. Even before she spoke, he knew the answer. Her body tensed tighter than a bow string, her dread communicating itself to him before she ever said the words.

"They would not even try the machines, Geoffrey. And now the notes are due, plus the regular bills." She looked up at him, her confusion and hurt clear in the dappled light. "They would not give me a chance."

"Good Lord, Caroline," he breathed, his world collapsing in on him. "It has been less than three weeks. Even you could not destroy your entire inheritance in that amount of time."

"I have not," she said, her tentative smile adding fuel to the hunger burning in his blood. "I still have hopes that my other investments will pay off. But Mr. Ross says I should not expect anything soon."

Geoffrey breathed a silent sigh of thanks. She was not completely ruined. "What else have you invested in?"

"Oh, they are quite reasonable investments, I assure you."

A tickle of fear shivered through him. "What are they, Caroline?"

She grinned at him, but the expression seemed forced. "They are scientific in nature. Actually I am quite a patroness of the sciences."

"Of course," he agreed dryly, the tickle of fear growing to a tremor of alarm. "What are these investments, Caroline?"

"Being a scientist myself, I count myself a good judge of investments. I can tell when something is worth pursuing, my lord, even if others might not think so."

The tremor was now a pounding. "Caroline."

"They may seem odd—"

*"Caroline!"*

"An underwater ship."

He blinked at her, then said the obvious. "Ships are supposed to float on top of the water."

She frowned. "This is an entirely new type of ship."

"Sunken ships have been around for generations."

She stiffened against him, lifting her chin with hurt pride, completely unaware of the way her hair caressed his neck with the movement. "It is clear you have no appreciation for this type of scientific advancement."

He ground his teeth, his frustration mounting exponentially. "What else have you invested in?"

She paused, biting her lip. "Leonardo DaVinci."

He blinked, not sure he'd heard her right. "Caroline, DaVinci has been dead for many years."

"I know that," she snapped. "He left behind some drawings, designs for a…" Her voice trailed away.

He closed his eyes, not sure he wanted to know. "What, Caroline?"

"A flying machine."

This time, he groaned out loud. She was like a child, throwing away good money on any toy that caught her fancy. Good lord, it was amazing she and her father had a groat between them.

He lifted his arm, absently rubbing against the headache that pulsed at his temple. "Anything else?" he asked.

She shrugged, producing a quiet explosion in his body that only added to his tension. "The rest are open-ended contracts with various scientists. I supply them funds, and they…" She paused to lick her lips, the moisture glistening red and full in the rosy light. "They have agreed to allow me to share in the profits from their inventions."

"Good lord," he breathed. He could not have imagined anything more open to abuse by charlatans and thieves than such an agreement. But then he forced himself to think more rationally. Caroline was a good judge of character, or so he hoped. Perhaps she had gotten lucky. Perhaps these scientists were well on their way to something valuable. "What are these other gentlemen working on?"

"Electrical experiments with frogs and other dead animals."

He clamped his mouth shut. The urge to laugh hysterically was almost overwhelming, but he could not do it. Not only because it would hurt Caroline's feelings, but because if he once gave into this farce, he would never recover. His mother would lock him in Bedlam for the rest of his life.

"Geoffrey?" she asked, twisting slightly in his arms. "Are you all right? You look almost purple."

"Really?" he drawled. "Perhaps all I need is a shock from your electricity machine."

She frowned at him, her expression an odd mixture of concern and insult. "Science is the future of mankind, Geoffrey. Electricity is an important new discovery with almost limitless potential."

"Tell that to those frogs you're shocking."

"Geoffrey! That is unfair!" She shifted again until she faced him directly, though her body still pressed intimately close. "They are already dead. And I cannot tell you how difficult it is to get the appropriate types of dead animals here in London. Why, they have even had to import some from Hadleigh."

"I do not doubt it for a moment." Geoffrey sighed. The whole thing would be funny if it were not so serious a situation for Caroline and her father. "This Mr. Ross of yours. Is he the one who has advised you on your investments?"

"Oh no," she answered, her expression earnest. "Mostly he has advised against them."

Three cheers for the young Mr. Ross. "That explains why he is so twitchy."

Caroline bit her lip and glanced away. "He is not usually so panicky, Geoffrey. Only recently, and because he feels badly because he told Mr. Loots about my situation."

"What?" Geoffrey was so shocked he nearly toppled them both right out of the tree. Good lord, the boy must be greener than he looked, which put him about the maturity of a toddler. To make such a mistake…He sighed. It was the blind leading the blind. No wonder Caroline made such a disaster of it all. With no one to guide her, to explain things to her, she just went merrily ahead until…

He cut off his thoughts, not wanting to think of the worst that could happen. "What does Mr. Ross suggest you do?"

She exhaled, her whole body slumping with the movement. "He says I have to marry. If my husband sells the dower property, we can hold off the foreclosure. At least for a while. That is why Mr. Loots is here."

Geoffrey felt the heat in his body slowly die to ashes. "You are going to marry Loots?" he asked softly. "In order to get your dowry?"

She shoved against him hard, throwing him backward until his head cracked against the tree trunk and his cravat caught and tore on a dead branch. "Of course not, you lout! How could you say that? I shall m-mma…" She stopped abruptly, swallowed, then continued in a lower, calmer tone. "I shall speak with Harry. The sale of the dower will cover part of the debt. Harry's family has enough to handle the rest. That way, Papa will be able to keep Woodley Manor. And he will not notice if a few acres of land and most of our sheep are sold off." Her voice shook, but her gaze was steady.

"Surely there is something you can salvage," he offered.

Caroline shook her head. Then she turned to him, her expression filling with such love and hope that he knew the sight would haunt him forever. "Not unless you can think of someone else who might want to marry me."

He closed his eyes. How he wanted to say the words. The past three weeks, he'd hungered for Caroline as he had never craved anything or anyone else ever. He dreamed of her at night, yearned for the sight of her by day, and ached constantly for her touch. Being with her was insanity itself. He never knew what to expect next, never knew where she would be or what she would do, but she made him laugh as he had not done for a long time. She showed him that life could be lived to its fullest, even when beset by responsibilities and burdens and the oppression of high society.

He wanted to marry her. He wanted to spend the rest of his life second-guessing her unpredictable mind.

But he could not.

He had his family to think about, his honor. His sister and his mother both depended on him. How could he seize his own happiness at the expense of theirs? There might have been a way before. He had even discussed the matter with his own man of affairs. But now, with the added burden of her debts, their marriage would see the end of not only his family, but hers as well. He simply could not do it.

"Caro—" he began.

"Never mind." Her voice was a clipped whisper. "I understand. Besides," she said, her voice brightening with false cheer, "I was just saying how much I missed Hadleigh. Now I shall get to spend the rest of my life there."

She was trying to be brave, but the tremor in her body told him how much she dreaded the thought. She loved London, loved the anonymity she could assume. The city gave her the freedom to visit mistresses, to kiss men in gardens, and do all the other outrageous things she seemed born to do. But this was no game, and she was no longer a woman with enough wealth to indulge herself. Like him, she had someone else's welfare to think of besides her own. Marriage to him would only land them both in debtor's prison.

He closed his eyes and drew her close, letting his face settle again into the silken blanket of her hair. And when the scent of lavender filled his senses, he lifted her chin, kissing her with all the hunger and passion he held inside. She returned his caress willingly, eagerly, meeting his touch with her fire, his hunger with her need.

His hands began to move of their own accord, and soon he reveled in the feel of her breasts, full and aroused in his hands. She gasped as he pinched her lightly, erotically, and he began to kiss her again, more fully, more deeply, more sensuously than ever before.

"Geoffrey…" The word was half surprise, half plea. But there was no rejection in the sound, no fear. And it set his heart pounding as he found more innovative ways to kiss her, touch her. Love her.

Thanks to him, Caroline was no longer an innocent. And yet, her kiss retained a simplicity, an honesty that burned through his mind and body.

She loved him. He knew that now. This was no childish fantasy brought on by lust, cooled by distance, or worse yet, easily satisfied with a substitute. Caroline was a mature woman who knew her mind and her heart. And she offered them to him, without restrictions, without fear.

Awe suffused him as the magnitude of what she gave him sunk into his soul. She loved him. And for that, he worshiped her.

He dropped kisses along her neck like silent prayers, and she arched into him, receptive to his offering. Though their location restricted movement, he managed to loosen her gown enough to slide her bodice down before raising her chemise until he could murmur endearments to her glorious breasts. She gasped when he held them in his hands. She quivered when he inhaled their sweet perfume. And when he at last allowed himself to taste their magnificence, she opened herself fully to him, whispering his name in a breathless chant.

His body clamored for her. As he eased her skirt higher, stroking her long legs, the need to bury himself within her nearly overpowered him. Indeed, she reached for him, silently begging for exactly what he craved. But this time was not for him; he would seek no satisfaction in her body. Caroline would never be his, and so he would not defile her in such a way.

Instead, he captured her mouth with his, laying her down as he eased her legs apart. Again she reached for him, and he nearly acquiesced, so great was his hunger. But in the end, he denied himself for her sake, using his fingers instead to please her, plunging them into her as she trembled with the force of her need.

She cried out, but his kisses muffled the sound. And while her sweet nectar moistened his hand, he penetrated her more deeply, he rubbed her more fully and caught her moans of ecstasy in his mouth.

At last, with a final joyous exclaim, she splintered, bestowing her blessing upon him. He nearly wept with the beauty of the sight, even as he held her tenderly, adoringly.

In time, her breathing returned to normal. In time, her flushed skin paled and her kiss-swollen lips returned to a dusky rose. And in time, she reached for him, kissing him with all the love in her soul.

"Geoffrey," she whispered.

"Shhhh," he returned, unable to stop himself from kissing her hair, along her brow, and then to her eyes and nose and lips.

"But you—"

"I am content," he lied. He would never be content, never feel complete without her. And yet, there was nothing he could do. If he indulged his passion, ignored his family responsibilities, tossed aside everything he held dear now, they would both be left with nothing tomorrow. They would drag their families down with them as well. And even worse…"Men and women have separate quarters in debtor's prison," he murmured against her lips. "We wouldn't even be together there."

Caroline nodded, and he tasted the salt of her tears. She understood as well as he exactly what was at stake. "At least say you love me," she said. "Just once. I swear I shall not hold you to it."

He did not answer. He could not. He merely gazed at her, memorizing every curve and hollow of her face from her dreamy blue eyes to her perfect red lips. But she would not leave him an honorable way out.

"Geoffrey?" she pressed. "Do you love me?"

He clenched his jaw, knowing the answer, but hating it all the same. Yes, he loved her. He had loved her from the first moment she crawled backward into his mother's music room. He loved her kissing experiments and her interest in pleasing him. He loved everything about her, even when she was hiding in a silly tree.

But he could not tell her that. Her only hope for happiness lay with Harry, and for that he would have to crush her now, to take her fragile love and throw it away. He had to do it. It was the only honorable thing.

And since he held honor above everything else, he flattened his expression and lied.

"I am sorry, Caroline. I do not love you. And I never shall."

# CHAPTER 11

Caroline shivered.

Her tree haven felt cold. Dusk in London could be quite chilly, and she had been alone up here for hours now. Geoffrey's kisses were over, and the protective embrace of his arms had long since vanished.

His last words to her had been "I am so sorry." Then he'd disappeared into the house. She'd thought at first he would leave, go find his heiress, and wash his hands of the bluestocking who had disrupted his life. But then as the sun dipped below the horizon, someone lit a candelabrum in the library. She only noticed it because a man carried the light to the window, then stood, staring out at her elm tree.

It was Geoffrey. He had taken off his coat, his hair was mussed, and he rubbed his temples as if trying to massage away a headache. Even his cravat, that starched wonder that resisted even the most wrenching of her sobs, dangled about his throat like one of Cook's wet noodles. He looked rumpled, exhausted, and utterly adorable.

He had not abandoned her.

He was in there with Mr. Ross trying to find a solution for her.

She ought to be with him. She ought to help as best she could. But for the first time in twenty-one years, she was willing to admit defeat. In this area, at least, Geoffrey was much better equipped to solve her problem. If it were a matter of sheep husbandry, well then, she would be right with him making the correct decisions. But as it was cloth manufacturing in depressed Staffordshire—something she'd already failed at—she remained hidden away in the all-too-comforting embrace of her elm tree.

Until now.

Now, she was bored, lonely, and, most of all, tired. It was time to fight for her future again. For her and Geoffrey. Because after spending a magnificent hour with Geoffrey in the bowers of her tree, she knew that Harry simply could not measure up.

As for Geoffrey's statement that he did not love her and never would, well, men never knew their own minds, especially on matters of the heart. He was just being silly, and she intended to tell him so.

Why else would he work with Mr. Ross if not to find a way for them to be together? He had to love her. He just had to.

Caroline looked down at her hands as she carefully shredded a bright orange leaf. She might as well admit it to herself, she thought glumly. Her financial fiasco coupled with Geoffrey's bald statement left her in doubt, questioning her own mind and assessments.

Could it be true? Could he really not love her?

No, she told herself firmly. He loved her. He did.

But the seed of doubt had grown into a tree almost larger than her elm. And so she remained hidden away.

"Caroline! Good lord, girl, but this is outside of enough. That awful Mr. Loots left more than an hour ago. It is high time you came out of the boughs."

Caroline sighed and parted the branches to look down at her aunt, bundled in three shawls against the wind, which played havoc with her high coiffeur.

"Yes, Aunt Win. I was just coming down."

"Good. Then I want a complete explanation, my girl. Complete."

Caroline nodded, too depressed to argue. Still, she moved slowly as she negotiated her descent while trying not to further mangle her thin muslin skirt.

"You will not marry that mushroom, Caroline. I simply will not countenance it." Her aunt's voice was strong, almost shrill as it cut through the evening gloom.

"Which mushroom is that?"

"Do not be impertinent," she snapped. "That Mr. Loots. I do not care what your father thinks of him, I simply will not countenance it."

"No, Aunt Win."

"I told him as much, but he simply patted me on the head and told me to be a good gel. Me, a good gel! Imagine the audacity."

Caroline could, and it made her cringe.

"I simply will not allow that man into my family. He is a…a toad!"

Caroline raised her eyebrows as she jumped the last few feet to the ground. "Aunt Win, such language."

The lady drew herself up to her most imposing height. "Well, I cannot support such conduct."

"No, Aunt Win." Caroline's words were automatic, falling soothingly from her lips while she turned, her gaze once again drawn to the lighted window where Geoffrey worked. "Aunt…"

"Hmmm?" The lady was busily wrapping two of her woolen shawls around her young niece.

"Have you ever known Lord Tallis to lie?"

Her aunt paused mid-motion, turning Caroline around so that she could peer into her face. "No, I have not. Geoffrey is a most honorable young man. Why do you ask?"

Caroline's gaze slid away, drawn back to the library window. A blast of chill air cut through the thin fabric of her dress, making her teeth clatter a bit as she spoke. "But he *might* lie, would he not? If he thought a lie would save someone? Perhaps make the future more bearable?"

"Save someone from what?" Aunt Win frowned as she tugged her niece toward the kitchen entrance. "I suppose he might lie if he were captured by Napoleon."

Caroline shuddered at the thought of Geoffrey at war. Meanwhile her aunt increased her efforts to bring her inside. But Caroline's feet traveled slowly, her thoughts still centered on the man seated at her desk. Now that she drew closer to the house, she could see him through the window, his broad shoulders bent over Mr. Ross's columns of figures, his angular face all the more harsh in the flickering candlelight.

But she was not allowed time to study him as her aunt grabbed her by the shoulders, shaking her slightly, her grip hard and uncompromising. "Just what did the boy say to you?"

Caroline looked into her aunt's eyes, seeking reassurance in the familiar blue gaze. It was hard to say the words, and her voice broke as she finally voiced her biggest fear. "He said he did not love me. And he never would."

Aunt Win clicked her tongue. "Oh, dear. What did you say?"

"I called him a nodcock."

Her aunt's eyes sparkled with mirth, but that did not quite erase the worry in her austere face. "Then what happened?"

Caroline brushed a tear away under the guise of pulling the hair from her eyes. "He kissed me on the forehead and left. Oh, Aunt Win, why would he lie like that?"

The older lady did not answer directly. Instead, she finished the job of tucking back her niece's hair, her touch gentle and reassuring. "You think he does love you?"

"I…" Caroline stopped, swallowed, then squared her shoulders. She had to know the truth. About everything. "Aunt Win, did you ask Geoffrey to sponsor me? To introduce me around and make me…make me fashionable?"

Her aunt paled, and Caroline knew the answer even before she spoke. "Caro, dear—"

"No, do not apologize. I understand."

"It was—"

"You had my best interests at heart," Caroline interrupted, babbling rather than letting the tears spill over. "And naturally Geoffrey could not refuse one of his mother's dearest friends. I understand it all perfectly."

But she did not. She did not understand anything anymore. Had Geoffrey squired her about from a sense of duty? Was it loyalty to his mother and Aunt Win that brought him to her side? Or had it been affection, maybe even love?

Surely his kisses had not stemmed from some moral responsibility. But then she did not know much about kissing. Other men had tried to take liberty with her person before, and they certainly had not loved her. According to her aunt, men always took advantage of what was available. It was some unwritten code that men, even gentlemen, attempt a discreet kiss or two.

Perhaps that was all Geoffrey had been doing, nothing more. The only difference was that she'd returned his kisses. And she'd forced him into more.

Was that what had happened? She turned and looked back at her tree. Their most recent experience supported that terrible conclusion. Weeks ago, she made him take her virginity. And now that the damage was already done, she thought he would willingly repeat the experience. But he had refused her up there. She had done everything she could to get him to join her in a dalliance, but he had refused.

Would a man in love ever refuse such an opportunity?

"Caroline!" said her aunt sharply, and apparently not for the first time.

Caroline blinked her tears away, her focus returning to her aunt with what she hoped was a semblance of calm. "Yes?"

The lady frowned, then released a heartfelt sigh. "Come along inside. It shall be time for dinner soon and you need to change. We can sort it all out then."

Caroline complied because there was little else for her to do. By unspoken agreement, they avoided the library, moving up the back stairs to Caroline's room. She wanted a bath, a good long soak where she could sort out her thoughts. But she had barely crossed the threshold of her bedroom when the front door knocker sounded, echoing ponderously through the house.

"Oh, dear," moaned her aunt. "That would be Harry."

Caroline looked up in surprise. "Harry? Why ever would he be here?"

Aunt Win knotted her hands in her shawl. "When that Mr. Loots arrived, I was distraught. I—"

"You cannot mean you summoned him. Aunt Win! Whatever am I to say?"

"You cannot just see him?" Aunt Win threw up her hands in disgust. "I only summoned him because I thought you might want him here."

"Harry is the last person—"

"Wait." Aunt Win held her up hand, demanding silence while she apparently tried to reason something out. It was an odd thing to see. Aunt Win did not pace. She did not wring her hands, or do any of the other things Caroline often did when deep in thought. She merely stood still, her eyebrows knitted in concentration. "What about the other gentlemen of your acquaintance," she suddenly said. "Have you the slightest interest in any of them?"

Caroline bit her lip, bringing up mental pictures of all the assorted gentlemen she'd met over her last months. Many of them had piqued her interest, especially those she had met through Geoffrey. They were interesting or charming or simply delightful to be around...yet none of them stirred her heart as Geoffrey did.

And she had kissed many of them, so she knew her conclusion was correct.

"No, Aunt Win. There is not a one."

"Then we are back to Harry or Geoffrey. I refuse to even contemplate that horrid—"

"Don't fret, Aunt Win. I will not marry Mr. Loots."

Aunt Win nodded, apparently satisfied. "Good. The question now is how to find out if Geoffrey is in love with you." She cocked her eyebrow at her niece. "Am I correct that you want Geoffrey should he offer?"

Caroline blushed. There had been many times when she prayed her aunt could have a logical mind, but never in her wildest dreams would she have guessed the woman would turn scientific at this moment. She was methodically examining all of Caroline's options and devising an appropriate plan.

To be honest, it was most refreshing. Suddenly Caroline's hopes began to soar. At last she had someone— a woman—to guide her when her own objectivity was hopelessly lost. She lifted her chin. "Yes, Aunt, I love him." Her words had the ring of finality about them. She loved Geoffrey, and no doubt would until her dying day.

"Very well." Aunt Win pursed her lips. "I cannot say he is the wisest choice with his finances in such a deplorable state. But then you never were one to do things the easy way." Caroline was not given time to object as her aunt continued thinking aloud. "We must endeavor to discover if Geoffrey feels similarly about you."

Caroline nodded. That was the burning question in her mind.

"The best way to do that is to bring Harry up to scratch."

Caroline blinked. This was not exactly the scientific methodology she was used to. "I beg your pardon?"

"Harry must propose in front of Geoffrey," Aunt Win continued. Then she sent a sharp look at her niece. "Am I correct in assuming your financial position has recently become somewhat, um, untenable?"

Caroline felt her stomach clench, and she was barely able to force out the word. "Yes."

"Good. That will make Harry all the more boorish. If Geoffrey truly loves you, he will discover some brilliant way to keep you from him."

Caroline's mouth went dry, not daring to hope. "You mean he will offer for me?"

"Or kill Harry at pistols at dawn. Then he shall have to marry you because of the damage to your reputation," continued her aunt cheerfully. "You would have to live on the Continent, of course, but then I think you might enjoy it there." Her aunt grinned. "Either way, you marry Geoffrey."

Caroline gaped at her aunt. She could not be serious, could she? Geoffrey in a duel? Not to mention the abuse of poor Harry. Why, the very thought gave her chills. "Aunt Win—"

"Try to push Harry into priggishness. That always sets my teeth on edge, and it cannot fail to do so with Geoffrey." Aunt Win took a quick turn about the room. "I will have Thompson put him in the library where he can start getting in the way. By the time we are done here, Geoffrey will be ready to put a bullet through Harry's brain just for a bit of peace."

Caroline twisted her fingers in a tiny tear in her muslin skirt, making it that much wider and deeper. She had expected forthright logic from her aunt, not such coldbloodedness. "Please, I cannot like such deviousness."

Aunt Win crossed the room, taking her niece in her arms and giving her a warm, maternal hug. "I know, my dear. But that is why you have me. For the first time ever, I finally feel like a mother."

"But—"

"And remember to act meek. Men always like to protect a defenseless woman."

Caroline frowned, feeling completely disoriented. "But you always say you detest a simpering woman."

Aunt Win put her hands on her hips. "Well, of course *I* do. But I am not a man. Why else do you think women do it if not to please these dolts we call gentlemen?"

"But—"

"Hush, now. You must trust me." Aunt Win turned away, throwing open the doors to Caroline's wardrobe. "We must find you a gown that will make Harry cringe and Geoffrey pant."

"Aunt Win!" Caroline exclaimed, her cheeks heating at such explicit language. But the dear lady merely chuckled.

"Caro, I thought you were raised in the country. Surely you have seen two stags competing for a doe."

Caroline's entire face felt on fire. Young ladies, even bluestockings, were not supposed to know of such things. "Actually," she hedged, "I spent much of my time with Father and his chemicals."

Aunt Win shrugged as she inspected first one gown then another. "Sheep, then. Or pigs. Heavens, even frogs. Oh, never mind, dear. You shall get a firsthand view of two men at daggers drawn, and believe me, nothing is ever so comical a sight." Then she turned around and grinned. "I do love being female. It gives one a unique perspective into the vagaries of the male. Mind that you pay attention. It can only help as you grow older." She reached out and drew Caroline closer. "Come and let us pick out a gown."

Caroline had no choice but to comply with everything. She had no alternative plan, and so for once, she decided to rely completely on her aunt. The most she felt capable of doing was assisting in dressing herself.

In the end, they settled on a gown of rich sapphire satin that Caroline had been saving for the day when she was finally allowed out of white. It clung to her curves with a sensuous whisper and shimmered in the candlelight like a gem set before a flame. When she looked into the mirror, Caroline could hardly credit the image as her own.

"But Aunt Win this is much too forward. It will send Harry into spasms."

"Exactly," Aunt Win returned with a happy sigh. "Now come along. We have a few questions to answer."

Caroline bit her lip, taking a deep breath in the constrictive gown. She felt strange, as if she were disassociated with her own body. She was not the beautiful sensuous creature she saw in the mirror. And she certainly was not bent on manipulation and seduction. She was a silent ghost, a witness, wholly separate from these odd proceedings.

Then with a slight shock of surprise, she felt herself glide out into the hallway, moving down the stairs with a seductive grace and an almost wicked, secret smile.

Geoffrey's eyes felt like sandpaper. Scratchy and aching, they hurt even with his lids closed. But that was nothing compared to the throbbing in his temples. Lord, his own family's finances were difficult to begin with. But this? This was like trying to untangle a rope blindfolded with one hand tied behind his back.

Whoever had taught the woman accounts?

No one had, of course. He was stuck with neat little columns and rows with odd letters that made no sense. Like: Mg, Ca, Fe: 2. What did that mean? But that was nothing compared to her list of investments. Underwater ships and flying machines were the least of them. Many times, she had simply given money to people—men and women alike—and thought of them as investments rather than charity.

Geoffrey sighed and rubbed his tired eyes. He could have dealt with the conundrum of her finances, could have managed, if it were not for that obnoxious, pompous boor of a pup, Harry. The idiot was constantly poking his nose into things he had not the least clue about.

Good lord, how the man droned on and on!

Geoffrey stilled, suspending his breathing for a moment as he listened. Harry was not babbling about his dogs right now. In fact, he was not saying a word.

The room was silent.

*She* was here.

Geoffrey straightened in his chair. He knew that fresh lavender scent anywhere. He also knew from the abrupt silence in the room that something was different about her presence.

Geoffrey turned and opened his eyes…and felt his jaw go slack, even as he scrambled to stand at the entrance of a lady.

Caroline was naked! Or rather, she was not naked; she was worse than naked. She wore a dress that fitted her like a second skin, lifting her sweet bosom, pulling in tight around her narrow waist, then dropping in elegant waves that outlined her long, sensuous legs. Lord, he knew underneath her silly white gowns, Caroline hid a body that could drive a man wild, but never had he thought to see her gowned in such a way to advertise those attributes.

He did not know whether he should throw a blanket around her or throw her over his shoulder and carry her upstairs. One glance at the other men in the room told him he was not the only one with those ideas. Poor Mr. Ross had his mouth hanging open, his eyes filled with the all too typical mixture of lust and worship so characteristic of the young.

Harry, on the other hand, was practically purple with moral outrage. "Good Lord, Caroline, have you lost your mind? Get upstairs right this instant and into a dress more appropriate to your years."

Geoffrey cringed, and he saw from the sudden clench to Caroline's jaw that she was none too pleased about the comment. Geoffrey relaxed, folding his arms in anticipation. He could not wait to witness Caroline putting the pompous ass in his place.

"Of course, Harry," she said meekly. "I will change immediately."

Geoffrey was so shocked he nearly fell down. Then he stared at the apparition before him. This looked like the same Caroline. Why, she even smelled like the blunt, forthright woman he had come to adore. But she certainly was not acting like her. This girl was standing with her hands meekly folded in front of her, her eyes downcast like a scolded child.

Geoffrey glanced to Harry, wondering at his reaction. He had to suppress a grin, for the man was slack-jawed with astonishment. Perhaps Caroline did know how to handle the boor. But then the obnoxious puppy got a hold of himself, shut his mouth with a snap, and proceeded to puff himself up to further heights of self-important posturing.

"Quite right, Caro. You will do well to clothe yourself more circumspectly in the future. I told you not to listen to your aunt. She is a bad influence."

"Yes, Harry." The strange Caroline-imposter turned to go, her movements listless, but her aunt carefully blocked the exit. Instead, Mrs. Hibbert grabbed her niece's arm and pushed her forward.

"Unfortunately," said her aunt in a pleased tone, "there is no time for such trivialities, dear. We have guests. I am sure they understand—"

"I most certainly do *not* understand, Mrs. Hibbert," Harry blustered, clearly riding high from his success with Caroline.

"Well, I did not think you would," the aunt snapped, stepping forward. "But if you would just wait a moment, then I am sure Caroline will explain everything. Right, Caroline?" She turned around, swinging her arms in a wide arc, knocking ledgers and papers off the desk in one of the most blatantly obvious tricks Geoffrey had ever seen. "Oh, dear," she exclaimed, with false shock. "Caroline, dear, will you pick them up for me?"

Caroline still hovered in the doorway, appearing desperately ill at ease. She was several steps from the spilled items and the least logical person to retrieve them. Apparently she knew that as she frowned at her aunt. "But, Aunt Win—"

"Pick up the papers, Caroline."

"Please allow me," Mr. Ross piped in, his voice unnaturally high as he sprang to his feet, but Mrs. Hibbert roughly shoved him back in his seat. Geoffrey could see the boy wince under the strength of the woman's talons, but to the pup's credit, he did not say a word.

"Oh no, Mr. Ross. Caroline can do it."

Geoffrey frowned, unable to fathom the point of this little drama. It was not until Caroline came forward, kneeling down to retrieve the papers that he finally understood, and his mouth went dry at the sight.

Caroline's dress was cut fashionably low. So low, in fact, that when she bent down, he saw much too much of her delectable assets. Geoffrey had touched those particular assets before. He had taken unconscionable liberties with those very assets. But the sight of them now shot through him like lightning. They were creamy and lush in the candlelight, rising and falling with her breathing, alternately pressing against the constraints of her bodice, then falling away until he could almost see their dusky rose tips.

It did not matter that this was obviously a ploy. All he knew was he would give anything to touch those soft mounds again. To kiss and fondle and suckle...

"Good God," Harry sputtered behind her. "Have you no shame?" He obviously knew what was happening, even if he was not given quite the most opportune view.

Caroline glanced up at her aunt, her expression confused, and Geoffrey almost groaned out loud. She had no idea what she was doing to every man in the room. Her thoughts were obviously on the papers and ledgers she retrieved, meticulously straightening each page of figures and arranging them in their appropriate order.

Yet hours ago, she had come apart in his arms, and he had wanted her as if his very life depended on it. He still did.

"Oh, get up, Caro," Harry growled. "You can be so stupid at times."

Geoffrey did not miss the pain flickering across Caroline's expression. She did not flinch, like most women, but her eyes closed briefly, her lashes standing out against her pale skin, and then it was over. She opened her eyes and stood, her movement simple and graceful. As if she deserved such rude treatment.

The very thought had Geoffrey clenching his fists, devising times and ways for him to flatten the obnoxious Lord Breton. But he could not do it. At least not here and now. So Geoffrey leaned forward over the desk, pinning Harry with the force of his gaze. "I will thank you to treat the ladies in this room with the proper respect." His voice was low and threatening and had the gratifying result of silencing the entire room.

For a moment.

Harry was nothing if not stupidly oblivious to his own obnoxiousness. "And I will thank *you* to stay out of this. I do not know why you must poke your nose into my fiancée's affairs, but I do not like it. And I definitely will not tolerate any further interference."

Geoffrey felt his ire raise another notch. He felt his muscles tense, his fists lifting up from where he had planted them on the desk, and suddenly he was judging the quickest method to get around the furniture so he could give Harry a richly deserved drubbing.

Suddenly Caroline stepped between them, her back poker-straight as she faced Lord Berton. "I am not your fiancée, Harry," she said softly.

Geoffrey heard Mrs. Hibbert's annoyed sigh filter through the tension to him.

"Well, we have not announced it, of course," Harry blustered, "but—"

"And," Caroline continued, "you may not want me after you hear what I have to say."

The room was dead silent, but Geoffrey would not have heard a runaway carriage over the roaring in his ears. She did not intend to tell Harry, did she? Not only Harry, but Mrs. Hibbert and Mr. Ross? She would not tell them what they had been doing in the damned tree. What they had done in his home. She couldn't, could she?

She would be ruined! He would have to marry her, then. His conscience and his honor would demand nothing less.

The roaring subsided as quickly as it had come. His honor would demand nothing less, he thought dumbly. He would have to marry her.

It was like a weight rolled off his shoulders, and he was suddenly free. The thought of being forced to marry

Caroline made him feel oddly, inexplicably lighthearted for the first time in years. He almost started laughing.

"I have done something very stupid, Harry," Caroline began. And though she never raised her voice, the room seemed to echo with her words.

Geoffrey felt a smile pull at his lips.

"I have invested in a factory and lost all my money. The only way out is to marry. I know you were counting on my dowry to start your stable, but now it has to cover my debts." She looked down at her hands, and Geoffrey's gut clenched at the sight. He knew she was hiding her tears. "I am so sorry," she finally whispered.

Geoffrey, too, looked down. She had not told them. She had not forced him into marriage. Heedless of propriety, he dropped into his chair despite the fact that there were ladies standing in the room.

She had not told them.

He need not marry her.

The stone rolled back onto his shoulders.

"Everything, Caroline?" Harry sputtered. "In a factory?"

Caroline nodded.

It would have been easier on Geoffrey if she had been acting. She was such a bad liar he could have spotted a performance a mile away. Except he knew how much her failure tore at her, knew how much she wanted to be his heiress.

And how much he wanted her to be his heiress.

But she had lost it all, and now she must pay the consequences. Looking at her, he saw how pride alone kept her back straight and her posture erect while Harry gathered his breath. Geoffrey wanted nothing more than to go to her and enfold her in his arms, kissing away her pain, but he knew he could not interfere. This was Lord Berton's moment. This was the time when Harry would create the atmosphere that would color their marriage for years to come. Geoffrey had to keep silent, though the hounds of Hell tore at his gut, urging him to interfere.

He wrapped his left hand around his fist and planted them firmly on his right thigh. *You will not interfere*, he ordered himself. He would simply watch.

Harry paced the room. He slapped his gloves into his right hand, turning in tight little circles of annoyance. "An ape leader, bluestocking, and now poor to boot. I shall be the laughingstock of the county, not to mention London."

Geoffrey saw Caroline's shoulders stiffen, and he flinched at Harry's cruel words though she barely moved. Follow her example, he ordered himself. *Be silent. She is better off with the pompous ass. At least he will not land them in debtor's prison.*

"This is what comes of letting a woman run a man's business," Harry continued. "Factory, indeed. Lord only knows what other harebrained investments you have thrown your money away on."

Geoffrey clenched his teeth. It was no more than he'd said to her a few hours ago, had in fact said for the last three hours, but to hear it with such condemnation, and from a jackass to boot…He did not know how Caroline could stand it.

He knew he certainly could not much longer.

"I should have taken a hand earlier. I can see I shall have to watch you carefully in the future. Every groat you spend will have to go through me."

Caroline lifted her chin, and her voice was firm, if a bit soft. "This was an investment, Harry. It has nothing to do with sheep. You know I handle those expertly."

Lord Berton took another turn, ending up directly in front of Caroline, towering over her with such disgust in his eyes. "I know nothing of the kind, my girl. Nothing at all. Gad, but what will my father say? Lord, you are in for it now." He took another tight turn. "Best we get married quickly before he orders me to throw you over completely."

Caroline's eyes widened, and Geoffrey could not tell if her stricken expression was for fear of Harry's father or the thought of marrying such a stuffed poppinjay.

"You…you still wish to marry me?"

"Well, I cannot in honor abandon you now. I promised, though damn if you are not getting the better bargain, Caro." He spun around again and glared at her churlishly. "And do not forget it."

"No, Harry," she responded mechanically, her voice a bare whisper.

Geoffrey stared at Caroline, seeing the endless expanse of her life spread before him. Already she looked beaten. Her shoulders were stooped, her fingers twisted together at her waist. Suddenly her dress looked odd on her, as though all the life had been leached out of her, and the brilliant gown only emphasized the woman's lack.

What would she be like in five years? Or ten? Twenty? Caroline would not be one of those women who ran to bitterness and petty evils. No, she would turn in on herself, coiling into tighter and tighter knots of pain until there was nothing left of the vibrant woman he knew. She would become one of those washed-out, cringing nothings, and the very idea made him ill.

As if reading his thoughts, Mrs. Hibbert finally spoke up, her voice clear and hopeful as she gave him his opening. "Is there another way, Geoffrey? Surely you might find some alternative for Caroline?"

He nearly said it. He nearly proposed right then and there. Anything would be better than Harry and the future that awaited her there.

But then he remembered debtor's prison. He had been there once in his life, years ago when he went to pay his father's debts. There were women there too. In the other section. Wives, mothers, and daughters in filthy rags, reduced to penury. Some from gambling debts, others from circumstances completely out of their control, many from the cent-percenters. But all had that bleak look of hopelessness. Most especially his father.

And it had killed Geoffrey to see it.

Everyone else believed his father broke his neck riding to hounds. But Geoffrey guessed the truth was far different.

He believed his father had been so sick from the wasting illness he contracted in prison that he rode out with the specific intention of taking his own life. His father had taken that leap, knowing he would fall off his horse and probably tumble sideways into the river. In his weakened condition, he would have contracted pneumonia. Fortunately, God was merciful, and Geoffrey's father fell on his head, saving him that trouble.

How could he risk Caroline having that sort of future? How could he live with himself if he reduced her to that? At least with Harry she would survive. She would even have a title. There would be food on the table and no gullgroupers pounding at the door.

"Geoffrey?" repeated Mrs. Hibbert. "Can you not think of any other solution?"

Geoffrey looked up, seeing neither Caroline's hopeful expression nor the wide vulnerability of her beautiful eyes, but the haggard, gray women in debtor's prison.

"I…" The words clotted in his throat, suffocating him. "I—"

"Marry me!" Everyone started, even Geoffrey, as Mr. Ross jumped up from his seat only to land on his knees before Caroline. "You must marry me!"

Geoffrey frowned. The boy, apparently overcome by the tension and emotions in the room, had obviously snapped. But no one stopped him as he grabbed Caroline's hand, wringing her fingers as he babbled to her palm.

"I have been afraid to speak before, Miss Woodley, but I cannot tell you how much I have admired you from afar. All these years, thinking, dreaming about you at night."

Harry groaned.

"Yes, I knew you were far, far beyond my reach. Please, Miss Woodley, I make a good living. Mr. Loots has paid me quite handsomely. We could have children."

Mrs. Hibbert gasped.

"I have saved most assiduously. I have—"

"Silence, puppy?" Harry bellowed.

Mr. Ross stopped speaking, his mouth frozen open, his gaze hopping like a terrified rabbit between Harry's red swollen face and Caroline's bemused one.

Then Harry took an angry step forward. "Get out of here, you toady! She is my wife!"

Geoffrey expected the boy to bolt. After all, that was the way with impetuous rabbits. But the youth surprised them all by standing, squaring his shoulders as he faced up to the slightly older, much larger nobleman. "She does not have to marry you if she does not want to. I, at least, appreciate her charms."

*Three cheers to you*, thought Geoffrey bitterly.

Mr. Ross turned to Caroline, his eyes wide and earnest. "I would worship you, Miss Woodley. I would clothe you in garments of gold, would kiss your feet, would—"

"Oh, Lord," Mrs. Hibbert moaned, as she collapsed into a nearby chaise, her shoulders shaking with hysteria or melodrama, Geoffrey was unable to tell.

"Stuff and nonsense!" Harry blustered, but the boy would have none of it. He continued, saying things that by rights should have been recorded for a farce. The whole scene would have gone over marvelously in the best London playhouses.

Through it all, Caroline stood stock still, an island of silence and sanity orbited by this madness. She did not look at Harry's shaking jowls and blustering motions or even at Mr. Ross's soulful worship. She looked at Geoffrey, and in her expression he saw it all.

She loved him.

He had realized it before, when they were in her tree. But once again the knowledge overwhelmed and humbled him.

She *loved* him. She loved him with the depth and maturity of all her twenty-one years. She loved him with the certainty of a woman who knew her own mind, who had run her father's estate for the last nine years, and who had the courage to explore passion and marriage with scientific zeal. She loved him so much she was willing to go through this ridiculous charade just in hopes of getting him to propose; he saw that now.

She loved him.

But he could not love her. Not without throwing both his family and hers into poverty. It was not moral. It was not sensible. And most of all, it was not honorable, no matter what his heart told him.

So he did the only thing he could. The one thing his honor demanded.

While Mr. Ross was still on his knees importuning Caroline, and Harry still gesticulated with wild, increasingly passionate movements, Geoffrey grabbed his hat and left.

# CHAPTER 12

Geoffrey wanted to buy her factory.

Caroline stared at the letter from his man of affairs, at the neat rows of tiny black letters marching in pristine elegance across a backdrop of white, and she nearly cried aloud at the pain.

He wanted to buy her factory.

But he would not marry her.

In fact, rumors recently connected him with a dark-haired heiress whose beauty was spoiled by the fact that she never spoke. It was said her lack of conversation was equal to his empty coffers, and together they would make an excellent pair.

Caroline could not think about it, did not wish to know of it. She felt numb from head to toe, unable to understand anything but one inescapable fact.

Tomorrow she would be wed. To Harry.

He was coming for her in an hour. They were to elope for Scotland. So whether or not Geoffrey wed his painfully shy heiress mattered very little, since he would still be beyond her reach.

She would be irrevocably tied to Harry.

Poor Mr. Ross was heartbroken, but Caroline had remained firm. She would not ruin the man's life when it was clear he was the victim of a youthful infatuation. Somehow she had convinced him to express his devotion to her by searching for a buyer for the dower property.

In the meantime, she waited for Harry.

Caroline dropped the letter on her desk and wandered to the window. She gazed longingly at the elm tree in the backyard, but knew she would never again seek solace in its boughs. Harry had never approved of her tree-climbing. Once they were wed, she would no longer seek that private refuge out of respect for his sensibilities.

Besides, after the ecstasy she had shared with Geoffrey in that very tree, she doubted she could manage entering that silent haven without remembering. And regretting.

She shifted closer to the window, and her foot knocked against her valise. At least she was eloping, she thought with a sigh. That had always been one of her secret fantasies. A desperate dash across England in the dead of night, her love at her side, holding her tight every anxious inch of the way. The very thought sent a tremor down her spine.

She ought to be thrilled.

Except that Harry chose to depart at noon. They would travel in easy stages to Scotland, stopping along the way at Hadleigh. All the proprieties were being observed, including taking Aunt Win as chaperone. If the formidable woman ever returned from the Mantua makers, that is.

And Geoffrey, of course, would be nowhere near.

Caroline let her head drop against the windowpane, feeling as if the weight of dead dreams were pulling her to her knees. She raised her gaze, intending to take one last final look at her tree when she saw something odd.

Was that a boot?

Caroline pressed her face to the window, her heart accelerating to a rapid tattoo. There was something in her tree. And it was definitely a man's boot. Could someone be sitting in her tree? Someone like Geoffrey?

Caroline did not think. She tore out of the library and dashed outside, slowing only as she made it to the tree trunk. But before she could speak, she heard a man's voice. It was deep and gravelly, and although it contained the same ring of authority as Geoffrey's, she knew instantly that the person in her tree was not the man she loved.

It took barely a moment more to realize that the man was not alone.

"Sophia," the man said. "I cannot think this is a good idea. Especially in your condition."

"Oh, do not be such a prig, Anthony. You are enjoying this as much as I."

Caroline bit her lip, trying to quell the disappointment that rippled through her body. Geoffrey was not waiting for her. It was simply a servant couple trysting in her tree. She felt tears blur her vision and angrily blinked them away as she focused on the argument going on just above her.

"You are in a delicate condition—" the man said.

"Oh, hush," said the woman repressively, although Caroline could swear she heard a note of mischievousness in the words. "This shall be our last English tree for a very long time, and I for one intend to enjoy it."

"But…"

Then there was only the sound of leaves rustling as the couple no doubt occupied themselves in a similar way to how Caroline and Geoffrey had only a few days before. It was not until Caroline heard the woman's soft sigh of delight that she herself choked on a sob. She had thought she was resigned to her fate, thought she could go quietly with Harry, giving up Geoffrey without the smallest of tears.

She knew her responsibilities—to her father, to Harry, and most especially to her future children. She could not abandon any of them willy-nilly, casting them all into debtor's prison. Yet until she stood beneath her tree and listened to the sounds of two people in love, she had not realized how desperately wrong her decision was.

She could not marry Harry. Not even if the other choice was indeed incarceration. It was wrong to marry him, to promise to love, honor, and obey him, when all the while she loved another, honored another, and had absolutely no intention of obeying Harry in any event.

She would simply have to find a way.

With that in mind, she began to climb her tree, her entire consciousness consumed with reasoning out a new scheme to marry Geoffrey. It was not until she banged her head against a rather hard masculine thigh that she remembered the couple in the boughs.

"Oh!" she exclaimed.

"What the devil!" he said.

"Look, Anthony, a visitor," the woman remarked, then she leaned forward to get a better look at Caroline. "Good afternoon. You must be Miss Woodley."

"G-good day," Caroline stammered, unsure how to proceed.

"Sophia, please," groaned the man as he tried to slide the woman off his lap. His companion, however, seemed blithely unaware of his intentions, although she did giggle a bit as he tried to move her.

"Anthony?" she exclaimed in mock reprimand.

Caroline watched the two of them with a mixture of confusion and envy. Her confusion was because they were dressed much too well and appeared much too refined to be servants from any of the neighboring houses. She was envious because they were so obviously in love. It was clear from the way the man's gaze seemed to caress his companion's fair face, even when he frowned at her. And though he clearly felt uncomfortable with the situation, he still had one hand entwined in her golden curls, as though touching her were the most natural thing for him to do. The woman herself practically glowed with happiness as she teased him.

Caroline was sure these two must tingle when they kissed and was on the verge of asking that very thing when the woman interrupted her.

"Please, please come up," she said as she scrambled backward away from the ladder. "Really, Anthony, you must move." Then the woman turned back to Caroline. "I must apologize for invading your tree, but Mama said you believe it is the most heavenly place in London, and I could not resist coming."

"Your mother?" Caroline echoed, baffled. This woman seemed so familiar, but Caroline was given no time to remember as she continued to speak almost without pause.

"We have come expressly for the purpose of speaking with you, you know. But I so wished to see your tree that I could not wait. And now that you are here, everything has worked out for the best."

"Sophia!" the man cried. "Be reasonable. We cannot discuss this in a tree."

"Why ever not?" she responded, forcibly pushing his legs out of the way to give Caroline room to climb up. "Mama says that Mrs. Hibbert says that this is Miss Woodley's favorite location. And I quite understand." She glanced at Caroline. "You do not mind us visiting, do you? I vow it must be the most wonderful place in all of London."

Caroline shrugged, her ease returning despite the odd situation. In fact, she began to like this irrepressible woman. "Why would I mind?" she asked. "You are here, I am here. I see no reason why we should move."

The woman shot a triumphant glance at the man as Caroline joined them on the platform.

"Well, now that we are all settled," the woman continued, "I suppose we should introduce ourselves."

It was at that moment Caroline at last realized with whom she sat. While they had used the names Sophia and Anthony, that had unfortunately not meant anything to Caroline. But now that she had a clear view of the woman, she recognized the familiar features. How could she have missed the woman's dimple, her high cheekbones, and most of all, the glimmer of merriment in her eyes?

"You are Sophia Rathburn," Caroline said. Then her eyes widened as she remembered what Geoffrey had said about his sister. "Geoffrey claimed you were the epitome of serene consequence and would never dream of climbing a tree." She frowned. "But here you are."

"Yes, well," Sophia announced with a casual shrug, "my brother does not seem to understand some basic elements of human nature." She leaned forward. "I am counting on you to explain them to him."

"But—"

"And I am Major Anthony Wyclyff," the gentleman said before Caroline could phrase her question. "At your service." He then performed a makeshift bow that was elegant despite their constrained circumstances.

"And you," continued Sophia happily, "are Miss Woodley, the woman who has sent my brother to Brooks' to gamble."

"I beg your pardon?" Caroline was shocked. Geoffrey had been vehement in his condemnation of high-stakes gamblers. She could not imagine him engaged in such activity. Warmth spread through her body as she considered it. Unless he was trying to win his fortune instead of marry it.

"I should hate you, you know," Sophia continued happily, her tone clearly indicating she felt no such animosity. "In fact, I should throw you straight out of the tree for torturing my brother this way. But then I realized that perhaps he deserved it. He was quite an obnoxious brother, always lording himself over me. So I suppose I should thank you for allowing me to get even with him."

Caroline could only shake her head as she tried to absorb Sophia's meaning. "I am afraid I cannot take credit…" Her voice trailed away as a glimmer of hope sparked within her. "You say he is feeling tortured?"

Sophia nodded, her smile becoming a sly grin. "Most decidedly so. Or so Mother claims. I have not had a moment's rest to speak with him." She glanced at the major, her eyes teasing, but Caroline barely noticed for disappointment knotted her stomach.

"If you have not seen him," she said softly, "then you cannot know if he truly grieves *for me*."

"Of course, I do. You *must* be the one who has cast Geoffrey into the dismals. I have met the other woman. She is much too drab to cast anyone anywhere. Except perhaps to sleep."

"Sophia!" the major admonished.

"Well, it is true," the woman shot back. "You said so yourself. So, if it is not the silent mummy-woman, it must be Miss Woodley."

Caroline spoke up, unwilling to allow herself to hope. "I cannot think that I—"

"You must be the one he is trying to win a fortune for," continued the woman.

"No. Your own dowry—"

"Is nothing to the point," Sophia argued emphatically. "Ergo, you must be the woman who has stolen my brother's heart."

Caroline could only frown at such convoluted logic. "Truly, Lady Sophia—"

"Call me Sophia. We shall be sisters after all."

Caroline could barely breathe for the sudden surge of joy Sophia's words brought. But then reality intruded, and she could not allow such erroneous thinking to continue. "I must tell you as a woman of science that your thinking is not entirely logical."

Sophia leaned forward, her voice dropping to an undertone. "Logic is overrated—even in science. My only question is if you love him."

Caroline could only stare. "What?"

Then Major Wyclyff spoke, his low tones bringing a welcome note of reason. "Sophia, please. You are flustering the poor girl."

Geoffrey's sister dropped her hands onto her hips and glared at him. "It is a simple enough question, Anthony. Does she love him?" Then she pinned Caroline with a disconcertingly direct gaze, "Do you love him?"

Caroline felt misery well in her soul. "Of course I love him, but I am to marry Harry, Lord Berton. That is why I came to my tree today, to find a way out of this coil."

"What coil?" exclaimed Sophia. "I see no coil except for two stubborn people who cannot admit they are desperately in love." Then she fluffed out her skirt while sending coy glances toward the major. "Believe me, Caroline, it is better to simply give in now rather than struggle. The end is the same, and…" She paused as her glance grew openly passionate. "I can highly recommend the end result."

Caroline could see that for Sophia and her major, at least, love was indeed a happy event. But unfortunately that had nothing to do with Caroline's own situation. Especially since Geoffrey still would not admit he loved her. And there was the matter of their families' debts.

"Perhaps," the major broke in, the rumble of his deep voice somehow soothing, "we should cut right to the heart of the matter." He turned toward Caroline, his expression kind. "I wish you to deliver a message to Tallis for me, if you please."

Caroline reached for a leaf that fluttered near her hand and began methodically tearing it to shreds. "Perhaps you should discuss matters with him directly," she offered softly. "I do not believe he will see me."

"Well," Sophia chimed in, "then you shall just have to find a way for him to notice you. Perhaps you could get drunk."

"Sophia!"

The woman shrugged, her eyes shimmering with mischief. "It worked for me."

The major cleared his throat, sent a quelling look at her, then turned back to Caroline. "I wish you to inform Geoffrey that Sophia and I are recently wed."

"Wed!" Caroline exclaimed. That would only increase the pressure on Geoffrey, she realized with horror. He would have to procure Sophia's dowry immediately.

"Yes," Sophia added, oblivious to Caroline's distress. "We escaped to Gretna Green in the most romantic of drives." She leaned forward conspiratorially. "It has always been one of my fondest dreams."

"Mine too," Caroline whispered.

"The dark carriage. The miles slipping away. The tension and excitement. It can lead to the most delightful—"

"Yes, well," interrupted the major, his face turning a deep red. "To continue—"

"I was continuing," commented his wife, clearly teasing her new husband.

"Sophia!"

"You wished me to deliver a message?" prompted Caroline. She began to feel dizzy keeping up with their banter. How would she ever find a resolution to this newest problem if they were forever distracting her with tales of their successful romance?

"A message," the major repeated, sending Sophia a look telling her to be silent. "Yes. Please inform the earl that Sophia and I shall be leaving for India directly—"

"That is Anthony's new appointment," interrupted Geoffrey's sister. "His orders came early, so we cannot stay for the formal event Mama planned."

"Oh, I should love to see India," Caroline said wistfully. "I have read it is the most beautiful of places."

Sophia's eyes twinkled. "I have always wanted to travel. It is, in fact, the only reason I married Anthony."

"Truly?" Caroline asked, not believing it for a second.

"Ladies! Could we perhaps remain on the topic at hand?"

Both women turned to the major, surprised, but it was Sophia who spoke. "I thought this was the topic. We are going to India."

"Tomorrow," the major added, his voice suggesting a wealth of underlying meaning.

"Tomorrow?" Caroline echoed. It took a moment for his meaning to penetrate her distracted thoughts. "Tomorrow!" If they were leaving tomorrow then Geoffrey would need Sophia's dowry tonight! "But Geoffrey cannot possibly find the funds so quickly."

Sophia clapped her hands, smiling from ear to ear. "I am so glad you understand."

"I…" Caroline did not know what to say, except perhaps that she did not understand at all.

"Perhaps I should make myself more clear," the major continued, his glare becoming more forceful as he tried to silence his wife. "I understand Geoffrey insists on paying Sophia's dowry despite her expressed wishes to the contrary."

Caroline twisted around so fast she nearly slid off the edge of the platform. "You do not wish for your dowry?"

Sophia shrugged. "I gave it to Geoffrey with the promise I would not wed. It is not his fault I am such a fickle creature."

"But…" The ramifications were just becoming clear to her. "Geoffrey said his honor—"

"I know," Sophia said, sighing. "And men can be depressingly pricklish about such matters." She cast her husband a severe look that was softened by the love in her eyes. "Why, take Anthony for example—"

"Therefore," the major interrupted, clearly cutting off any of Sophia's impulsive revelations, "I wish Geoffrey to hold Sophia's dowry in trust for us."

"Until we return from India," Sophia added.

"Which shall not be for at least two years," the major added.

"Or more."

Caroline stared at them. "Two years? But that is ages away." She suddenly started forward out of her seat, only to clutch at an overhanging branch to avoid falling. "This means he shall be able to marry whomever he wishes!"

"Precisely," the major said.

"Mama said you were clever," Sophia added. "Mind you, tell him immediately. Before he gambles away the rest of his money."

"Of course…" Caroline murmured, her mind whirling in a hundred directions. Now that Geoffrey was free, all she needed to do was find a way to cover her own debts, get rid of Harry, and convince Geoffrey not to send Sophia's dowry to India.

What could be easier?

"Well, Sophia," the major began with the air of one well pleased with himself. "Now that that's done, it is time we returned to our honeymoon."

Sophia dimpled, clearly dismissing all thoughts of her brother. "As I said," she commented in an aside to Caroline, "I highly recommend following one's heart. The consequences can be quite rewarding." Then she slid into her husband's arms as they prepared to climb down the ladder, out of the tree.

"Wait!" Caroline cried, catching Sophia before she could begin her descent. "I just have one question to ask."

"Yes?"

"Do you tingle when Major Wyclyff kisses you?"

Caroline did not realize how odd that question might seem until after she spoke it aloud. Fortunately, Sophia did not appear to mind. Her face took on a dreamy expression, and her gaze sought out that of her husband.

"It is more than a tingle," she said as a slow grin spread over her face. "I would say it is powerful enough to drive one to a madhouse."

Caroline descended from her tree soon after Sophia and Major Wyclyff took their leave. She had a good many things to think over before she spoke with Geoffrey, but first and foremost, she needed to explain matters to Harry. He would arrive any moment, and she owed it to him to break their engagement face-to-face.

If only he would hurry, she thought with a frown as she sat and waited at the window. She was anxious to get at least this part of her plan over and done with.

As if her thoughts had summoned the sight, Harry's closed carriage turned the corner onto her street. She would recognize his stylish conveyance anywhere. No other vehicle sported both gold and silver ornaments accenting a maroon crest. She considered the vehicle hopelessly ostentatious, but it fit Harry's personality quite well.

She knew she ought to wait for him to come inside the house, but she was too anxious. Besides, Aunt Win was due back from the Mantua maker's any moment now, and Caroline did not wish an audience. Her best option was to have their discussion in the privacy of Harry's carriage.

So with a quick smile for Thompson, Caroline dashed outside, rapped on the carriage door, and then swiftly slipped inside.

It was not until her eyes adjusted to the dim interior that she realized her horrible mistake.

Geoffrey shuffled the cards, feeling the now familiar shift of the deck beneath his fingertips. The sensations had become soothing to him, and for the first time in his life, he could understand his father's attachment to gambling.

Card play had become both an act of desperation and a comfort—and it had met with surprising success. He had won at piquet and whist and loo for the last three days, and in time, assuming his luck held, he could win a small fortune.

But time was the one thing he did not have.

Caroline had already left for Scotland with Lord Berton. He'd learned from his mother of her intentions, was even treated to their detailed itinerary. Clearly his mother had still held hopes that he would wed the impetuous Miss Woodley.

But he could not. Not without a fortune to pay not only Sophia's dowry, but Caroline's debts as well.

Geoffrey shuffled the cards, enjoying the rustle and slap as he cut and recut the deck. If only it were loud enough to push away the memory of Caroline's laugh, the vision of her smile, or the feel of her body pressed intimately against his.

But there was nothing in the world that could block out his memory. Not brandy nor cards nor light skirts. Although right now, he was considering all three.

"How much have you won?"

Geoffrey looked up at the familiar voice, feeling surprise pierce his obsessive thoughts. "Mavenford! Good God, I thought you were safely buried in York. What brings you back to town?"

"A damn fool." Though the other earl's voice was grim, his expression was warm and his smile supportive as he settled into the seat across from Geoffrey. "I hear you are hanging out for another heiress."

Geoffrey shrugged, unwilling to answer. It was bad enough knowing he had failed without laying open his wounds before one of his dearest friends—especially the friend who had taken his other bride, Gillian Ames, away at the altar.

Mavenford leaned forward onto his elbows, and Geoffrey could see his gaze narrow as he took in Geoffrey's mussed cravat, bloodshot eyes, and most of all, the fatigue that hung about him like a mantle.

"So," he drawled as he reached for the cards. "Care for a game?"

"I will not play with you, Stephen."

Mavenford did not pause, but began shuffling the cards, dealing out a hand of piquet without a hitch. "Why not?"

"Because I intend to win."

Stephen grinned. "Excellent. A monkey a point."

Geoffrey nearly choked on his brandy as he gaped at his friend. Five hundred pounds a point? Surely he could not be serious. But one glance at Mavenford's determined expression told him Stephen was in deadly earnest. "Have you gone mad?" he gasped.

Stephen glanced up, and Geoffrey could swear he caught the tiniest flash of a grin. "Perhaps. Gillian is increasing again, and I feel in an extremely giddy mood." This time Geoffrey was sure. Stephen was grinning.

Geoffrey frowned, unaccountably depressed by the sight of such wedded bliss. Gillian pregnant again? And by the looks of Mavenford, their relationship had never been more euphoric.

"Come, come," the earl said. "Will you play or not? Pick up your cards."

Geoffrey responded automatically, looking at his cards out of habit rather than thought. It was not until halfway through the first hand that he realized he had just agreed to incredible stakes. Five hundred pounds a point would have been worthy of his father at the height of his gambling career. Good God, Geoffrey realized with a start, he could lose everything!

"Do you know what I find most interesting?" Stephen asked, his voice congenial as he made a colossally bad play. "I know this man. He has friends, colleagues who trust him, and even more importantly, people who feel as if they owe him a debt they can never repay."

Geoffrey glanced up at his opponent. Not only was Stephen's play truly horrendous, but the man did not seem to care. "Uh, Mavenford, perhaps we should defer this game," he offered. "Your mind appears to be elsewhere."

"Hmm? Nonsense, old boy, just keep playing."

Geoffrey had no choice but to continue, though guilt ate at him. He could not quite decide if Stephen was totally distracted or if he had some devious stratagem in mind. For a moment, he almost suspected the earl was purposely losing, but he quickly dismissed the thought. Above all else, Stephen was a gentleman. To purposely lose would be tantamount to cheating, and no gentleman would taint his honor in such a way.

"To continue," Stephen said as he casually tossed aside a winning card. "I find it most amazing that a man with friends all about him can so blithely ignore them as if they were no more than manure on his boots." He glanced up, and Geoffrey found himself squirming beneath the cold finality in his friend's gaze. "I find that most ungentlemanly behavior. Most ungentlemanly indeed."

Geoffrey frowned, his gambling skills fading as he tried to both follow Stephen's odd conversation and remember the card play at the same time.

"Oh, bad move, Geoffrey," the earl drawled. "Perhaps you should quit if your mind is not on the game." Geoffrey breathed a heavy sigh of relief. At last a graceful way out of the game. He folded his cards, but Stephen's voice stopped him. "Of course, you did agree to play. It would not be sporting to stop now." Stephen raised his eyes, and again his stem expression chilled Geoffrey to the bone. "Most ungentlemanly."

Geoffrey swallowed. He had agreed to the stakes. He could not in honor back out now. He had no choice but to pick up his cards and finish out the game.

"Perhaps," Stephen continued, as he dealt the next round, "it is a young lady who has you so distracted."

Geoffrey flinched. He did not wish to discuss Caroline just now.

"I hear she is a most odd creature," Stephen drawled.

Geoffrey slapped down the rest of his cards, taking great relish in winning the hand. Then, when he spoke, he made sure his gaze matched the chill blue of Stephen's eyes. "Miss Woodley is not in the least bit odd. I would suggest you remember that in the future. Or perhaps you would rather call our friendship at an end."

Stephen's only response was an arched eyebrow. "Woodley? Hmmm," he mused aloud. "I was speaking of that other poor, silent creature. Pray forgive me."

Geoffrey frowned. Mavenford had mentioned Caroline, hadn't he? Or was it Geoffrey's own fevered brain that once again conjured up the girl's image at the most inappropriate time? He could not remember, and now Stephen was dealing yet another hand.

But this time, Geoffrey knew better. He could not keep playing. He was too distracted, too confused. With a sigh of regret, he pushed back his chair. "My apologies, Stephen, but I am afraid I cannot continue."

"Of course you can."

"Mavenford—"

"Sit down."

"But—"

"I have not released you from our wager."

Geoffrey's breath caught. He was not even sure who had won. His thoughts were so occupied with Mavenford's strange conversation that he had completely lost track of the points. And considering the amount of money riding on their play, it was perhaps one of the most idiotic things he had ever done.

"Stephen—"

"I shall release you on one condition."

Geoffrey tried to swallow past the lump in his throat. He had a great deal of respect for Stephen's intelligence. He was not in the least bit sure he could outsmart the earl if put to the test. But his only other alternative was to continue playing for five hundred pounds a point when his mind was completely occupied with the thought of a beautiful bluestocking intent on kissing experiments.

Geoffrey sighed and returned to his seat. "Very well, Mavenford, what is your condition?"

"That you answer one question. Do you love her?"

Geoffrey just stared at his friend, wondering if in fact he looked at an imposter. Stephen had become much more relaxed since his marriage, but this last question was the oddest remark in a long string of oddities.

"Mavenford?"

"Do you love her?"

Geoffrey shook his head, unwilling to say it aloud. "Love whom?"

Stephen merely raised his eyebrow, and Geoffrey was forced to look away. It was too difficult to answer when the situation was so completely hopeless. Caroline was on her way to Scotland, and Geoffrey was destined for a mute heiress.

"You do." Stephen's voice was low and intense.

Geoffrey lied, shaking his head no while his hands knotted into fists just below the table.

"You *do* love her," Stephen repeated. "Say it, Geoffrey. It is important to say the words aloud."

Geoffrey lifted his gaze to his friend's and saw Stephen would not relent. The man would hound him until he answered. "Yes, damn you! Yes, I love her."

"Whom?"

"Caroline!" Her name seemed to tear at him as he pushed it out, but still he continued. "I love Caroline."

Suddenly Stephen relaxed, dropping back against his seat with a contented sigh. "Then, you idiot, go marry her."

"I cannot!" The words exploded from him with the force of a comet. "Sophia needs her dowry, and Caroline has staggering debts. Marrying her would land us all in debtor's prison."

"Well, as to that, I suppose you will wish payment for our wager."

"What?"

"Our wager. Piquet. Monkey a point, I believe." Then, with perfect calm, Stephen pulled out his bank book and wrote out a draft for a staggering amount of money. "Will this cover your immediate needs?"

Geoffrey shook himself out of his stupor long enough to square his shoulders and frown at his friend. "I cannot accept that."

"Why not? It is a debt of honor. And I assure you, Geoffrey, there are many things I would do for you, but welshing on a bet is not one of them."

"But you cheated!" It was not until after he spoke that he realized they had attracted a good deal of attention. Almost a score of men scattered about the room were covertly watching their discussion, and Geoffrey quickly modulated his voice to a harsh whisper. "You deliberately lost to me. You cheated!"

Stephen merely shrugged, ignoring a comment that five years ago would have brought them to pistols at dawn. "If there is one thing I have learned from Gillian, it is that sometimes deception is necessary to break through extremely dense obstacles." His gaze left no doubt as to whom he thought was dense.

Geoffrey shifted uneasily in his seat. "You have already been more than kind. Five years ago—"

"Five years ago, you gave me the greatest gift in the world. You allowed me to marry the woman I love. Now I am simply returning the favor."

Geoffrey stared at the bank draft, a stark white page on the dark green of the card table. He could not take it. It was too…dishonorable.

"It is only pride, Geoffrey," Stephen said softly.

He lifted his gaze to his friend, letting his anguish shine through his eyes. "Pride is all I have left. Money, respect, even my labor, all have been stripped from me. What do I have left but my honor—my pride in who I am?"

Geoffrey let his gaze fall again to the bank draft, lying there like the last temptation. All he need do was reach out one finger. But he could not. If he did, he would lose the one thing he had left: his self-respect.

Then Stephen broke into his thoughts, his voice low and intense. "What does *she* give you, Geoffrey? What do you gain when you give up the last of who you once were?"

Images flashed through his mind, pictures of Caroline in all her moods. He recalled her pensive concentration that first night in his mother's music room. Then he saw her filled with the zeal of scientific discovery. He remembered the times when she was sad, passionate, embarrassed, or furious. And he felt his love grow as he adored her in all those myriad times.

But more than her beauty and her spirit, he remembered himself when he was with her. He was alive, active, and...happy. She drove him to the brink of insanity, and yet his life before meeting her seemed colorless and empty. She challenged his thoughts, pushed him into new situations and experiences, and brought him a joy he could not express. He was at his best when he was with her.

"What does *she* bring you, Geoffrey?" Stephen asked again.

"Herself." It was such a simple thing, and yet it was more than he'd ever imagined having.

"And is she worth your pride?"

Geoffrey looked up, feeling wonder fill him as he realized the truth. "She is worth everything I have and more."

"Then take the cheque and marry her."

Could it be possible? Geoffrey thought with a strange sort of wonder. Could he truly have found an answer? Not an answer to his financial problems, but an answer to the emptiness that had wormed itself so silently into his life?

With achingly slow movements, he reached forward and picked up the bank draft. He held the paper in his hands, feeling the crisp edges, seeing the dark, black words.

He expected to feel a great heaviness come over him as he lost his honor, the one thing he cherished above all else. But he did not. He felt so light, he thought he could fly. It was as if the last few weeks had not happened. The fatigue, the pain, even his befuddled thoughts faded until all that remained was the knowledge that he could marry Caroline.

He could marry her!

He looked up at Stephen and heard the awe that colored his own voice. "You are right. I have been a fool."

Stephen answered with a grin. "Just thank God you have friends to point out your failings."

Geoffrey laughed, then jumped out of his seat, slapping the other earl on the shoulder. "Care to be my best man?"

"I would be h—" But Stephen was not given the time to complete his answer as a loud commotion caught their attention. They stood near the hallway entrance, and they could hear muffled cries of outrage filter down to their room.

"I wonder what…" Then Geoffrey cut off his words, able only to stare in stupefied horror.

Gillian, the Countess of Mavenford, had entered the hallowed halls of Brooks'.

# CHAPTER 13

Geoffrey stared at the unheard of sight of a woman entering Brooks'. All around him, gentlemen expressed their outrage and horror, but all he could think was that Gillian looked good. She had always been a beauty, even when dressed less than fashionably. Now she seemed happy too. The haunted expression had left her eyes, and her body had matured, grown riper and fuller. She had indeed come into her own, and he could not be happier for her.

Or rather he could not have been happier unless she were *outside* Brooks'.

"There you are!" she exclaimed. "I was afraid I would have to search this whole place."

"Gillian!" Stephen exploded beside him. "A lady does not enter a gentleman's club!"

She turned, giving her husband a fond smile. "Then put it on the list of things not to do, Stephen. I have come to speak with Geoffrey."

"But—"

"Perhaps we should continue this discussion outside," Geoffrey suggested. He nodded to the doorman and was immediately rewarded with his and Stephen's hats. They were outdoors moments later despite the fact that

Mavenford and his bride were still quarreling like two magpies.

"I cannot believe," Stephen blustered once they achieved the front steps, "that you could have the effrontery to storm into Brooks'!"

"I tell you this is important! Geoffrey"— Gillian turned to him—"I have just been to see your Miss Woodley."

Geoffrey almost tripped down the front stairs. Gillian and Caroline together? It boggled the mind. No telling what sort of mischief or inappropriate discussions they might have had. "Good Lord." He gasped. "What did you discuss?"

"Absolutely nothing." Gillian pushed her way to his side. "Geoffrey, she has been abducted!"

"What?" Caroline abducted? The thought turned his blood to ice, but a moment later, he remembered Caroline's plan. "No, no," he breathed as he tried to force his heart back to a normal tempo. "She has only gone with Lord Berton. I shall catch them up."

Yet Gillian stepped forward, clutching his arm. "No, you do not understand. I have been to Lord Berton's apartments. Thompson gave me his address."

"Gillian, you cannot tell me you went into a gentleman's apartment!" cried Stephen, clearly becoming more exasperated by the second.

"Well, it is a good thing I did," she shot back at her husband. "I found him lying on the floor with a knot on his head the size of a goose egg."

Geoffrey felt his chest grow tight as a gnawing fear began to eat at his insides. "Lord Berton was knocked unconscious?"

"Yes." Gillian turned back to him. "I went there to find out where they were headed. I thought I could discover something from his butler or manservant." Suddenly she stopped, her eyes narrowing as she peered intently at him. "You do love her, do you not? You wish to marry her?"

Geoffrey ground his teeth. "Yes! Now tell me about Harry. Who hit him?"

"He mumbled something about boots or hoots or…"

"Loots?"

Gillian frowned. "Yes, maybe. He was not very coherent. I helped him to his bed, then came directly here. Who is Mr. Loots?"

A memory flashed through Geoffrey's mind of Caroline struggling in that boor's arms the evening when he discovered her kissing experiment. Apparently, he had not hit him hard enough then. He would make sure to complete the job this time! That vengeful image filled his mind, stoking a raw anger within him despite Gillian's attempt to attract him.

"Geoffrey! Who is Mr. Loots? Why would he accost poor Berton? And who abducted Miss Woodley?"

He heard the urgency in her voice, but it was only an echo of the alarm clamoring inside his own head. He quickly scanned the street for his horse. What was taking so long? He turned back to Gillian. "Did Thompson see where they were headed?"

Gillian nodded. "He thinks they headed for the Great North Road, but he cannot be sure."

"Scotland," Geoffrey said, his voice low and angry.

Stephen stepped forward, pulling his wife around to him. "You seem to have learned a great deal from this Mr. Thompson. Is he reliable?"

"Absolutely," answered Geoffrey before Gillian could speak. "House spy."

Stephen frowned. "But why would this Mr. Loots abduct Miss Woodley, if it was indeed him?"

Geoffrey turned back to his friend, dread sucking at his energy. "He did. And I intend to find out."

He at last spotted his horse being brought around from the mews. But before he could dash for it, Stephen caught his arm, restraining him. "What will you do?"

Geoffrey smiled, taking grim satisfaction in his words. "I intend to find them, kill him, and marry her."

"Geoffrey!" Gillian exclaimed, but she was cut off by her husband.

"Excellent," Stephen said. "I shall follow directly behind as soon as possible."

Gillian abruptly pulled the earl around to face her. "We shall follow him."

"Absolutely not!"

"You cannot leave me behind when I was the one who…"

Geoffrey did not wait to hear the end of their argument. He was already sprinting for his horse, his every breath, every muscle, every thought focused on saving Caroline.

Caroline stared at the enormous form of Mr. Loots and tried to ignore the ache in her head and the queasy, roiling feeling in her stomach. She could not manage it, so she closed her eyes again and concentrated on the mundane. She was lying on her side against the velvet squabs of Harry's carriage. She could hear the rapid pounding of the horses' hooves as they seemed to career down a road at an incredible pace.

But what was she doing here? And with Mr. Loots?

She carefully tried to piece together her fragmented memories. She recalled speaking with the Wyclyffs in her tree and her momentous decision to marry Geoffrey no matter what. Then…

The carriage!

Caroline frowned. She remembered a handkerchief pressed to her face and a strange smell. It had been sweet, cloying, almost burning. Ether!

Now she remembered. She had entered the carriage intent on speaking with Harry only to be surprised by Mr. Loots and quickly subdued by an ether-laden handkerchief.

Caroline nearly groaned out loud. Of all the ridiculous situations. How would she ever tell Geoffrey that they could marry if she was being carted off by Mr. Loots?

She could not, of course. And so she would tell her traveling companion. After all, he was her father's dearest friend and a fellow member of the Chemical Society. She need only appeal to his logic and all would be well. He was a scientist, after all.

With a low moan, Caroline pushed herself upright, gritting her teeth against a nearly overwhelming nausea.

"My dear, you are awake. Please, please, be careful. We would not wish you to be ill all over poor Lord Berton's fine carriage."

Caroline blinked, trying to clear her blurry eyes. Once she accomplished a semblance of normal vision, she lifted her chin to regard Mr. Loots in the exact manner she used when her father was being unusually dense.

"Mr. Loots, truly it is nice to see you again, but I am afraid I must take issue with your method."

"Nonsense, my girl," he said heartily. "This is the most perfect method possible."

"I am afraid I cannot *agreeee*!" Caroline's last word became a small cry as the carriage jolted over a rut, and she had to clutch at the seat to steady herself. Mr. Loots, however, seemed as congenial as ever, and for the first time in a long while, Caroline felt her temper slipping.

But she had to remain calm, she reminded herself. She was dealing with a scientist, after all, and logic would be her savior. But first she must formulate an argument. Again she smiled up at Mr. Loots.

"Please, would you explain what is your intention in this mad ride?"

"Why, of course, my dear. I am rescuing you."

Caroline frowned. "I am unaware of a situation that required rescue."

He leaned over and patted her hand. "Your financial situation, my dear. You do remember?"

"Of course I remember," she snapped. Then she bit her lip. It would do no good to be irritable. "I thank you for your assistance, but I have that particular problem solved."

Mr. Loots's eyes grew wider as he stared at her in astonishment. "You do?"

"Absolutely. Major Wyclyff does not wish for Sophia's dowry, which means my dowry may go toward covering my debts." Then she frowned, her thoughts running ahead of her. "Of course that is only the first three payments. December could become quite awkward." She paused, counting off assets on her fingers. Then she gave up with a shrug. "Never mind. I am sure I shall contrive an answer." She smiled up at her companion. "So you see, there is no need for this daring rescue. You may order the driver back to London." She leaned back and waited for him to do just that.

To her shock, Mr. Loots did not do as she wished. He simply laughed and patted her knee. "Ah my dear, you are a delight. Now just relax and rely on me."

"But I do not wish to rely on you," she said, almost stomping her foot in frustration. "I have the matter well in hand."

"I am sure you do," he said with a condescending smile. But still, he did not move.

And so, Caroline decided, she would simply have to do it herself. Pushing out of her seat, she prepared to bang her fist hard on the top of the carriage to get the driver's attention. But she had no sooner raised her hand when Mr. Loots roughly shoved her backward.

"Mr. Loots!" she exclaimed. "I do not—"

"Be quiet!"

"My gravest apologies, Mr. Loots, but I am afraid I cannot—"

"I said, be quiet!" He punctuated his words with a slap across her face. It was not painful. In fact, she had experienced worse from sheep during shearing season. But still her cheek flushed hot with mortification and the stinging imprint of his hand. She looked at her companion, noting the ruddy color of his fleshy face and the way his eyes narrowed to pig-like points. Mr. Loots would not hesitate to strike her again, she realized with a jolt. And probably with much more force.

Caroline frowned. "But you are a man of science," she said, trying to reconcile that thought with the man before her.

"I am a man who recognizes a good patent."

"I beg your pardon?"

He groaned, as if tiring of her questions. "Your father, gel. He has put his patents in your dowry."

Caroline shook her head, clucking her tongue as she sometimes did when Aunt Win irritated her. "My father has not made out any patents at all. I have been trying to make him sign the papers for more than a month now."

Suddenly, Mr. Loots laughed, loud and hard, and Caroline nearly covered her ears as the sound was not particularly nice. In fact, it was insulting. "That," he chortled, "is what comes of leaving money to women."

"But—"

"He made the patents for his formulas years ago. But I was the one who suggested he add them to your dowry. He gave them to me. And then I carried the letters to your solicitor."

"But Mr. Ross—"

"Mr. Ross is a fool. He has no idea about them." Then he grinned, obviously enjoying his own cleverness. "I had it planned from the very beginning. They are safely attached to your dowry, and you and I are going to Gretna Green where we will be married."

Caroline folded her arms, thoroughly annoyed with this nonsense. "I will not agree, Mr. Loots. I have no wish to marry you."

He leaned forward, his tiny eyes dark and threatening. "You will, Caroline, or I will kill you right here and forge the papers. Either way, the patents fall to me, and I shall know how to use them."

Caroline stared at him, perhaps seeing the real Mr. Loots for the first time. She had no doubt he would carry out his threat. He had the air of a man intent on his goal no matter the cost. He had obviously been planning this for a very long time, perhaps as far back as his initial entrance into the Chemical Society.

Caroline shook her head, unable to fathom a mind that would pretend an interest in chemical matters, then use a friendship with her father to discover a way to make money. It was obvious he cared nothing for science. He simply wished to make himself rich.

She stared at the gargantuan man across the seat from her and lifted her nose in disdain. Then with as much force as she could muster, she delivered the most stinging insult she could conceive. "You, sir, are no scientist."

Then she lapsed into silence as his arrogant laugh filled the carriage.

She tried to escape at the next inn when they stopped to change horses. She waited until Mr. Loots was distracted and tried to bolt from the carriage.

She barely made it out of her seat before he cuffed her back into place.

She tried everything she could think of. She pleaded the need to use the necessary, and he pointed to a chamber pot on the floor of the carriage. She tried to make herself ill, but she had a disgustingly healthy constitution, and he quickly saw through her pretense. She even tried to jump from the carriage while they were moving, but he anticipated her yet again.

At last she decided to wait until he slept. Subsiding into silence, she waited with thinning patience for him to nod off. Except that the man never seemed to weary. His pig-like eyes stayed alert throughout the entire day and well into the evening.

The only aspect of his personality that slipped away was his manners. When he spoke to her, it was only to give orders, and she was forced to obey in silence, praying that some opportunity might appear for her to escape.

While she sat there, racking her brain for any possible means of escape, her thoughts kept revolving around one person—Geoffrey. She did not wonder what happened to Harry; Mr. Loots had described the boy's unfortunate injury in detail. She barely spared a moment for Sophia or Major Wyclyff, or even of what Aunt Win would think when she returned to find Caroline gone.

The only constant in her thoughts was Geoffrey. He was not with her. He had, in fact, abandoned her to Harry. There was no possible reason to hope he would save her from Mr. Loots now. But still she hugged his image to her heart, using her love for him to comfort herself.

Somehow she would escape and go to him. Somehow she would find a way.

It was after ten on that drizzly night when Mr. Loots finally allowed them to stop. The carriage pulled into a cobbled inn-yard to change horses. Usually Caroline and Mr. Loots stared at each other like angry beasts until the team was exchanged for another. But this time, Mr. Loots grabbed her arm and pulled her toward the door.

"We stop here for the night," he said, his voice cold.

"Good," she responded, thinking she could sneak out while he slept. "I am bone weary," she added, hoping it might convince him she would sleep heavily all night.

"Well, you shall not get any rest tonight. We cannot make Scotland until tomorrow at the earliest, but I intend to ruin you tonight."

Caroline froze, halfway down the carriage step. "Ruin me?"

Behind her, Mr. Loots sighed as if frustrated by a recalcitrant child. "Try to think logically, my dear. Even if that milksop Harry catches us, he will not want damaged goods. So it is supper and bed, my girl. And no whimpering from you, or it shall take ten times as long to complete the business."

Caroline stared at him. He was asking her to think logically? When he was the one abducting her for some silly patents? She shook her head. She would never understand the unscientific mind.

"Perhaps," she offered sweetly, "we should keep going until Scotland." At least if they kept driving she would not have to fear his unwanted attentions. Or at least she hoped she would not.

She started to turn around, but he pushed her the rest of the way out of the carriage. Then he nimbly followed, keeping his hand on her arm to prevent her escape.

"This way, my dear," he said congenially.

The innkeeper met them at the door, bowing and scraping as he led them into a private parlor. One glance at the obsequious man and Caroline knew she could not hope for help there. The man would not even look at her, but pandered exclusively to Mr. Loots.

Obviously, her captor had planned this abduction very well. Caroline's low spirits sank even farther. It was beginning to look as if Mr. Loots had thought of everything.

All too soon the innkeeper left them alone in the small parlor. Caroline looked around, stepping closer to the merry fire in their cozy room, wishing the flames could burn away the chill that settled into her bones. They could not, of course, because the ache was born of fear, and so once again she set her mind to finding an escape.

Nothing. Not even a window. And with Mr. Loots between her and the only exit, she had little hope. Even the furniture appeared too heavy to easily wield as a weapon. She would simply have to rely on her wits.

"Come and eat, my dear," called her captor, gesturing to a sumptuous sideboard already laid out by their innkeeper. "You will need your strength for tonight."

Caroline tried not to grimace as she wandered over to inspect the fare. Surprisingly enough, it appeared excellent and smelled even better. Her stomach growled, and she picked up a plate, deciding she would think better on a full stomach.

It was not until she sat down that he leaned over and patted her hand in a disconcertingly paternal gesture. "I would not truly have killed you, but it is easiest to establish things early on. You must listen to me."

Caroline opened her mouth to respond, but he held up a finger, forestalling her comment.

"Truly, my dear, you will soon adjust. And as for tonight," he added with a shrug, "it is not so bad. In fact, you might even enjoy it."

"Somehow I doubt you are correct," she said dryly, but he merely chucked her under the chin before turning his attention to his food.

Caroline had no choice but to do the same. But as she nibbled at her food, her thoughts were whirling with a possible plan. It might work, she thought, but first she had to allay his suspicions, perhaps put him in a better frame of mind.

Accordingly, she focused on becoming more congenial. She smiled, ordered herself to be polite, then ventured a single conversational sally. "If you do not mind my asking, Mr. Loots, what exactly do you plan to do with my father's patents?"

He lifted his head and frowned at her, one fat chunk of beef halfway to his mouth.

Caroline bit her lip. It would appear that Mr. Loots's favorite dinner companion was a silent one. She lowered her gaze to her plate and ate without speaking, making sure she kept her head down and her expression demure.

They passed a silent hour this way. But as the wine bottle dipped lower and lower, Mr. Loots became more animated. With his belly full, the wine gone, and a new bottle of brandy within reach, he became positively spirited.

Very soon, Mr. Loots merrily chattered away, speaking of his plans for her father's patents. "It is all quite simple, my dear," he began. "Take your father's cleaning formula…"

Caroline did not make the mistake of interrupting. Instead she listened intently, at first for his benefit, then later for her own. She was shocked by her own ignorance. She had no idea her father had developed formulas for cleaning grease out of wool or another for killing sheep lice. She knew, of course, that they had performed many experiments with explosives, but she had no idea that he had actually developed a stable formula for them, or that he had perfected a strange type of glue for metals.

Her interest, as well as his, had always been in the effects of certain chemical combinations. It never occurred to her that the results of his rather esoteric experiments were marketable.

But apparently, Mr. Loots had spent a great deal of time thinking of it. And for the first time ever, she began to appreciate Mr. Loots's own brand of genius. No wonder the man was wealthy. And with her father's patents, he might very well become one of the richest men in the country.

"Well, what do you say to that, eh, my gel?" he asked with a hearty chuckle as he wound up one of his schemes to sell her father's improved glue.

"I find it fascinating," she answered truthfully. "I would never have thought it possible."

"But it is, my gel," he exclaimed heartily. "Soon I shall be very, very rich!"

Now was her opportunity. He was in an excellent mood; cheerful and, hopefully, amenable to suggestion. "Actually, Mr. Loots, it occurs to me there is perhaps an alternative to our marriage."

"Alternative?" He frowned into his empty wineglass. "I have all the alternatives I require."

"Ah, but you have not heard my suggestion." Caroline set her own glass aside untouched. "You truly do not wish to be saddled with an unwilling bride. And I assure you, Mr. Loots, I am most unwilling."

He brushed her objection aside with a single wave of his large fist. "You will not complain when the money starts coming."

Caroline lifted her chin. "Oh, but I shall. Most vehemently." She leaned forward and dropped her voice as she confided in her captor. "You see, I am in love with Geoffrey, the Earl of Tallis."

Mr. Loots shook his head. "No money, that one. None at all."

Caroline frowned. "Yes, but that should not matter at all to you. You see, if I marry Geoffrey, I shall gain control of the patents."

"Not you," he grumbled, as if impatient with her logic. "Your husband. And I will be your husband."

Caroline shook her head, wishing he would be quiet for just a moment so she could explain. "What if I marry Geoffrey and then sell you the patents?"

Mr. Loots smiled the way one does at an ignorant child. "Why should I pay for something I can have for free? I am to be your husband, girl. Best get used to the idea."

"But you *are* paying for me, Mr. Loots. I am to be your wife, and believe me, I shall be a very *expensive* wife."

Her captor frowned at her, and she was delighted to see she had at last caught his attention. "You cannot be," he said. "You dislike jewels, clothes, and fripperies. That is one reason why I settled on you. You are the most inexpensive woman I have ever met."

Caroline smiled, at last seeing her opening. "But I intend to change, Mr. Loots. In fact, I expect if you force me to marry away from my heart, I shall become very expensive indeed."

Mr. Loots shifted in his chair, his face flushed with anger. "You will not! I will lock you inside."

Caroline shrugged. "Then you will have to pay for guards, for I am very good at escaping. Mind you, guards can be very expensive, especially as you will need them twenty-four hours a day for as long as we are married."

"But—"

Caroline began to smile as she warmed to her theme. "I shall sneak out in the dead of night, waking jewelers from their bed just to buy strings of diamonds and emeralds."

"I will not pay!" he said, banging his fist on the table.

"But you must pay!" she responded cheerfully. "Everyone will know we are wed. If you wish to maintain your business standing, then you must honor your debts." She grinned at him. "And as your wife, my debts are yours."

"I will put out to the shopkeeps that you are not to be extended credit."

"And I shall make up reasons why you treat me so badly."

"But you would not dare," he blustered. "I will beat you."

"And for every bruise you give me," she declared firmly, "I shall buy something new. Perhaps a new dress." She tapped her fingers on the table as she thought. "No, that is not expensive enough. A horse? Ah, I have it!" She clapped her hands. "A new house. We shall have scores of houses. Hundreds even."

"But what would you do with hundreds of houses?" he cried, his face turning a rather shocking shade of purple.

"I believe I shall give them to the poor. Yes, come to think of it, I find that a most wonderful idea." She smiled and threw wide her arms. "Mr. Loots, I believe I should like you to beat me."

"Absolutely not!" he cried, cringing away from her in his seat.

Caroline let her arms drop to her sides, pretending disappointment. "Well then, Mr. Loots, perhaps you might reconsider purchasing those patents?"

She watched him study his empty wineglass, his face pursed into a sullen pout as he raised the most significant objection. "You cannot sell those patents unless you are wed. They are part of your dowry."

Caroline took a deep breath, hoping that at last she could convince her captor. "As I have said before, I intend to wed the Earl of Tallis."

He shook his head, his jowls quivering with the movement. "But you are ruined. Even if I have not had my way with you, no one will believe it. No one will marry you." Mr. Loots glowered at her as if this whole situation were her fault. "There is no help for it. I shall have to marry you." He spoke as if he were about to cut off his right arm.

Caroline did not take offense. She knew that for him, his money was more dear to him than his right arm, and she had just threatened to spend all of it. So she leaned forward, gently patting his arm in the same manner he had used not an hour before. "Do not fear, Mr. Loots. I shall find some way to contrive."

He looked up, his dark eyes widening with hope. "Do you truly believe you can?"

She nodded, allowing all her faith to shine through her expression. "Absolutely. Geoffrey will come up to scratch as soon as I return to London."

"Then, I accept!" Mr. Loots jumped out of his seat, and before she could react, he threw his arms around her and pulled her into a rough, rather avuncular embrace.

At that very moment, as Caroline struggled to find breath against Mr. Loots's massive chest, Geoffrey burst through the door.

# CHAPTER 14

It was a long and difficult ride, but Geoffrey spared nothing. Not his horse, not any expense, and most especially not himself. All that mattered was to catch that demon Loots before any harm could come to Caroline. But as every second ticked by, as every mile sped beneath his horse's pounding hooves, Geoffrey felt his heart beat a little faster, his blood grow a little colder.

Night was coming.

Would Loots push on toward Scotland? Or would he choose the quicker, more hideous route of stopping and raping Caroline so that she had no choice but to marry him? Part of him hoped the fiend would try. It would give him time to find them before they wed. And no matter what happened to Caroline, he would marry her and spend the rest of his life making up for walking out on her three days ago.

But the other part of him—the biggest part—could not bear the thought of that man touching her, of any other man touching her. His mind played out scenes of ravishment he could not prevent. He witnessed horrible struggles ending in tragedy. And the idea of Caroline's misery was heart-stopping. He urged his horse to greater speeds despite the rain and the chill, and he prayed he would locate them soon.

He found them just before midnight. He almost missed the secluded inn, tucked away as it was behind a grove of trees. But Lord Berton's carriage was hard to miss, and Geoffrey spotted the distinctive crest even through the open doors of the carriage house.

Some angel had left a lantern on, seemingly just for him, illuminating the side panels of the carriage in just the right way. It was a singular stroke of good fortune, and one he intended to thank the Lord for every day of his life.

He dismounted almost before his heaving beast skidded to a stop. Then he was inside the tiny inn before he could draw another breath. He intended to open every door, search every corner until he found Caroline.

The tap room was empty except for the innkeeper, and he quickly skirted it, sparing only a moment to flip the man a coin and tell him to stay out of his way. Then he moved to a closed parlor door.

He shoved it open, ignoring the outraged cries of the innkeeper and was horrified to see his nightmare playing out before his eyes. He saw Caroline struggling in the grip of that monster's tight embrace.

Like a dam giving way, Geoffrey loosed his full fury. Ripping the large man's arms off his love, he let fly with his right fist. It landed on the fiend's jaw, and Geoffrey felt the satisfying crunch as bone gave way beneath his onslaught. Loots had barely enough time for a cry of fright before Geoffrey released all his pugilistic ability in a frenzied rain of blows.

Somewhere in the distance, he heard Caroline's voice, but he ignored it. He had seen she was unharmed in that split second before he landed his first blow. Now all that mattered was that he finish Mr. Loots so the blackguard would never threaten her again.

It was not until he felt Caroline's arms wrapping around him, pulling his fists down and away, that he hesitated enough to hear what she said.

"Geoffrey! Oh, stop! Stop! Please, Geoffrey."

He stared hard at the whimpering mass of bloody terror beneath him and decided that, for the moment at least, the man would stay down. So he spun around, grasping Caroline as he scanned her again from head to toe.

"Is there anyone else?" he asked, his breath still coming in short bursts.

Caroline shook her head, then seemed to realize something. "No one. Oh, Geoffrey, you came! You saved me!"

She threw herself into his arms, and he caught her, tightening his hold on her as she pressed so wondrously against him. He felt her strong and whole, her every curve, every miraculous, heated inch of her delightfully alive in his arms. He kissed her, pressing his lips to whatever he could touch—her hair, her neck, her face, her mouth. And with every movement he claimed her, with every press of his lips he made her his.

When he could draw breath, he clutched her arms and looked her straight in the eyes. "You will marry me."

"Oh yes, Geoffrey!" Her eyes were dancing in the firelight, but fear still gripped him.

"You will marry me as soon as I can find a cleric," he said, needing to hear her acceptance again. She did not disappoint him.

"Yes, Geoffrey."

He tightened his hold on her, drawing her closer. "Then I will work night and day in your factory while you herd my sheep, and some way, somehow, we shall stay out of debtor's prison."

"Oh yes, Geoffrey."

Then he kissed her, hard and thoroughly, as she arched against him, softening in his arms. From somewhere behind him, he heard a noise as Mr. Loots stirred. Quickly breaking away, he spun around, ready to plant another blow right in the wretch's face. But Caroline intervened, using her body to stop him.

"Oh no, Geoffrey! You must not hurt him!"

It took a moment for her words to penetrate, but when they did, he stared at her in shock.

"What?"

"I have the most wonderful news! Mr. Loots is going to buy my patents, and we shall be rich!"

"What?"

She reached up and wrapped his tight fist in her hands, trying to draw his arm down. "He has the most wonderful plans," she said, her face animated with delight. "I am sure they will bring us lots of money. So you see, it was actually most fortuitous that he abducted me."

He gaped at her. "What?"

"At first I was most unhappy with him," she said, still trying to make him lower his arm. "He wanted to do the most horrible things."

Geoffrey's fist jerked, but she quickly intervened before he could strike, stroking his fist as if it were a nervous puppy.

"I spoke with him, Geoffrey! I told him I would spend all his money, which I assure you, I would have. And so you must not hit him now."

He glared at the quivering lump that was Loots. "What?"

Caroline sighed. She was pressed so closely against him, he felt the breath leave her body in an exasperated push. "Will you please put your fist down and let me explain?"

He frowned, sending another glower at the bloody lump. But eventually, at Caroline's insistence, he let his arm drop.

"Good. Now listen, Geoffrey, I have the most delightful news to tell you." She was practically bouncing on her toes, she was so excited. "Your sister is leaving. She is already married and sailing tomorrow!"

Geoffrey blinked. He frowned. He stared. And then he exploded. "What the devil has that got to do with anything?"

Before Caroline could begin her response, the door burst open. First Geoffrey's mother, then Mrs. Hibbert, and finally a rumpled-looking Mr. Woodley stumbled into the room. The innkeeper would have joined them as well, but the absent-minded Mr. Woodley accidentally slammed the door right in his face.

"Good heavens, Geoffrey," his mother exclaimed, as she bustled forward. "You have blood on your shirtsleeves!"

Someone groaned. At first he thought it was the whimpering Mr. Loots, but then Geoffrey realized he had actually made the sound. In fact, he was making quite a few unhappy sounds as his mother began fussing over him. He would not have minded as much except Caroline chose that moment to slip out of his arms to run to her aunt and her father, greeting them with exuberant good cheer.

"Aunt Win! Papa! Whatever are you doing here?"

"Rescuing you, of course," her aunt responded calmly. "Thompson sent word to me immediately after realizing something was not right. I collected Lady Tallis and your father, and here we are!"

"Don't see the bother," Mr. Woodley grumbled. "Looks as if young Tallis has it well in hand."

"Oh yes," Caroline enthused. "He was most wonderful. Except I had already rescued myself."

"What?" Geoffrey said that, although he might have been talking to the prostrate Mr. Loots for all the good it did him.

"There is more," continued Caroline. "I have the most wonderful news about Geoffrey's sister, Sophia. But first, Papa, why did you not tell me about the patents?"

"Patents?" Mrs. Hibbert exclaimed, dropping her hands on her hips. "What patents?"

"Yes, my dear, what patents?" Mr. Woodley echoed.

Caroline merely folded her arms and looked stem. "The patents in my dowry, Papa. Mr. Loots abducted me so he could control them."

Geoffrey felt another surge of anger coil through him. The man had abducted her! When he got hold of—

This time it was his mother who stopped him. "Don't, dear," she said soothingly. "You shall only get more blood everywhere, and I am in a new gown."

Geoffrey forced his hands to relax and concentrated on the odd sight of Mr. Woodley blushing. He had the distinct feeling that Caroline and her father were discussing something he needed to understand.

"Oh, goodness," muttered her father. "*Those* patents. I had quite forgotten them. Did you need them?"

"Albert, really!" Mrs. Hibbert cried. "Did we need them?" She cuffed him soundly on the shoulder. "Of course, we need them. We have been in an uproar for a week now trying to find money." She quickly spun around to Caroline, a mercenary gleam in her eyes. "I take it these patent things are valuable."

"Oh yes," Caroline responded. "In fact, Mr. Loots is going to buy them from me, but only if I can marry Geoffrey. Which is why we really should not beat poor Mr. Loots anymore."

Geoffrey's head was spinning. It was hard enough to think with everyone in the room speaking at once, but then to have Caroline refer to her abductor as "poor Mr. Loots" was outside of enough. He lost control of himself. He began to bellow.

"Out! All of you out!"

"But Geoffrey!" his mother exclaimed.

"I must say, young man," Mrs. Hibbert began.

"Quite right," Mr. Woodley agreed. "Have some experiments that cannot wait now that Caro's fine. Come along, Winnifred. Leave it to my daughter. She has always been a sensible girl."

"Really, Alfred!"

"Out!" Geoffrey roared again.

The only one who moved was the trembling Mr. Loots as he tried to crawl toward the door. Seeing the tiny movement, Geoffrey stomped down with his boot, placing it barely an inch from the man's nose. "Not you," he growled. Then he reached forward and snatched Caroline's arm, hauling her back toward him. "And not you either. Everyone else, out!"

He saw reluctance on the older women's faces as they showed stubborn determination to meddle in everything. But he was stalwart, glowering at them with all the power in his aristocratic body. Finally, he heard their combined sigh.

"Very well," Mrs. Hibbert said, but then the door burst open again, this time to admit three more people. Gillian bustled forward immediately, trailed by a worried-looking Stephen and a gaunt man whose thinning hair had been plastered to his face by the rain.

"Excellent, Geoffrey," Gillian cried as she wormed her way to the front. "I see you have things well in hand. Er, rather in foot." Then she turned to Caroline, her face wreathed in a charming smile. "You must be Caroline. I have been waiting an age to meet you. We have so much in common."

Then she began to draw Caroline away, but this time Geoffrey was prepared. No one would ever separate him from her again. He kept his hold on her firm, preventing her escape with Gillian. "Not now, Gillian," he said firmly. "You may rip my poor male pride to shreds with Caroline later."

"But—"

"Later." That was Stephen. His voice was low and firm, and after a mute glance of protest, his wife released Caroline's arm.

"Oh, very well. But I promise, we shall talk at length later." Then Gillian slipped back toward her husband, ignoring both Stephen and Geoffrey's combined groan.

Then he heard another voice, the only one he did not recognize. It was low and rich, and it took a moment for Geoffrey to realize that it came from the dripping, gaunt man. "Perhaps I should wait outside…"

"Yes," Geoffrey said.

"No!" Stephen said.

The man looked uncertain.

Then Stephen pushed his way forward, firmly setting aside Mrs. Hibbert when she would not move of her own accord. "Geoffrey, allow me to introduce the Reverend William Appleton. He hails from London and is a dear family friend. Reverend Appleton, this is the Earl of Tallis."

The gaunt man bowed as much as possible given the press of bodies. Geoffrey returned the greeting with a flourish. Finally, someone he actually wanted to see.

"And," Stephen continued, as he pulled a slightly rumpled piece of paper from his pocket. "This is a special license." Stephen smiled. "I have come to take you up on your offer of being best man."

Geoffrey grinned. At last things were making some sort of sense. "You are the best of fellows," he said, clapping his friend on the shoulder, his good humor suddenly restored.

The good reverend was just moving toward the center of the room when once again the door flew open, shoving Mr. Woodley backward, who tripped over Geoffrey's mother before landing in an ungainly heap on top of the cleric. Both men went down, nearly on top of Mr. Loots, while the two older women let out squeals of alarm. Geoffrey dove forward, trying to rescue the minister, but was hampered by the many different arms and legs all trying to do the same thing.

Meanwhile, his maneuvering forced him to make a serious tactical error: he released Caroline. In truth, she had been holding tight to him, so he had not expected her to suddenly disengage from his side as she gasped in shock.

"Harry! My goodness you look awful!"

In truth, she merely released Geoffrey, but in the press of bodies, she was jostled aside as the wet and muddy Lord Berton shoved his way forward. He was clearly in a towering rage, not to mention wet from the rain outside and sporting a swelling cheekbone that would likely turn into a dark and ugly bruise.

"Caroline, this is outside of enough!" he bellowed. Indeed, his yell was so loud, it had the awesome power of stunning everyone into silence. Unfortunately, the quiet lasted barely long enough for the various women in the room to draw breath.

"My goodness, young man—" began Geoffrey's mother.

"You are not needed here," cut in Caroline's aunt.

Gillian also pressed forward enough to frown at the newcomer. "You cannot possibly believe this is her fault."

Worst of all was Caroline's slight mew of sympathy as she gestured toward the growing bulge just below his right eye. "Oh, Harry, Mr. Loots did not say he beat you. Merely that you were knocked unconscious."

"He did not have that when I saw him," spoke up Gillian in tart tones.

"Hush, dear," said Stephen to his wife. "Have some sympathy for the lad. He's about to be jilted."

"Harry, old boy," piped up Baron Woodley congenially. "Would you be so kind as to drive me back to London? Have an experiment to finish, you know."

Lord Berton didn't answer.

Meanwhile, Geoffrey found himself completely cut off from his love, pressed against the sideboard and what appeared to be the remains of an excellent mutton. All he could do was glare across the room at this latest interloper, while the dispassionate part of his mind recognized that young Berton was about to explode. A vein throbbed visibly in the boy's right temple, and his skin was turning an alarming shade of scarlet—except for the part that was already purple.

"Hush, everyone," cut in Caroline. "Please, hush. Aunt Win, do move aside. You are stepping upon poor Reverend Appleton's coat. Now, Harry, take a deep breath. We all wish to hear what you have to say."

"No, we do not," grumbled Geoffrey as he reached out to assist the minister in gaining his feet. Unfortunately, no one was listening, least of all Harry who had finally drawn his own breath in order to begin lambasting Caroline.

"I warned you!" he blustered. "I told you that my father would not support further evidence of madness."

Geoffrey straightened, his spirits rising as his frustration found another outlet. Grimly, he released the cleric, pushing his way toward the churlish boy. "And I will not support another crass—"

"Please, Geoffrey," interrupted Caroline as she gave him an imploring look. "Let me handle this. Please?" She spared a moment to glance at everyone in the room.

Once again, Geoffrey had no choice but to rein in his temper, folding his arms across his chest even while Stephen sent him a commiserating look. Berton drew breath to continue. "I had to convince my father, Caroline. *Convince* him that you were worth the bother. That we could not, in honor, throw you over."

"Of course, Harry." Caroline hung her head, looking the picture of humble contrition, while Geoffrey ground his teeth at the sight.

"And what happens on the very day we are to be wed? Madness, that's what! Total madness. Huge men coming to my door to beat me senseless."

From his place, boxed in at Geoffrey's feet, Loots let out a slight gurgle of objection.

"Strange women demanding answers," Harry continued.

"I tended to your head!" snapped Gillian from the side. "Though I'm afraid I could not cure you of boorishness."

"An insane ride in beastly weather after my carriage!"

Aunt Win straightened at that, her eyes shooting sparks of indignation. "Your *carriage*! My God, Harry you cannot—"

"And now this?" interrupted Harry. "You are all insane! The lot of you! Having a party like this on my wedding day. Why, the nerve!"

Caroline stepped forward as much as possible in the constrained room. "It has been awful for you, hasn't it, Harry? You are wet and muddy—"

"He's ruined my gown, you know," whispered Geoffrey's mother to her dear friend. "Just look at the mud."

"And that bruise is going to look terrible," continued Caroline.

"Slipped in the mud on the way in," muttered Harry. "Banged my head on the damned posting rail."

"Oh my, Harry, I am so sorry. And I am afraid you are quite right. Apparently there is madness in my family, madness that I cannot hide any longer." She sighed and looked tearful. "I fear I am just like my mother, prone to strange starts, running after my heart without thought to your comfort."

The entire room exploded into a cacophony of objection to that statement, but Geoffrey barely heard it. All he could hear was a roaring in his ears as Caroline glanced back at him, shooting him a heated look of such passion that he immediately took a step toward her. Unfortunately, he could not get to her without once again toppling the cleric. And before he could deal with that obstacle, Caroline had turned back to her childhood friend.

"Therefore, Harry," Caroline continued. "I fully understand that you must throw me over. You cannot have madness in your family. Think of what your father would say."

"Outraged, that's what he would be. Outraged." The boy genuinely looked unhappy.

Caroline gripped his hands. "Go home, Harry. And tell your father that you have jilted me." She smiled winningly at him. "He will likely be so pleased that he will buy you that stallion you wanted. You can play with Mathilda, or whomever you like, until you truly want to marry and are not simply doing a favor for an old bluestocking friend."

Harry brightened, straightening up with boyish eagerness. "Do you truly think so?"

"Absolutely. And I insist. But first, why don't you spend the night here? I believe Mr. Loots ordered a room. Why don't you take his. It's the least I can do." Then she stretched up and kissed him lightly on the cheek before turning him around. As everyone shuffled to make way for his departure, Gillian softly applauded.

"Oh, well done. I knew I would like you."

"Gillian," whispered Stephen right back at her. "A lady shouldn't indulge in such blatant manipulation." To which all four women in the room released distinctly unladylike guffaws.

Geoffrey did not care. He took advantage of the opening that removed Harry from the room to dive his way across the still prostrate Loots and grab hold of Caroline once again. She turned into his arms with gratifying eagerness, wrapping her sweet arms around him.

"Are we done with interlopers?" he asked.

"Oh, I do hope so," she answered as she lifted her sweet lips toward his.

But he resisted temptation. Instead, he twisted her around, still within the circle of his arm. Then, with his free hand, he grabbed a hold of the somewhat embarrassed-looking minister.

"Reverend Appleton, if you would please. Everyone, this will only take a moment."

The explosion of noise and protest was nearly deafening, but Geoffrey did not hear any of it. He assumed that Stephen, as best man, would handle them. His only thoughts were for Caroline as he once again turned toward her.

"I have never had a chance to properly ask you."

"That does not matter…"

He cut off her words with a simple shake of his head. "It does." Then he dropped down on one knee, drawing her forward by just her fingertips. "Caroline Woodley, will you do me the greatest honor by becoming my bride?"

"Well, of course, Geoffrey," she said, her smile warm and loving as she gazed down at him. "But do you not want to know—"

"Shhh," he said, rising up to draw her into the circle of his arms. "I do not care."

"But my debts, the patents, Mr. Loots—"

He pressed his fingers to her lips, feeling the hot caress of her breath. "Not another word until 'I do.'"

Her eyes widened into silvery blue pools. He once thought a man could drown in those eyes. Now he knew he already had, and it was the happiest thought he ever had.

"I love you, Caroline."

"I love you, Geoffrey."

Then as one, they turned to the minister. It was a matter of minutes to speak their vows, but it was as if his whole world changed in the space of a heartbeat. He was irrevocably tied to Caroline. He had a mountain of debts and years of hard labor before him. Yet he had never been happier or felt more free.

When it was done, he kissed her soundly, firmly, and thoroughly. Then he smiled at her, savoring his last moment of peace. With a deep breath, he let it go, bidding adieu to his former lonely existence. Thoughts of peace, honor, and order faded away without regret.

"Very well," he said turning to the room at large. "Now the chaos and mayhem may begin."

And it did.

*The End*

*Turn the page for an
excerpt from*

# NO PLACE
# FOR A LADY
The Regency Rags to Riches Series
*Book One*

Jade Lee

---

*London, England, February 1807*

"'Ey, Fanny! 'Ow bout a diddle wi' me?"

Fantine Delarive winked as she swiveled her hips past a group of leering men, her smile friendly as she focused on the biggest of them all. "Ye ain't got enough t' diddle wi', Tommy boy. Talk t' me when ye grow a mite more."

She tweaked his cheek as she served him his ale. Then she passed on through the dingy pub, trading insults and affectionate pats with the customers.

They all knew her here, recognized her face, called her Fanny, but not a one knew the truth. They would never guess she had played maid to a princess or caught a French spy. They would never believe she could speak Spanish or cook a goose fit for the king. Nor would they credit that she planned to do such things again and again until she was too old to blow a kiss at an aged lord.

They would never believe what she had done, and she could never tell. So she teased the clientele like a two-bit tart, playing her role with consummate skill, because deep inside she did not truly credit it herself.

"Fanny!" called the keep, his gravelly voice carrying easily over the din. "'E wants ye. Tomorrow. Tea."

Fantine hitched her hip up to the edge of a bar stool,

allowing a near-blind old man to feel the curve of her knee, but no more. "Tomorrow, tea," she echoed. "Guess I better put on me fancy togs. Not that I keep 'em on fer long!"

Then she laughed as loudly as the rest at her crude joke.

"Good morning, my lord. I trust you slept well."

Marcus Kane, Lord Chadwick, looked up, a single bite of egg poised precisely on his silver spoon. "Whom would you trust with such information, Bentley?" he asked dryly.

"Not even my sainted mother," the dough-faced man replied with a bland expression.

"Just so long as it is not *my* sainted mother," Marcus responded. "I trust that you have seen Paolina safely transferred from my bed to her own."

"Safely settled in, my lord."

A dozen possible responses came to mind, but Marcus washed them down with a sip of tea. His secretary would not understand a one of them, and so he did not waste his breath. Instead, he opened the morning paper knowing he could easily divide his attention between the news and Bentley's itemized list of the coming day.

He was wrong.

"I have canceled your appointment for tea with your sister, citing urgent matters with the Scottish estate."

Marcus's eye caught on a column detailing William Wilberforce's latest speech to the House of Commons, but at his secretary's news, he lifted his gaze.

"Do I have urgent matters at the Scottish estate?"

"No, my lord. But you do have an invitation to Lord Penworthy's home. The tone appeared somewhat urgent."

Marcus arched his eyebrows. He had not spoken with Penworthy since Geoffrey's funeral nearly three years ago. They had, of course, corresponded over political matters and seen one another in the House of Lords, but this was something else entirely. To be invited to his former mentor's house, and so abruptly, indicated something of supreme import.

Marcus set his napkin aside and rose from his chair.

"Thank you, Bentley. I now recall why I pay you so exorbitantly."

———◆———

**No Place for a Lady**

**available in print and ebook**

# THE
# THE REGENCY RAGS TO RICHES SERIES

Jade Lee, a USA Today bestseller, has two passions (well, except for her family, but that's a given). She loves dreaming up stories and playing racquetball, not always in that order.

When her pro-racquetball career ended with a pair of very bad knees, she turned her attention to writing. An author of more than 30 romance novels, she's decided that life can be full of joy without ever getting up from her chair.